Critics Rave About
R

TEMP

"Robin T. Popp off_____work offering a highly _____ over-flows with high action drama. Very highly recommended."
—MyShelf.com

"HOT...Popp's Night Slayer adventures branch out into new territories for even higher stakes in this latest chapter."
—*Romantic Times BOOKreviews Magazine*

"Mesmerizing and had me on the edge of my seat for the entire ride! Robin T. Popp is fast becoming one of my favorite authors of this genre!"
—RomanceReaderAtHeart.com

"Gritty, fast-paced suspense combined with an intense, intimate relationship. The characters from previous books make welcome appearances."   —ARomanceReview.com

SEDUCED BY THE NIGHT

"Popp spins a suspenseful yarn and many will enjoy this take on vampire romance."   —*Publishers Weekly*

"One of the best...[a] highly original twist on the vampire genre...Popp weaves threads of her former sci-fi genre into this vamp series to give a stronger base in reality. It sets the Night Slayers apart from all the other vampire books...Popp is a talent to stay."
—SR.TheBestReviews.com

more...

OUT OF THE NIGHT

Also by Robin T. Popp

Out of the Night
Seduced by the Night
Tempted in the Night

LORD
OF THE NIGHT

ROBIN T. POPP

FOREVER

NEW YORK   BOSTON

Copyright © 2007 by Robin T. Popp
All rights reserved. Except as permitted under the U.S. Copyright Act of 1976, no part of this publication may be reproduced, distributed, or transmitted in any form or by any means, or stored in a database or retrieval system, without the prior written permission of the publisher.

Cover design by Diane Luger
Book design by Stratford Publishing Services, Inc.

Forever
Hachette Book Group USA
237 Park Avenue
New York, NY 10017
Visit our Web site at www.HachetteBookGroupUSA.com

Forever is an imprint of Grand Central Publishing.

The Forever name and logo is a trademark of Hachette Book Group USA, Inc.

Printed in the United States of America

First Printing: December 2007

10 9 8 7 6 5 4 3 2 1

To Adam, Dakota, Mihka, Garrett, and Marlaine—
for understanding and for being there.

Acknowledgments

As always, I'd like to thank:

Fellow writers Donna Grant, Georgia Tribell, and Mary O'Connor for letting me rant and rave under stress.

Agent Michelle Grajkowski—who assumes the role of big gun or cheerleader as needed and with finesse.

Editors Karen Kozstolnyik and Michele Bidelspach—whose judgments I trust and whose talents I appreciate.

My readers—as always—you make it all worth the effort.

LORD
OF THE NIGHT

Prologue

As soon as he stepped out of the woods behind his family's ancestral castle, Erik Winslow smelled blood. His vampire senses had no trouble detecting the sweet coppery scent hanging thick and heavy on the air. He scanned the wide stretch of lawn that lay before him, searching for the source, but saw nothing.

Driven by a growing fear, he raced across the yard and around to the side where he stumbled to a stop, met by a sight he would never forget. The blood-drained bodies of the Winslows' manservant, Vince Renault, his wife Sarah, and their young son Robbie lay ghostly pale in the moonlight.

Erik dropped to one knee beside the boy's body and pressed his fingers to Robbie's throat. There was no pulse. He went over to the boy's mother and found she was dead as well. Twin round holes on the side of both their necks revealed how they'd met their deaths—vampires. Creatures of the night. Like Erik—and yet nothing like him. Erik revered human life while these murdering bastards preyed on it.

He went to kneel beside his friend. From the slashes across Vince's face, arms, and torso, it was obvious he'd fought desperately for the lives of his loved ones. As he was a seasoned vampire slayer, it would have taken more than one vampire to defeat him.

Pressing his fingers against Vince's throat, Erik was shocked to discover a pulse, one so faint and erratic that death loomed near at hand.

"Vince?" He touched the man's shoulder, hoping to rouse him—if only long enough to discover what had happened.

The manservant's eyes fluttered briefly before opening. There was a glazed, wild light in the eyes that searched Erik's face. "Er-ik." He struggled to make himself heard. "Sarah? Is she...?"

Erik fought the urge to look at the other two bodies. "She didn't make it."

"Robbie?"

"I'm sorry."

"Oh, God." Vince's expression crumpled with grief. "My fault."

"Easy now," Erik said as Vince struggled to sit up. "You need to rest while I get the doctor."

Vince shook his head. "Kacie?"

Erik looked around for Vince's five-year-old daughter but saw no signs of her. Nor did he see Gerard, his great-nephew several generations removed, which was not good.

When Erik had left the castle earlier that evening, the two families—Gerard's and Vince's—had been together.

"Find my daughter," Vince rasped as he struggled to grab the front of Erik's shirt.

"I will."

"Promise me... you'll take care of her," Vince gasped urgently. He released Erik's shirt and held his hand up expectantly.

Erik gripped it in his own without hesitation. "I promise."

As soon as the words left his mouth, Vince's hand went slack. His eyes closed and he sighed for the last time.

There was no time to mourn the passing of his friend. With the sense that the nightmare wasn't yet over, Erik jumped to his feet and continued to the front of the castle.

As he rounded the corner, he saw more dead bodies. This time, they were vampires. Erik continued running until the sound of fighting drew his attention to a place on the far side of the lawn. His relief at seeing Gerard alive was quickly replaced with grave concern. His great-nephew was an accomplished swordsman, but even he could not defeat four vampires at once.

Erik started forward to help but stopped short at the sound of a soft whimper.

Turning to identify the source, he felt a cold stab of fear rip through him. Deep in the shadows, almost hidden from view, Lily Winslow, Gerard's wife, lay dead. Beside her, their young daughter Jessica battled a vampire for her life. Beyond them, another vampire sat hunched over a body. Two small legs were visible, kicking violently as Kacie Renault struggled—impotently—to save herself.

Both children were moments from death.

Erik pulled his sword from the sheath at his back and

raced forward. As soon as he was within range, he plunged the blade into the back of the creature attacking Jessica, piercing its heart, then shoved the creature aside as he continued to run, his full attention now on the scene before him.

Loud, wet, sucking sounds, mingled with the faint choking cries of the young victim, fed Erik's rage so that by the time he reached the vampire he was consumed by a blind fury. Weaponless, he attacked the creature with his bare hands. When the rage had subsided and rational thought returned, the vampire lay dead at his feet.

There was no time to think about what he'd done. He looked around, praying Gerard was still alive. To his relief, he saw his great-nephew, wounded but alive, hurrying over to his daughter. Three of the four vampires he'd been fighting lay dead on the ground; the fourth raced across the lawn toward the nearby woods. As Erik watched, the escaping vampire was joined by several others.

Erik knew that if he didn't stop them soon, they would disappear and he might never find them again.

As he was about to start after them, a soft keening noise at his feet changed his mind.

Bending over young Kacie, he checked her pulse and found it faint but steady. She would need medical attention, but she would live. Feeling the weight of her gaze on him, he looked into her face. The whites of her eyes shone like bright beacons and a fine trembling shook her small body. Erik, not used to being around young children, knew he needed to do something but was hesitant to act. After all, to a terrified child, he would look like one of the enemy.

The soft whimpers grew louder and Erik couldn't ignore

the small girl any longer. Calming himself so his eyes no longer glowed with their unnatural crimson light and keeping his mouth closed so his fangs wouldn't show, he reached for her. To his surprise, she moved readily into his arms and buried her face in his neck. It had been a long time since Erik had offered comfort to anyone—much less a child—and he wasn't good at it. Still, he stroked her back and murmured words of comfort.

Around them, the night fell silent until only the four dead bodies and the sounds of two weeping children gave testament to the tragedy that had occurred.

In that moment, Erik made a vow. Someone would pay.

Hours later, after the town's physician had come and gone, Erik left his apartment in the castle's dungeons and went upstairs to find Gerard sitting in the family room, looking worn and defeated.

"How are they?" He asked, going to join him.

"The doc gave them both sedatives. They're sleeping."

"How are you?"

There was a long moment of silence. Erik saw Gerard shake his head, fighting to keep his emotions under control. "We were all here, in the family room, enjoying a quiet evening. None of us realized young Robbie had gone outside until we heard his scream. Vince and I grabbed our swords and hurried out." He paused, his eyes taking on a faraway look. "There were so many of them. For every one I killed, two more came at me. I didn't even know Lily, Sarah, and the girls had come outside until..." He took a shuddering breath and dropped his head into his hands. "Oh, God. I can still hear her screams."

"I should have been here," Erik said, guilt weighing heavily on him.

Gerard looked at him, eyes bright with tears. "I'm glad you came when you did. Otherwise, Jess and Kacie would be dead, too."

Erik's thoughts focused on Vince's daughter. "What's going to happen to Kacie now that Vince and Sarah are gone? They didn't have any family left and I made a promise..." He let his words trail off because he was in no position to raise a small child. He hoped Gerard would want to help. After all, while he and Vince had been close, theirs was nothing compared to the relationship Gerard and Vince had shared. Giving up Kacie would be like losing another member of the family.

"In his will, Vince made me her guardian."

"Good."

Both men fell silent for several long seconds, lost in their respective thoughts. "Tonight is the first time either of the girls have seen me," Erik said finally. "With everything that happened, I doubt they'll remember me. It might be best if we left it that way."

"What are you saying?" Gerard looked confused.

"I just think it might be best, under the circumstances, if they don't know about me."

Gerard shook his head. "No—keeping who and what you are a secret isn't fair to them or to you."

Erik gave him a sad smile. "Maybe not, but I think you'll agree that it's necessary. Right now, those girls need to feel safe—especially in their own home. Finding out they have a vampire living below them isn't going to accomplish that."

"Are you thinking of moving out?"

Erik heard the worry in Gerard's voice and shook his head. He and Gerard had been friends from the moment he'd met Gerard as a small boy growing up in the same castle. He'd watched him grow up and taught him to use the sword. "No. I'll stay below and be here any time you need me."

Gerard sighed. "All right," he said, finally nodding. "I can make up some excuse why the girls can't go into the lower levels for now. But when I think the time is right, I *will* tell them about you." He stood up, signaling the end of the discussion, and walked to the front door. Erik followed him outside.

The bodies still lay where they had fallen. Erik stood back as Gerard approached each one in turn to make his final farewells. When he saw Gerard withdraw several small wooden stakes from his coat pocket, he stepped forward.

"No," he said, closing his hand around Gerard's fist. It was bad enough the man had lost his wife and closest friends. "I'll do it."

For once, Gerard didn't try to argue. He surrendered the stakes, stood, and gave Erik a grateful nod before walking off. Erik stared at the bodies. If they weren't staked, in two nights they would rise from the dead. Not as primes like Erik, who had been killed by a chupacabra and retained his intelligence and capacity for rational thought. But as progeny—created by vampires—quickly losing their intelligence; degenerating until they were nothing more than bloodsucking creatures that killed indiscriminately for food. They would become the parasites of the vampire world. That, in Erik's opinion, was a fate worse than the one he'd inherited. At least he could pretend to still be human.

He steeled his emotions. It was hard enough staking victims he didn't know. These humans had been his family and friends for the past fifteen years. Losing them under any circumstance would have been bad, but this was heart-rending. Erik set about his grisly task and had just staked the last body—that of ten-year-old Robbie Renault—when he sensed the presence of Michael, Sedrick, and Ty.

"We came as soon as we heard your call," Michael said as all three hurried toward him.

The three vampires had been his friends, both in life and in death. Because all four had been killed by the same chupacabra, they shared a psychic link. It was through this link that Erik had summoned them.

Standing, he quickly told them what had happened. "I want the ones who did this...the ones who got away," he demanded after he finished. "Find them and bring them to me."

Michael, leader of the local lair, stared at him, clearly surprised. "You don't think it was one of my primes, do you?" Erik made no comment and Michael gasped at his silence. "That's absurd."

"Is it?" Erik asked. "I don't know anymore. I don't live in the lair, nor do I spend time with your primes. Maybe you have insurgents who don't like the rule about not feeding off humans."

Sedrick opened his mouth to argue but Michael held up his hand. "We'll look both within the lair and outside it to find your killers. We *will* find them."

"You have three nights."

"Three nights!" Ty gasped. "Erik, be reasonable."

But Erik was beyond reason at this point. Justice—meted

out by him—must be served. "Three nights," he repeated. "Or the pact is off."

"What?" Michael looked angry as the others stared at Erik, eyes narrowed.

"You heard me. If you don't bring me their killers, then I will not only kill every vampire I see, I will actively start hunting them, be they prime or progeny, feeding off live-stock or humans. I'll kill them all," Erik snarled. "This was *my* family and I will not rest until I have avenged their deaths—as I would avenge any one of yours."

Chapter
1

Hocksley, England
The present

The rain shower that swept through Hocksley earlier that evening had soaked the surfaces of the centuries-old storefronts until they glistened like new. Puddles of water reflected moonlight across the empty cobblestone streets, casting an eerie glow over a town that, at this hour of the night, seemed as lifeless as the eyes staring up from the severed head at Erik Winslow's feet.

In death, Sedrick's face bore little resemblance to the man Erik had known. So little that, at first, Erik hadn't recognized him. When the realization hit, it was accompanied by a sharp stab of shock and grief. Sedrick had been a close friend.

Trying to find the same calm detachment he once wore into battle, Erik picked up the severed head and placed it gingerly on the lap of the headless body. Slipping his arms beneath the corpse, he was about to lift when his gaze fell on the small silver knife lying close by.

Resettling the body, he took a moment to study the weapon without picking it up. The short blade was open and covered in blood. Erik briefly wondered if this had been the instrument of Sedrick's death, but quickly discounted it as being too small to make the clean cut through tendons, tissue, and bone. This knife, with its polished silver handle and small blade, was more decorative than functional, though in the right hands he supposed it could be deadly.

Logically, it would have taken a sword to sever Sedrick's head, which limited the pool of assailants considerably. The average person didn't normally carry a sword, which meant that Sedrick's killer was an actual vampire slayer. Since Erik and Gerard were the only known slayers in Hocksley and neither of them had killed Sedrick, there was a new player in town.

Erik had no idea who it was, but the knife might be a clue to the killer's identity.

About to pick it up, Erik stopped when he felt the hairs along the back of his neck prickle. He stood and moved in front of the newcomer, hoping to block the view of Sedrick's body. "Michael," he began, grabbing his friend's arms and pulling him to a stop.

"Where is he?" Michael asked, sounding both worried and guarded. "Where's my brother? I heard his cry through the link and then nothing. I've been searching for him ever since."

His voice trailed to silence as he stared beyond Erik's shoulder. Erik saw the worry and fear in his eyes and gave up looking for an easy way to deliver the news. "Sedrick's dead."

"No." The strangled sound was filled with pain as Michael pushed past him. "Why?" He cried, falling to his knees beside the body. "Who would do this?"

"I don't know," Erik admitted, struggling to keep his emotions under control so he could think. With four hundred years of fighting experience under his belt, Sedrick had been a formidable opponent. That meant his killer was that much more skilled.

"Gerard?" Michael turned to glare at him.

Erik gaped in return, not liking how quickly Michael implicated his great-nephew. He shook his head. "Impossible. Gerard's been out of town for the last couple of days. This has to be someone new."

He watched Michael's gaze rake over his brother's body and then fix on the ground by his side. "What's this?" He bent and picked up the knife, turning it over in his hands. "Do you recognize it?"

"No." Erik felt anger seething just below the surface, threatening to explode. Who dared to come into his town and kill his friend? "Whoever did this will pay," he promised.

"But not by your hand," Michael warned him. "His death is mine to avenge."

Erik nodded, watching as Michael wiped the knife clean using a piece of Sedrick's shirt. He closed the blade and tossed it to Erik, who caught it in midair. "I will search the lairs for his killer, but I will trust you to search among the humans."

Erik fisted his hand around the knife. "If he's human and still lives, I will find him."

For an instant, Michael's gaze softened. "You are a true

friend." There was nothing more to say, so Michael lifted Sedrick's body into his arms and let Erik settle the severed head on top before walking off.

Pocketing the knife, Erik continued down the street. There was still time before the sun rose to search for Sedrick's killer. As Erik knew all too well, avenging his friend's death wouldn't bring him back, but it *would* bring a certain satisfaction.

When Erik finally returned to the Winslow castle hours later, he went directly to his dungeon apartment through the castle's back entrance, using the modern electronic keypad to deactivate the locks. He'd had plenty of time to perfect his living quarters and short of a large meteor striking the castle, his apartment was impenetrable.

The main room was a large, open area with only a counter separating the kitchen from the living room. He crossed to the refrigerator and removed a container of pig's blood purchased from the local butcher. It wasn't as potent or satisfying as human blood, but Erik had grown used to it over the years. He did, however, keep several bags of human blood, secured from a blood bank, in the freezer for emergencies.

After he finished eating, he went down the short hallway to his bedroom where he removed his black leather jacket. Next he eased off the harness that held his sword across his back and draped it over the back of the chair.

Moving about the room, he flexed his arms to ease the tension and aches. He felt old; when he paused to look in the mirror, he expected to see gray hair and a face withered with age. Instead, the same face he saw every morning stared back at him—youthful, with a half-moon scar at the lower corner of his right eye and dark brown eyes that matched the color of his shoulder-length hair.

He absently scratched the back of his head and reflected how there had been a time when he'd been more aware of his appearance, enjoyed that women seemed attracted to him. Now there were more important things to worry about in life.

He reached into his pocket and pulled out the knife. He'd not found Sedrick's killer, which meant tomorrow he'd have to start all over again. The town of Hocksley was small, located in a remote part of Northumberland, along the eastern coast just south of Scotland. Not many tourists came through their area and there weren't many residents, so he felt positive that he *would* find the killer.

Laying the knife on his dresser, Erik started to undress, moving with a bone-tired weariness brought on by more than the coming of dawn.

Every time someone he cared about died, a piece of him died with them. He would have thought that by now there would be nothing left, yet the ache in his chest over Sedrick's death told him differently.

Despair filled him as he thought of his life, now measured by the number of loved ones lost rather than by the passing of years, and the thought of ending it all flashed through his head with the same intense longing it did every day just before dawn. He could think of no better way to meet his end than by standing on the edge of the cliffs he loved, listening to the ocean's waves crashing against the sheer wall of rock, and watching the sun rise over the horizon until the sun turned him to stone. Oh, how he missed seeing the sun, feeling its heat on his face.

The misery inside him turned into a physical pain, nearly choking him. He was tired of this endless existence.

Instead, he crossed the room to his bed and lay down. He had too many responsibilities; too many people were counting on him. Death would have to wait.

The next night, after Erik woke and sated his hunger, he carried the knife to his study and called the nearest medical facility, which was located in the next town. There was always the chance that Sedrick had injured his killer before he died. Unfortunately, there was no listing of a patient being treated for severe cuts, scratches, puncture wounds, or significant blood loss.

Next, he called Myrtle's, Hocksley's only inn, to get a list of any out-of-towners. There weren't that many and he resigned himself to going into Hocksley in order to check out each guest personally.

He left the knife on his desk and returned to his bedroom where he donned his sword and jacket. Then he left.

The Winslow castle had been built near the top of a cliff, virtually surrounded on three sides by a sheer drop into the ocean—not that one could walk out the front door and fall off. There was at least a good two to three hundred meters between the castle's front door and the cliff's edge. On the fourth side, a dense wooded section of land separated the castle from the town of Hocksley.

There were two ways to get to town: by car, taking a road that meandered along the edge of the cliff before finally looping around to town; or by foot, along the well-worn path through the dark and gloomy forest. The first way took about thirty minutes and the second took half that time. Erik headed for the woods.

Once he arrived in town, Erik navigated the streets until he reached the tavern district. There had been a time when the residents of Hocksley wouldn't go out after dark because of the vampires. But over the years, familiarity had bred contempt and the people now seemed to think that while there might be some truth to the old legends, there wasn't anything to worry about.

As he drew near the inn, he heard the sound of drunken laughter coming from within. Drunks, with their impaired judgments and slower reflexes, made easier targets for vampires. Therefore, the inn was the perfect place to find vampires and, by extension, those hunting vampires.

Erik selected the building across the street and scaled its outside drainpipe to the rooftop. Perched on the edge, he could see down into the street below.

For an hour or more, all was quiet. When the first drunk patrons stumbled out of the door, Erik went on full alert. He didn't have to wait long before movement in the shadows below caught his attention. *Vampire.*

The door opened a second time and a figure stepped out. This one was dressed in dark clothes and moved with the stealth and grace of a hunter. Erik kept his eyes on him, curious to see what this newcomer might do. Odds were that this wasn't the slayer he was looking for, but when the figure started after the vampire, Erik dared to hope.

The figure reached behind himself and something glinted in the moonlight. Erik took a longer look and felt a burst of excitement. There was only one reason why anyone would carry a sword these days and that was to hunt vampires.

Following the figure with his eyes, Erik ran quietly along the rooftop, keeping himself out of sight from those below. When he reached the end of the building, he didn't slow down but simply held his arms out for balance and dropped neatly to the cobblestone street, absorbing the shock of impact with his legs.

Immediately, he took off running, following the muffled sound of hurried footsteps up ahead. At the end of the block, he paused to listen and heard the noise of a struggle coming from the darkened alley beyond. He hurried to the entrance and saw two figures fighting.

The swordsman obviously had skill. He countered every move of the vampire's attack, using his free arm and sword together to keep the vampire's razor-tipped claws from raking his arms or face. Erik hurried forward, reaching down his back to draw his own sword. His intention was not clear even to himself. The vampire was clearly a progeny and Erik had no intention of letting it live. The slayer, of course, couldn't have known that. When Erik got there, the slayer had just finished piercing the progeny through the heart and turned to face Erik.

For a second, neither moved. Erik took in the slayer's smooth, almost boyish complexion, the dark knit cap pulled low over his head, the slender build concealed beneath dark clothes—and the gloved hand holding the sword with practiced ease. This was a swordsman who knew how to use his weapon; he had the obvious skill to take off a man's head.

Erik's anger, simmering beneath the surface, roared to life as he faced Sedrick's killer.

Lunging at his opponent, Erik came up short when the slayer blocked him. The impact of the swords clashing vibrated up his arm. Erik quickly stepped back and lunged again. Once more, the slayer met his attack. Again and again. Like a well-choreographed movie, they lunged, parried, and blocked each other's moves.

Erik sensed they were falling into a pattern, and on his next attack he changed his strategy mid-strike, catching the slayer by surprise. The tip of his sword sliced through the upper sleeve and Erik knew he'd drawn blood when he caught the smell of the sweet coppery scent. The wound appeared to throw the slayer off his game because his sword dipped and he seemed suddenly unsure of himself.

Erik took advantage of that momentary weakness to grab the slayer's sword arm at the wrist. He shoved the slayer up against the nearest wall, using his own body to pin him there. Before Erik killed the slayer, he would hear his confession.

With one hand holding the slayer's sword arm to the brick wall, he pressed his own sword arm against the man's throat, applying enough pressure that the killer took the hint and stopped struggling.

Then Erik caught the faint powdery scent of perfume and took a closer look. What he'd taken to be a boyish face was, upon closer inspection, surprisingly delicate. Like a woman's. At the same time, he noticed the rounded curves of the body he was pressed against.

As he grappled with his shock, the woman tried to free herself from his grip. Erik was impressed with her strength, but held her easily. When she raised her leg to knee him in the groin, he twisted his body and took the blow on his thigh instead. The pain was slight, but it did much to remind him of why he held her.

It rankled his admittedly old-fashioned chauvinism to think this woman might have bested Sedrick. He moved closer, allowing himself to draw her scent deep into his lungs, hoping to rattle her as much as she had rattled him. "You're playing a dangerous game, pet. Someone is likely to get hurt."

"I think that someone is going to be you."

The voice, more than the words, shook him badly. All thought of this being Sedrick's killer vanished. "Kacie? Bloody hell," he swore, unable to stop himself. "When did you get home?"

Instead of answering, she strained against the arm pinning her to the wall, arching into him. A sizzle of pure male awareness shot through him, as did the thought that Kacie Winslow was surprisingly well-developed. Why was it he had never noticed that before?

"Get your hands off me," she spit at him when he didn't immediately release her.

His laugh held no humor. "Right, so you can run me through with that sword of yours? Not likely." If he'd thought that three years away from home would have changed her, he was wrong.

"I won't run you through," she promised between gritted teeth.

"No, probably not, although not because you won't try. Skills a bit rusty, are they? Well, that's to be expected. Not much opportunity to use a sword in the field of *accounting,* is there?"

She muttered a curse under her breath and shoved against him again. He almost groaned aloud because it had been too damn long since he'd held a woman in his arms and while Kacie's tongue was still as sharp as ever, parts of her were round and soft. "Best you stop that, love," he growled, "or I might change my mind about letting you go."

"You're not scaring me, Erik. I know you don't feed off humans." Her tone was contentious.

"I'm not as neutered as you think I am." He gazed into her hazel eyes, letting his own take on a reddish glow. "In your case, I might make an exception."

Her mouth opened, but she bit back whatever she had planned to say and held still.

"That's better," he growled. He stepped back slowly and took his hands away, but not before relieving her of her sword. Though she glared at him, she didn't try to take it back. "So…the prodigal daughter returns. Does your father know you're here?"

"Gerard is *not* my father."

Erik tamped down the irritation he felt on his nephew's behalf. "He adopted you. He raised you as his own."

"Yes, well, signing a piece of paper doesn't alter one's DNA. My *biological* father—as you recall—was killed by a repugnant piece-of-shit undead."

The "like you" was implied and he inwardly winced at her grouping him with those who'd killed her family.

Noticing again the sweet coppery scent in the air, he remembered her injury. "Let's see that cut." He sheathed his sword and gently took hold of her arm to get a better look.

"It's nothing." She tugged to free herself and he reluctantly let go.

"It's not nothing," he assured her. "It needs stitches. Let's get back to the castle and I'll sew it up."

Distaste for the idea was written all over her face. "Right. I think I'll go to Doc Turner and let him do it."

"Doc Turner's dead."

"What?" She looked dazed. "When did that happen?"

"The winter after you stopped coming home."

"I'm sorry to hear that," she mumbled, more to herself. "Dead dead?"

He felt like rolling his eyes, but didn't. "No one turned him into a vampire, if that's what you mean. He was eighty-six and died in his sleep."

She gave him a defiant look. "Then I'll go to whoever took over his practice."

"That would be no one."

She looked aghast. "Are you telling me that there's no physician in this town?"

Erik enjoyed giving her a nasty smile. "Of course there is. There's old Hank." Veterinarian and town drunk.

"Fine. Where can I find him?"

"Let's see, at this hour, we can probably find him at the pub, well into his cups."

She turned on her heel and started off in the direction of the pub.

"Forgetting something?"

She turned and he held out her sword, forcing her to walk back for it. When she was close enough, he gripped her uninjured arm above the elbow. "I'm not letting that old boozer mutilate your arm. I'm afraid you're stuck with me."

"I don't want you touching me," she said, trying to pull away.

"Too damn bad." They'd been bickering like this since she'd turned sixteen and realized her new fencing instructor was a vampire, not the human she'd mistaken him for. It had set the tone for the next five years. He'd taught her everything she needed to know to be the best vampire slayer around and she'd been an apt student. When she'd gone off to college, he wondered if she would continue her training and was pleased when she had. For the first four years away, when she came home during holidays and summers, they fell back into their routine. Then, when she'd started her Master's program three years ago, she simply stopped coming home. She looked at him now with undisguised contempt and he resigned himself to the fact that the situation between them was never going to change.

"Come on," he said. "The stink of your blood is filling the night and soon every vampire in town is going to come sniffing for the source. So unless you want to fight them all, let's go." Still holding on to her, he pushed her to start walking.

She refused to move her feet. "You can't make me go with you," she challenged. He saw her preparing to strike out at him and with a jerk, dragged her close enough to keep her off balance.

As the familiar tension crackled in the air between them, Erik's eyes shone a little brighter and he smiled, revealing his fangs. "Want to bet?"

The trek back to the castle was made in silence, but Erik didn't mind. He was too preoccupied with searching the night for the presence of other vampires to make small talk.

Once they reached the castle, Kacie tried to go in the main door, but he steered her to his private entrance. She'd never been in his apartment and standing on the threshold he wondered if she might refuse to step inside, but she didn't.

"Pull up a stool," he told her after he closed the door behind them. Instead of moving to comply, she stood gazing around the room. With the couch, throw rug, and seating arrangement, it looked just like the rest of the castle.

"Where's your coffin?"

He stared at her, aghast. "You're joking, right?"

She shrugged. "You're a vampire and vampires sleep in coffins."

He gave her a dour look. "Maybe in the movies. Not in real life." He walked into the kitchen to retrieve a box of first aid supplies from the cupboard, which he set on the counter a little harder than he'd intended. Feeling her gaze on him, he looked up to see her staring at him expectantly, eyebrows raised. "A bed," he said with exasperation. "I sleep in a bed. Like you—except mine isn't made of nails." He gave her an unpleasant smile at which she merely rolled her eyes.

She went back to surveying the room, stopping when her gaze fell on the far wall. "Where does that lead?" She gestured to the heavy door.

"To a hallway that connects with the castle's main stairwell."

She nodded and said, "So *that's* the door."

"What do you mean?"

"When I was a kid, I asked Gerard what was down here. He wouldn't tell me. Just said to stay away because it wasn't safe. I got curious and decided to find out for myself, so I went exploring. I found this door, but I could never get it open."

"I keep it locked." He gestured to the bar stool, wanting to take care of her arm and get her out of his apartment as soon as possible. "Come sit down."

She gave him a sharp look. "I told you, I'm fine—"

"Don't argue with me, Kacie. If the wound is left untreated, it's going to get infected."

"I'll clean it myself when I get upstairs," she said stubbornly.

"Is that right? And are you also going to stitch it closed?"

She shot him a defiant look. "I'll use butterfly bandages."

He found himself staring into the eyes of the angry teenager she once was. Back then, she'd viewed the world and everyone in it with contempt. No, he amended, not everyone. Just him. "Those might work for some of the smaller cuts," he said, trying to hold on to his patience, "but not that deep one. It needs stitches." He was starting to sound like a broken record, which just added to his irritation.

"Do you know what you're doing?"

"Yes; now sit down."

She stared at the stool and Erik stood patiently, waiting for her to make up her mind. Finally, she sat.

He turned to pull the first aid supplies closer and when he turned back, she had removed her dark cap. Rich, auburn waves fell about her shoulders, much longer than Erik remembered. The change in her appearance was astonishing. She looked softer. More feminine. When he met her gaze, he found himself drowning in her rich hazel eyes. Stunning.

Get over it, Winslow. This is Kacie. She hates vampires—and she hates you.

He cleared his throat and walked behind her so he could stand on her injured side. Pulling out his knife, he cut through the fabric of her bloodied sleeve and carefully peeled it away from the edges of the wound. The sight of the gash defiling the otherwise smooth perfection of her skin was sickening. He muttered an oath because he had done this to her.

Kacie jerked at the sound he made and leaned away. "Have you fed tonight?" she asked warily. "Because I'm not sure I want you hovering over my bloodied arm if you haven't."

He hadn't—and her blood was a siren song, calling him, luring him closer. He ignored it, bringing four hundred years of well-honed self-discipline to bear. "I have no interest in your blood," he lied, pleased his voice sounded so normal.

Reaching into the cabinet behind him, he took down a bottle of whiskey and poured a healthy amount of the amber liquid into a glass. For a moment, he considered drinking it himself, but instead handed it to her. "Here. It'll help deaden the pain."

She took it from him and downed the entire contents in two swallows, leaving Erik somewhat surprised.

He waited for the alcohol to take effect, busying himself by getting a damp cloth and dabbing at her arm with a gentle touch until most of the dried blood was gone. She was lucky. It was a neat, clean—albeit deep—cut, but it could have been so much worse.

Shaking himself, he took out a sterilized surgical needle and threaded it. He hesitated. He'd sewn up a lot of wounds in his time—on warriors, knights, and slayers. All men. Despite her caustic tongue and slayer garb, the woman before him was both feminine and delicate. The last thing he wanted to do was inflict more pain on her—or worse, do a poor job of suturing and leave her with a ragged, ugly scar as a constant reminder of this evening.

"Try to keep your arm relaxed, at least as much as you can," he advised. Taking a breath, he applied pressure to the needle and pierced the edge of the wound. Her flinch was accompanied by a quick curse, but after that she impressed the hell out of him by sitting quietly while he worked. She might not have been so trusting if she'd known the war that raged inside him.

Standing so close to her, her powdery fragrance washed over him, intoxicating his senses. Her skin felt as soft as satin and he couldn't help but notice the way her full breasts rose and fell with each breath she took.

Erik tried to look away and when he failed, told himself that his interest was merely the result of not having been with a woman in . . . he tried to think back to the last time and realized the fact that he had to think about it meant it had been too long.

He focused on the stitching.

"All done," he said several minutes later, after tying off the last knot.

She studied his work with a critical eye. "Nice job. Thanks."

That surprised him. "You're welcome." The silence between them grew awkward, so he occupied himself with putting away the supplies. When he heard her move, he looked over to see her walking across the room, her attention on the pictures hanging on the wall. They were the pride of his collection; works by Da Vinci, Renoir, Van Gogh, and Rembrandt, to name a few. He'd purchased them from the artists personally and they remained undiscovered to the rest of the world.

He went to join her. "They're fantastic, aren't they?"

She jumped a little at his question, as if he'd caught her deep in thought. "They're nice."

"Nice?" He couldn't believe he'd heard her correctly. He pointed to one colorful work on the wall. "That's a Monet."

She looked at it. "Very nice."

"Kacie, the weather is nice. A cool breeze on a hot day is nice. *These* are artistic marvels," he exclaimed in frustration. "These have been painted by some of the most talented artists the world has ever known."

Her scowl said that she was as exasperated with him as he was with her. "Fine." She turned her attention back to the paintings, stopping in front of each one in turn to study it more closely. "Ooohhhh. Aaaahhhh. Stupendous," she mocked. "I've never seen anything like..." Her words trailed off as she stopped before a landscape painting. "Is that a McLaughlin?" Her tone took on a breathless quality that immediately piqued his curiosity.

"Yes. Are you familiar with his work?"

"Yes," she admitted. "Dad—Gerard—gave me one of his pictures years ago. A sunset. It was...really terrific. I've acquired several more in the last couple of years—whenever I could afford to. Prints, of course, not originals."

He was floored by her admission and she seemed suddenly self-conscious in the silence that fell between them. "If we're done here, I should go." She went back into the kitchen to retrieve her sword from the table.

He nodded and headed toward the door that led into the castle so he could unlock it. "You can go out this way," he told her. Now that the more immediate concern of her injury had been seen to, it was as if his mind had been freed to start thinking again—and he didn't like the direction of his thoughts. "Why didn't you tell Gerard you were coming home?"

"Who says I didn't?" She asked, her voice cool and impersonal.

"He would have told me."

She seemed to consider that and then shrugged. "It was a last-minute decision. I'm moving to the States with Ben—my boyfriend—my fiancé. I left some things here—clothes, shoes, you know, personal things—that I wanted to take with me."

The announcement floored him and he wasn't sure how to respond to it. Gerard would be crushed when he learned, but it wasn't Erik's job or business to try to talk her out of it. Hell, he hadn't even known she had a fiancé. "Gerard's out of town—at an armory convention, showcasing his work. He'll be upset to have missed you. He should be home next week—if you can wait."

"I don't know." She looked conflicted and busied herself adjusting the drape of her jacket over her arm. As she did, a flash of silver caught his eye and he took another look. It was her belt buckle. Made of hammered silver, it was larger and more ornate than he would have expected her to wear. There was an odd shape or pattern to it across the middle. It shone with the darker, dull gray of unfinished metal and looked out of place in the larger design; almost like a piece was missing.

Erik started. His mind was putting together a picture he didn't like. "Did you get home today?"

"No. I got in yesterday."

The bad feeling got worse. "Did you happen to go into town last night?"

A peculiar expression came to her face. "Yes. Gerard doesn't have any food in the house and I got hungry."

"Did you run into any problems?"

She shrugged. "Nothing I couldn't handle."

She started to leave, but he held out his hand. "Wait here a second. I'll be right back." He hurried to his study and grabbed the knife from the top of his desk. When he got back to the living room, he studied the handle. It was made of the same hammered silver as her belt. With a sinking feeling, he held it out to her. "Did you lose this last night?"

She gave him a surprised look as she reached for it. "How'd you get it?"

"I found it in the street. Next to the body of a dead vampire." He waited a heartbeat. "Did you kill him?"

She was too busy examining the knife to look at him. "Of course I did."

She said it with such nonchalance, Erik could only stare at her as she slid the closed knife into her belt buckle, where it completed the design, perfectly camouflaged. She turned then and started to leave, but he couldn't let her go.

Grabbing her arm, he pulled her to a stop, receiving a pained look. "What?" she demanded.

"I just want to make sure we're clear on this. You killed a vampire last night—with that knife."

"Of course not," she bit out. "That would be impossible." He felt a rush of relief—that didn't last. "I lost the knife in the fight, so I killed him with my sword."

She glared at him and tried to pull her arm from his grip, but he refused to let her go. All he could hear was the ringing in his ears. "You killed him." *Sedrick*. Erik felt sick.

"Yeah, I killed a vampire," she bit out, raising her sword until the tip pricked his throat. "Now—let go of my arm before I have to kill another."

Chapter
2

Kacie stared into Erik's eyes, watching as they took on the crimson light that meant danger. She had no idea why he should be upset that she'd killed a vampire when he was the one who'd taught her how to do it. But he was—and it pissed her off. She let her body grow still— the calm before the storm—and waited for his next move.

"You have no idea what you've done," Erik growled as he released her.

"I think I do," she bit out in return. "I rid the world of a bloodsucking monster." With Erik standing so close, every fiber of her being hummed with awareness. "If you have a problem with that, you can go to hell."

She reached back for the doorknob, grateful he'd already unlocked it, and pulled open the door. Hurrying down the hallway, she didn't slow her pace as she stormed up the stairs, fuming. She was as mad at herself as she was at him.

Killing that crazed vampire last night had been—

exhilarating. She'd felt alive for the first time in years.
That's what made her mad, because she'd thought she'd
said good-bye to that life. The vampires. The killing. She
had a chance to leave it all behind and start over in America—with Ben and a normal life involving a day job, running numbers in a spreadsheet, a small house, a husband,
and two point five kids. Not that Ben had said one thing
about getting married once they were in the States—but
Erik didn't need to know that. Neither did Gerard. As far
as she was concerned, they'd lost the right to hear the truth
the day she discovered they had both lied to her.

She continued up the stairs to the second level, thinking that Erik hadn't changed. He was still the most rug-
gedly handsome man she'd ever laid eyes on. Memories
rushed to the surface and she was sixteen again. Gerard
had taught her and Jessica everything he could about
vampires and using a sword and had turned their training
over to a new instructor.

Kacie still remembered seeing him that first time. Her
pulse had quickened and she'd developed her first teenage
crush. She cringed, thinking of how she'd flirted with him.
At sixteen, she was ready to experience romance; love.

Her skills had blossomed under his teachings, surpass-
ing both Jessica's and Gerard's. Fueled by her hatred of
vampires, she was a natural slayer—though never as good
as Erik, who was always stronger, faster—deadlier. At the
time, it had added to his sex appeal.

The memories darkened as she remembered the day
she'd learned the truth. After six months of training—and
six months of Erik refusing to take the hint that she was
interested and willing—she'd finally decided to press the
issue. After returning from an evening of hunting, she'd

only pretended to go inside. When Erik left, she slipped out to follow him and was stunned to see him disappear through the back door of the castle.

She'd waited several minutes for him to reappear and when he didn't, she'd collected her courage and knocked on his door. He'd answered it wearing only his jeans. Her young eyes had feasted on his muscled chest covered with dark hair. It had taken almost a full minute for her to realize she was staring.

Her gaze had flickered to the large, capable hand holding a cup from which he'd obviously been drinking. She'd followed the line of his arm, savoring the sinewy strength, up to his broad shoulder. When she'd finally looked at his face, he was staring at her with eyes alight with a heated crimson glow and lips so red it took a moment for her to realize they were covered with blood.

In that moment, she'd been overwhelmed with emotions of disgust and self-loathing. Vampires were vile, abhorrent creatures. They'd killed her entire family. They'd killed Jessica's mother. She'd spent her life learning to hunt and kill them. How could she not have known what he was? Worse, how could she have had a crush on him?

The crush had quickly turned to hate and loathing. He had betrayed her trust—and so had Gerard. She'd thought that was the only offense Gerard was guilty of, but she'd been wrong about that as well.

She reached her room and, once inside, leaned back against the door, bone weary. The pale yellows and greens of the wallpaper and comforter were the same as the day she'd left and belied the dark nature of her thoughts.

Pushing away from the door, she dropped her jacket on a chair and picked up the soft cloth she'd left on the edge of the bed. She used it to wipe down her sword blade as Gerard had taught her. *Take care of your weapon and it will take care of you.*

When she was done, she carefully slid the sword into its scabbard and then went into the bathroom to brush her teeth and wash her face. She thought about showering but felt beat up, both physically and emotionally, and just didn't have the energy. Even the thought of pulling her suitcase out of the closet and digging through it for night-clothes was beyond her.

Stripping out of her clothes, she climbed into bed, reveling in the feel of the cool sheets sliding across her bare skin.

Taking a deep breath, she made herself relax. Immediately, her thoughts turned to Ben Thompson. Using her uninjured arm, she reached for her cell phone where she'd forgotten it earlier on the bedside table. A quick check showed there were no missed calls and no voice messages. She supposed Ben was too busy spending time with his family to call her. It didn't matter.

Putting the phone back, she closed her eyes and waited for the dark curtain of sleep to fall. As the seconds ticked by, nightmare images from the past, buried during the day, surfaced and began nibbling away at her fatigue.

Trying to head off the inevitable, she summoned The Voice. It was the faceless, bodiless voice from her child-hood, lulling her to sleep with the soothing words, "Go to sleep, little one. I'll protect you." She replayed the sound bite over and over in her head, wishing she could hear it as clearly now as she had then, when it had seemed so real.

After several minutes, she knew that not even the sooth-ing sound of The Voice was going to relax her enough to avoid the nightmares that so often plagued her sleep. She resorted to her backup plan and grabbed the iPOD off the bedside table. Putting in the earplugs, she turned the music loud enough that she could barely hear herself think— which was, of course, the whole point.

Erik woke just as the sun set. He'd slept later than usual because after Kacie had left him, he'd stayed awake trying to figure out a solution to the catastrophe that had become his life. Even now, fatigue pulled at him, but he forced himself to get out of bed. No amount of sleep was going to make this situation go away.

Kacie had killed one of his closest friends. Last night he'd wanted to wring her neck so badly that the only reason he hadn't was out of respect for Gerard and Vince.

Now, his need for vengeance was tempered by the realization that he was partially to blame for Sedrick's death. If he had been honest with Kacie when he was training her and told her about the pact he'd made with Michael's lair—introduced her to the members—then perhaps Sedrick would still be alive.

Feeling the weight of his own guilt in his friend's death, Erik dressed. He needed to talk to Michael, but first he wanted to make sure Kacie didn't go out tonight. He could just imagine how *that* conversation was going to go over.

He left his apartment and hurried through the hallway to the stairwell, taking the stairs two at a time. When he reached her bedroom door, he stopped and listened. From the other side, he heard the steady rhythm of her breathing. He raised his hand and knocked, then listened for a response. When none came, he knocked louder. When there was still no response, he tested the doorknob and found it unlocked. He went in.

Kacie lay stretched out beneath a sheet that outlined her perfect body. He tried to pull his gaze away, but couldn't. The change in her was startling. She'd put on weight since he'd last seen her and it had turned the almost boyishly slim figure of the teenager into a curvy feminine form that was sure to draw male gazes everywhere. His eyes strayed from the swell of her breasts rising and falling with each breath to her hair spread about her head like a halo. She looked like an angel.

Angel of death, a bitter inner voice corrected.

Moving closer to the bed, he caught the sound of music and noticed the earplugs she was wearing. She'd definitely picked up some bad habits while away at school, he thought. Leaning forward, he stared at the peaceful expression on her face. She looked so innocent, so vulnerable. An unwelcome sense of protectiveness rose up in him.

He thrust it away and touched her good arm. It was a feather-light stroke, meant to waken her gently, but she lurched upright, catching him off guard. She grabbed his hand and in a move that *he'd* taught her, twisted his arm as she came off the bed, forcing him to one knee. Then he couldn't have moved if he wanted to.

"Christ, Kacie. Put on some clothes."

"Erik!" She screeched. "What are you doing in here?" She released him abruptly and scrambled to the other side of the bed, where she grabbed the corner of the sheet and pulled it up to her neck with one hand while reaching for her sword with the other. The corner she clutched wasn't wide enough to cover all of her and Erik's gaze drank in the sight of one exposed breast, tipped by a dusky rose nipple that was hard and distended from the chill air.

He knew he should look away—or at least pay attention to what she intended to do with the sword—but God help him, he was only a man.

He felt a part of his anatomy stir to life and cleared his throat. "I'm sorry if I startled you. I knocked but you didn't answer."

"That doesn't give you the right to come into my room," she muttered, still struggling with one hand to cover herself with the sheet. She stepped to the side in an effort to wrap it around her, unaware that by doing so she had stepped in front of the mirror. Now he had a very enticing view of a long, toned back and slender waist that flared into shapely hips—and a butt he'd love to—

"At least have the courtesy to look at me when I'm talking to you," she growled.

"My apologies," he said, doing his best to sound contrite. Reluctantly, and with great effort, he dragged his gaze to her face. "What were you saying?"

She harrumphed. "Was there a reason you sneaked into my room?"

"I beg your pardon," he said indignantly. "I did not *sneak* into your room." He was fighting, unsuccessfully, the urge to peek at her reflection. "I knocked and when you didn't answer, well, then, yes, I came in, but I wasn't sneaking."

"Is that right?" she asked disbelievingly.

"Absolutely. I came to check on you." He gestured to her injured arm.

"Well, as you can see, I'm just fine."

"Pet, from what I can see, you are more than fine."

He had no idea what compelled him to say this, but the minute the words were out of his mouth, her eyes opened wide in surprise. Turning to follow the direction of his gaze, she saw her reflection in the mirror. Instantly, her face grew pink. "Get out!" she shouted, trying to pull more of the sheet around her.

He got to his feet, all too aware that his pants had become much too tight, but made no move to leave. "Not so fast. We need to talk."

"About what?" She raised the sword as if she planned to use it soon.

"Do you always sleep in the nude?" It wasn't what he'd meant to ask; it just slipped out. Then it was too late to take it back.

Kacie gave an inarticulate cry and lunged for him. Erik had no doubt that this time, she meant to do him bodily harm. Using his preternatural speed, he raced out of her room, pulling the door shut behind him. "I'm going into town," he called through the door when she didn't come after him. "I want you to stay inside tonight."

"Go to hell."

Despite the certainty that she had no intention of minding him, he smiled and walked off.

If it was possible, Kacie felt her face grow even hotter and silently cursed herself as she put her sword back in its scabbard. Then she walked into the attached bathroom and considered sticking her head in the toilet and drowning herself. Only a small part of her humiliation was because she'd let a vampire sneak up on her while she slept. The majority of it was due to the fact that Erik had seen her naked. Even now, she couldn't believe it had happened.

She quietly groaned and turned on the shower. When the water was warm enough, she stepped beneath it. Between sore muscles and her injury, the ache in her arms was twice as bad, but the pain helped take her mind off—other things. Like the way Erik had looked at her. It had been confusing, seeing that hungry look on his face. Had he been a man looking at a woman? Or a vampire considering his next meal?

That thought was unsettling.

She finished showering, dressed, and left her room, grateful that Erik wasn't around. It was going to be embarrassing enough to face him again and she was in no hurry to do so.

She went into the living room, not really sure what she wanted to do. For several minutes she wandered aimlessly, reacquainting herself with the familiar objects and the memories they brought. Trailing her finger along the back of the old blue couch, she remembered when she and Jess were kids, how they'd race through the room and jump on the couch at the same time. They'd done it so often they'd eventually broken a spring. Gerard had threatened to throw it out, but the girls had begged him to keep it since it was their favorite.

There was a matching recliner sitting a little off balance beside it; also the victim of exuberant childhood antics.

On the mantel were the family photos. She picked up one of her and Jess, standing arm in arm. Though they wore smiles on their faces, their eyes held similar haunted looks—the kind that comes from finding out at too young an age just how harsh and unfair life can be.

Suddenly she really missed her sister. It had been three weeks since she'd last talked to Jess. At that time, Jess had been planning a trip to the States to deliver the latest Death Rider sword to Gerard's cousin, Admiral Charles Winslow.

It seemed that the United States, which had been vampire-free for hundreds of years, was suddenly suffering an epidemic of them. It had started two years ago, when the U.S. military accidentally discovered two unidentifiable creatures in South America that bore a marked resemblance to living gargoyle statues. Uncle Charles had recognized the creatures as *chupacabras,* but not before the creatures had attacked three men, turning two into vampires and one into a changeling—a half-vampire, half-human.

The entire group—chupacabras included—ended up in Washington, D.C., where a second changeling was created. At this point Uncle Charles had stepped in. He turned the changelings into Night Slayers and gave them the Death Rider sword—a sword that gives a slayer an almost mystical ability to kill vampires. Unfortunately, there was only one sword in existence and as the vampire population grew, a second sword was needed.

Gerard was the only one with the knowledge and skill to craft a Death Rider sword, and when he'd finished the second one, Jess had agreed to deliver it.

Thinking of Gerard reminded her why she'd come home—to say good-bye. There was no point in staying if he wasn't coming back in the next day or so. She'd move to the States and hope to schedule a trip to England as soon as she could—which could be difficult once she started a new job.

What a mess.

At that moment, her stomach growled and she realized how hungry she was. Knowing there was virtually nothing in the kitchen to eat, she decided to run into town. She remembered Erik's order that she stay inside and smiled. Who did he think he was? Her lord and master? Well, she did not take orders from him.

Going back to her room, she strapped her sword harness to her back and pulled on a jacket. Fortunately, the chill of the March air wouldn't make wearing the jacket too uncomfortable. Then she left the castle.

Outside, the moon was up and it lit her way as she crossed the clearing at the edge of the woods. As she entered the murky forest, she wished she'd thought to bring a flashlight.

"Going somewhere?"

Erik's voice floated out of the darkness, startling her. She looked toward the sound and saw the faint glow of his eyes where he leaned against a tree.

"What are you doing here?"

She heard him growl. "Waiting for you, of course."

"You didn't trust me to stay inside?"

"Unfair of me, wasn't it, not to trust you to mind me?" He pushed away from the tree and came up to her. "Now, where do you think you're going?"

"Into town for food, if you must know."

"Not tonight. You can afford to skip a meal."

She gaped at his rudeness. "No."

"I insist," he said more forcefully. "Go inside, Kacie."

"You can't make me." In one quick motion, she stepped back and pulled her sword, holding it ready.

"Please," he scoffed, coming forward and knocking her sword to the side as carelessly as if it were a rolled piece of paper. Before she could recover, he gripped her upper arms, the one hand pressing against the stitches of her wound. He tightened his grip, twisting the skin until she cried out in pain.

She felt the cloth of her sleeve grow moist and knew he'd opened the wound, making it bleed. "You son of a bitch," she exclaimed, pulling free. She shrugged out of the jacket enough to see her blood-soaked sleeve.

Erik reached out and pinched the damp fabric between his thumb and fingers. When he pulled his hand back, his fingers were covered in blood. He raised it to his nose and inhaled. "Ah, there is nothing sweeter than the smell of human blood." He licked his fingers and swallowed, groaning. "Yours in particular." His eyes grew brighter, their crimson light becoming a beacon in the night. "Go back to the castle, Kacie, where you'll be safe from the vampires—from me."

She noticed that his breathing had quickened and his fists were clenched tightly in an effort to control himself. For the first time in her life, she wondered if Erik might actually attack her.

Angry and wary, she backed away. He'd made it impossible for her to do anything until the bleeding stopped, so she turned and stormed back to the castle.

When she reached the main door, she looked back once and saw that he had disappeared into the night.

When Erik saw Kacie look back, he stepped behind the tree and closed his eyes. That small amount of blood he'd licked from his finger had been a taste, nothing more, but oh—how it made his body feel alive. How long had it been since he'd had human blood?

Too damn long.

He'd meant to hurt her; cause her a small measure of

the pain she'd caused him, though he argued inwardly that it had been for her own good. She wouldn't go to town with her arm bleeding. To do so would be like sending out a broadcast message inviting vampires to stalk her.

He risked another look at the castle and saw that the door was closed, and knew she was inside. Now he could continue with his original plans without worrying about her.

It took Kacie fifteen minutes to stop the bleeding, clean the blood from her arm, and change shirts. Ten minutes later, she was barreling down the path holding her sword in one hand and a high-candlepower spotlight in the other. She remembered Jess telling her about how such a spotlight had been used in Washington, D.C., to kill a vampire. She'd found this particular one in the laundry room. If Erik wanted to stop her now, let him try. She'd turn his ass to stone.

Erik walked through the streets of town, his thoughts in a chaotic tangle. He knew what Michael would do to Kacie if he got his hands on her. He'd done the same thing once, long ago, to avenge the deaths of loved ones. Even now, part of him seethed for justice. He wanted to avenge Sedrick's death. But he'd taken a vow to protect Kacie—he couldn't just ignore it.

What about the pact? If Sedrick's killer wasn't found, would Michael still honor it? Or would he break it as Erick had threatened to do? If he did, how many innocent people would die then?

He took a deep breath and tried to clear the emotions from his thoughts. He needed to be clearheaded and logical—now especially.

The prickling of awareness skittered across his mind like the shadow of a cloud passing above. He focused on it until he recognized the signature essence of the vampire lurking up ahead.

"Evening, Ty," Erik called out, announcing his presence. A moment later, a tall, gangly youth stepped out of a darkened storefront doorway. His hair was light blond, and despite being four hundred years old, he looked seventeen. His expression was grim as he walked up to Erik. When they were close enough, he clasped Erik's hand and pulled him forward for a manly hug.

"Erik, it's good to see you. How are you?"

"I've been better, and you?"

Ty shook his head. "It's bad business, that's what it is. I just can't believe it—Sedrick dead. I mean—really dead. I never thought it would happen to any of us." He paused to collect himself. "I guess I was being naive." He shook his head. "I don't suppose you've found his killer?"

"Not yet," Erik lied. He wasn't quite ready to share his dilemma with anyone. "How is Michael?"

Ty grimaced. "Not good. He and Sedrick were so close. Right now, he's focused on getting revenge. I don't know what'll happen later. Things are so different now with Sedrick gone."

The two fell silent, each lost in their grief and memories of the friend they'd lost. Finally, Erik held out his hand. "I've got to go," he muttered. He started to leave, but Ty gripped his hand a little tighter, holding on. When Erik looked into the boyish face, it seemed like Ty wanted to say something, but then thought better of it.

He gave a sad smile and released Erik's hand. "Be

careful." Then he turned and hurried away, leaving Erik alone on the street.

Erik started walking and his thoughts, as they did too often of late, turned to reflections on his past. Growing up as a boy, it had been inevitable that Erik, son of the Earl of Hocksley, would become friends with Viscount Ellington's sons Sedrick and Michael. The three boys had been born within months of each other, so being of similar age and coming from titled families, their education and interests had been the same.

Ty, on the other hand, was eight years their junior and the only son of a local village woman. Erik remembered the hushed whispers that had followed her around town when she became pregnant out of wedlock. It was only later, as Ty matured and began to bear a marked resemblance to both Michael and Sedrick, that the whole community learned of Lord Ellington's indiscretion.

Of course, in those days, it wasn't uncommon for a man to take a lover out of wedlock and Lord Ellington didn't care enough about Ty, his mother, or the gossip to see that they were taken care of or to send them away. Lady Ellington, however, had found it hard to ignore the fact that her loving husband had slept with another woman and fathered a child.

Michael and Sedrick knew that her failing health had had something to do with the young boy who had taken to following them around. This caused the beginning of the boys' relationship to get off to a rocky start. Over time, though, Ty's constant presence became expected and it wasn't long before all four boys were inseparable.

Erik stopped walking and glanced up. He'd reached Myrtle's, so he went inside. On top of his other problems, his business manager Penny had called him and insisted they meet in person tonight to discuss "issues." He wasn't sure what "issues" couldn't be discussed over the phone, but he had a suspicion.

The usual crowd was gathered and they all stopped what they were doing long enough to look him over when he walked in. Then, just as quickly, he was dismissed and they returned to their conversations and games of cards or darts.

Erik scanned the room for the thirty-something woman of classic beauty and short platinum hair, wearing an impeccably fitted suit. She should have stood out from the gathered crowd. He felt a flash of annoyance when he realized she wasn't there, because it meant he'd have to go to her room. Lately, she'd strongly hinted that she'd like to make their relationship more personal.

Moving to the stairs, he understood now why she'd mentioned her room number to him when they'd talked on the phone. It was going to be difficult to keep things strictly business while talking in her bedroom, which was no doubt her plan.

Heaving a resigned sigh, he went up to the second floor. He found the door easily enough and after knocking, waited for her to answer. Soon he heard the sound of approaching footsteps followed by the deadbolt being thrown back.

"Hello, love," she cooed, all smiles. "Thanks for meeting me. Won't you come in?"

Erik took one look at her appearance and almost allowed his jaw to fall open. Instead of the business skirt, blouse, and jacket he was used to seeing her in, she wore a clingy dress that hugged her curves so tightly, there was no doubt in his mind that she wasn't wearing bra or panties. "Penny, you look," he began, struggling for the right word, "great."

She flushed under the compliment. "Thank you."

"Are you meeting someone? Maybe I should come back some other time."

She laughed and it was a delicate sound. "Nonsense. I'm meeting you. Come in, won't you?"

He hesitated. "I thought we might talk downstairs."

She waved aside his suggestion. "It's much too noisy down there. Besides, no one will bother us here."

There was no way to politely refuse, so he followed her inside. She closed the door, turned, and approached him, lightly placing her hand on his chest and leaning up to kiss his jaw by way of greeting. In itself, it was a common enough gesture, but she didn't immediately step away from him as would have been expected. He looked down into her eyes, noticing the way her body pressed against his.

The temptation was nearly overwhelming. He thought of all the reasons he shouldn't take advantage of the situation, none of which had to do with Penny not knowing he was a vampire. He'd learned long ago how to keep that secret from his lovers.

When Penny tipped her head back with an obvious invitation on her lips, he found himself wanting to accept. Maybe being with Penny would take his mind off a certain someone else.

At the edge of the woods outside of town, Kacie found a place to stash the spotlight because it was too cumbersome to carry while she walked around. Besides, between the moon and the street lamps, there was enough light to see where she was going.

Moving with unhurried steps, she kept a wary eye out for vampires as she headed for the nearest pub. When she reached it, she was about to go inside when the door opened and a lone man stumbled out.

Kacie recognized him from their school days and watched as he staggered and nearly fell.

"Reggie, is that you?" she asked, rushing up to steady him.

He blinked several times, trying to focus on her face. Then a slow smile tipped his lips. "Kacie? Well, what do you know?" He used the arm draped around her shoulder to pull her close and when he breathed out, she twisted away, trying to avoid the warm breath that smelled of sour ale. "Are you back in town, then?"

"Yes," she said. "I've been working on my Master's at York. I—"

"That's wonderful," he interrupted her, leisurely studying her face. "That's great. Gee, you look good."

She felt herself blush and hoped he didn't notice it. "Thanks. You're looking well."

He pulled himself up a little straighter. "I try to stay in shape, but you know how it is."

Kacie nodded absently, half her attention on the empty streets around them. "Where are you headed, Reggie?"

"Home," he mumbled. "Hey—why don't you come with me? Nancy—you remember Nancy Wilson from school? We got married two years ago. Anyway, Nancy's at home with the baby. I know she'd love to see you."

Kacie considered going but decided against it. "I'm sorry, Reggie. I need to get back home. It was great seeing you, though."

"Yeah, you, too."

She let him pull her close for a hug good-bye and because they were the same height, their belt buckles clanked together with a resounding noise.

"What the—" Reggie pulled back and looked down. Then a slow smile split his face. "Hey, that's one of those special buckles, isn't it? With a concealed knife." He smiled when she nodded. "I saw it on the news."

The buckle had been a gift from Ben who, before they started dating, had been her tae kwon do instructor. He'd bought several buckles from a black market street vendor and had given her one, insisting she wear it whenever she was out alone at night.

"Can I see it?" Reggie asked.

Kacie hesitated, wondering just how drunk he was. At his eager look, though, she nodded. "Sure," she said, sliding the knife from its place in the buckle and handing it to him.

He let the moonlight play across its surface before opening up the blade. "That is one cool knife," he observed.

Kacie smiled. "I like it."

She saw a movement out of the corner of her eye and turned her head to see two men walking toward them. The first man appeared to be about Kacie's age while the second man was younger, perhaps sixteen or seventeen. They looked enough alike to have been brothers, Kacie thought. Both had the same pale blond hair and chiseled good looks.

She kept an eye on them as they walked, not recognizing either of them. As they drew closer, she noticed their attention was on Reggie and the knife. "Maybe I should put that up," she suggested quietly.

"What?" Reggie looked up, obviously surprised they

weren't alone. He started to close the knife and hand it back when it was snatched from his hand. The older man shoved Reggie hard in the chest, causing him to fall back against the teenager, who immediately snaked an arm across Reggie's throat. Despite Reggie's struggles, the youth held him easily.

"Let him go," Kacie demanded.

"I've seen this knife before," the older man said, completely ignoring her. "It was found beside my brother's body." He leaned close to Reggie, waving the blade beneath his nose. "Did you kill my brother?"

"Wh-what?" Reggie stammered. "No. I didn't kill anyone." He tried to back away from the knife, going as far as the younger man let him. "It's not even my kn..." He let the words trail off as three pairs of eyes turned to stare at Kacie.

"That's right," she said. "It's mine."

"Impossible," the man growled, his eyes taking on the crimson glow of a vampire's. "Whoever killed my brother had to have skill and strength."

In one fluid motion, Kacie drew her sword. "That would be me."

"She's only a woman," the younger vampire gasped, sounding incredulous as the older vampire studied her closely.

Kacie held her position, ready in case one or both vampires attacked. They were too intelligent to be progeny, which meant she was facing two primes. Adrenaline surged through her, as did the realization that she could very well die tonight. Suddenly, she wished she'd tried to patch the rift between her and Gerard years ago.

Just then, a shadow shifted at the mouth of the alley not far from them. "What's going on here?"

At the sound of Erik's voice, Kacie almost collapsed with relief. She fought the sudden urge to grin. Her would-be attackers would not stand a chance against the two of them.

"I'm glad you're here."

That was what *she* had wanted to say, yet it was the vampire holding her knife who actually spoke the words out loud. As the implication sank in that these vampires were Erik's friends, Kacie felt like the ground had just crumbled beneath her feet.

Chapter
3

I 've found Sedrick's killer," the older vampire informed Erik, his gaze never leaving Kacie's face.

"Is that right?" Erik asked in a voice that sounded much too calm to Kacie.

"Yes, but you already knew that, didn't you? How else would she have possession of the knife?"

"Maybe I asked her to wear it in order to flush out its owner," Erik suggested.

"Perhaps," the vampire conceded. "However, she's just confessed to the crime."

The lazy expression on Erik's face didn't change as he turned to regard her. "Has she? Well, that wasn't very smart of her." She heard the censure in his tone, but refused to react. She was already in a precarious situation without doing anything to make it worse.

"So, Michael, what do you intend to do now that you've found her?" Erik continued.

"Kill her, of course," Michael said as casually as if they were discussing the weather.

"In all the years I've known you, you've never taken the life of a woman," Erik pointed out.

"In this case, I'm willing to make an exception."

Erik gave her a cold, hard look and she felt the chill of it to her very core. "You should have stayed home." *Like I told you to.* He didn't have to say it out loud for her to hear the words in her head.

Beside her, Reggie cried out in pain as the vampire holding him tightened his grip. Distracted, Kacie turned her head to check on him and in that moment, Michael lunged at her. Her life should have been over there and then, but he never touched her. Instead, Erik was suddenly in front of her, taking the full brunt of Michael's approach.

Apparently, she wasn't the only one shocked by his action.

"What the bloody hell?" Michael exclaimed angrily, his eyes burning brightly in the night as Erik knocked him to the side.

"Michael, don't let your grief make you do something you'll regret."

"I will avenge my brother's death."

"I understand. I want to as well, but I can't let you kill her," Erik said.

Michael frowned. "This is *not* what we agreed."

"I know," Erik admitted with a pained sigh.

Michael's eyes narrowed. "Think carefully on this, Erik. Make sure you know exactly what you're doing. There are much bigger things at risk here than the life of one woman."

Kacie couldn't see Erik's face anymore, so she couldn't

tell whether he was regretting his decision to protect her or not, but she knew she didn't stand a chance without his help. "Erik—"

"Shut up, Kacie," he said, cutting her off. "I'm sorry, but I can't let you do it," Erik said to Michael, sounding a little too remorseful for Kacie's comfort.

A movement from the younger vampire had her swinging her sword instinctively in his direction. He held Reggie before him like a shield and she stayed her blade a hairbreadth from the tender, vulnerable skin of his throat. "Hurt him and I'll kill you," she warned. It would be so easy, but she didn't dare. The situation was precarious enough as it was.

"Either help me or get out of the way," Michael growled at Erik. "She forfeited her life the moment she killed my brother—or have you forgotten?"

"No," Erik growled. "I haven't, but the situation has changed."

"Has it? Sedrick is still dead."

"I mourn his loss, too," Erik said. "But it doesn't change the fact that if you want her, you'll have to go through me first."

"If that's the way you want it . . ." Michael rushed Erik before he even finished speaking and Erik stumbled back several steps before he could stop Michael's forward momentum. Then there was a flurry of movement as fists flew on both sides.

The younger vampire holding Reggie glared at her with dark, hate-filled eyes, but she held her blade steady, daring him to attack.

She risked looking away long enough to see what the other two were doing and saw that both were bleeding from cuts on their faces. Kacie inwardly winced at the dull smack of fists pummeling flesh and bone. She wasn't sure how long they could keep going at this rate, but it seemed like they had no intention of stopping.

She wondered why Erik didn't just pull the sword he kept strapped to his back—unless he'd left the castle without it. Kacie considered making quick work of both vampires, but the thought of skewering a teenager on the end of her sword made her squeamish. She knew he was older than he looked, but the knowledge wasn't helping her any.

As long as the young vampire wasn't attacking Reggie, she would wait. When Erik defeated his opponent, she would strike.

The night dragged on endlessly. At one point, Reggie passed out from the booze he'd consumed, but the vampire continued to hold him. Finally, the fighters' movements started to slow. She could only imagine how much pain they were both in. To make matters worse, dawn was approaching. If they didn't end the fight soon, they were going to have more serious problems to worry about.

"Michael—finish this some other time. We must leave," the younger vampire said, apparently having the same concern Kacie had. "Michael—the time."

"Give over," Michael demanded of Erik between heaving breaths.

"Never," Erik gritted out, sounding just as exhausted. He threw another punch, attempting to draw Michael back into the fight.

"You crazy git, you'd fight right up until dawn turned us both to stone, wouldn't you?"

"If that's what it takes to keep her safe."

Michael stepped out of reach of Erik's fists, shock and dismay written across his face. "You would end all our lives—over a woman?"

"For this woman, yes."

For this woman. The words echoed in Kacie's head. She didn't know who was more surprised by the announcement—she or Michael. Her thoughts raced, searching for the reason behind his statement. It certainly wasn't because he liked her. Then logic asserted itself. He wasn't protecting *her* per se; he was protecting Gerard's daughter.

Michael shook his head. "So—in the end, it was a woman who came between us after all." There was a wealth of sadness in his tone.

Erik said nothing.

"I never wanted to be your enemy," Michael said finally. "But you leave me no choice. We *will* finish this." He gestured to the other vampire and then raised his hand to his forehead, giving Erik a small salute. "The pact is off."

They released Reggie and he fell to the ground. Kacie made ready to swing her sword, but Erik grabbed her arm. "Let them go," he said. Something in his tone got past her anger and caused her to take a good look at him. Moments ago, he'd seemed strong enough to go on for hours. Now he looked ready to collapse.

"You don't look so hot," she said, running her gaze over him. "Are you hurt?" His eyes and lips were swollen and his knuckles were raw and bleeding.

"I'm fine," he muttered. "Maybe you should see to your friend."

She'd forgotten about Reggie, who woke after being dropped, and hurried over to him as he got to his feet. Putting her sword away, she started to reach for him, but dropped her hand when he shied away from her. "Are you all right?" she asked him.

"I'm ... no. What were those things?"

Kacie was conscious of the sky's soft glow, getting brighter as dawn approached. Erik had just saved her life and she owed him something in return. "You deserve an explanation. Unfortunately, I don't have time to give you one. Whatever your mind is telling you about those men—no matter how crazy it might seem—is probably the truth, or close enough to it—so pay attention. Go home and for the next couple of weeks, don't go out after dark. You get off work? You go straight home. No more stopping off for a drink first. Do you understand?"

Reggie nodded.

"Good. It was nice seeing you again. Now, go home and go to bed. When you wake up, this will all seem like a bad dream. Okay?"

He nodded again and took a step back. Then another. Finally, he turned his back to her and walked quickly away.

"Don't you want to make sure he gets home all right?"

Kacie looked at Erik and saw the lines of fatigue etched across his face. "No. He'll be fine." She glanced at the sky again. "We should go."

They headed toward the back path that would take them to the castle. For several minutes, she was aware that Erik was struggling to keep up with her. "Maybe I'd better help," she suggested.

He turned those dark brooding eyes on her, but shook his head. "I don't want your help."

His refusal was like a sharp slap across the face but she understood. Theirs had never been a relationship based on trust. "Just so you know, if that stubborn pride of yours

gets you turned to stone, I'll leave you here for the birds
to shit on."

His hard expression didn't soften, but after a second
he nodded. It suddenly occurred to her that she'd never
touched him before except for when they were fighting.
This would be different. This would be getting in close;
his body next to hers. His arm around her shoulders. It
was such an intimate position, she wasn't sure she could—
should—go there with him.

Swallowing hard, she closed the distance between
them. Erik never moved. When she was beside him, she
wrapped her arm around his waist and waited for him to
drape his arm across her shoulders. The warm weight of
it sent fissures of awareness racing through her. The heat
of his body warmed her against the chill of the night air.
It was impossible not to be aware of him. She cast a furtive glance at his face and then felt herself blush. He was
so close. If she turned her body to him just a little, he'd be
close enough to kiss. Her eyes fell to his lips. How would
they feel? Was he a good kisser? Her pulse raced at the
thought.

At that moment, she stumbled on a rock and they both
nearly fell. Kacie took it as a sign to keep her thoughts
focused on the task of getting him to the castle.

"How badly are you hurt?" she asked as they emerged
from the woods.

"A few bruises."

She knew it was worse than that, but didn't press
because they'd reached his door. "What's the pass code?"

"I've got it." He leaned forward and tapped something
into the keypad. Seconds later, she heard the mechanical
sound of a heavy bolt sliding back. As soon as the door

opened, she helped him inside. It seemed that the minute the door was shut and they were sealed away from the approaching dawn, he felt a little better. Though she ached from having supported his weight, she felt oddly bereft when he took his arm from around her shoulders and stepped away.

"I can manage from here, thanks." He glanced at her face. "Are you okay?"

Horrified to think he might guess how she was feeling, she went on the offensive. "Michael said that the pact is off. What pact?"

He sighed, lifting a hand to rub his temples as if his head hurt. "Kacie, can we do this some other time? The sun's coming up, we're both tired. Let's get some rest and talk tonight."

"I don't want to wait until tonight—I want to know what's going on with you and those vampires."

Erik's eyes grew bright with irritation, but she didn't care. She stood her ground and stared defiantly. "I want some answers."

"Why can't you leave well enough alone? You want answers? Fine. Here they are. *Those vampires,* as you put it, are my friends. Years ago, we made a no-feed, no-hunt pact. The vampires don't feed off the residents of Hocksley, especially members of the Winslow family, and in return, I don't allow the Winslow slayers to hunt them."

She looked at him, shocked and confused. "But we *did* hunt them. Growing up—we killed scores of vampires."

"Yes, we did. Mostly progeny, which are exempt from the pact because they're a threat to us all. The others were primes from other lairs."

"*Other* lairs? How many lairs are there?" She felt stunned. It had never occurred to her that there would be more than one in the area.

Erik shrugged. "I don't know, exactly."

She looked around as if she could see out the solid walls of his dungeon apartment. "They could be all over the place. They could be in our own back yard and we don't even know it."

"Relax. Michael's lair is the only one in the immediate area and his isn't that close to the castle."

"How do you know?" she asked sharply.

He didn't answer, but she saw it in his face. "You know where his lair is, don't you? How long have you known? Years? Decades?" His expression didn't change. "Centuries?" He blinked and she felt like she'd been hit with a board. "You bastard," she spit out. "You've known all this time and did nothing to destroy them?"

"It's more complicated than that."

"Not from where I'm standing," she bit out.

Erik sank to a stool by the kitchen counter, his exhaustion evident. "Not all vampires kill humans," he muttered. "I don't. Michael and the vampires in his lair don't. That's why we have the pact; it's a live and let live arrangement."

"Live and let live?" She repeated dumbly, her hands fisting in her hair to keep her head from exploding. "Then why is my entire family dead? Tell me that, will you?"

He sighed. "Michael's vampires didn't kill your family. Those vampires came from a different lair."

"How do you know?"

This time, his look was stark and cold. "Because that's what they told me—right before I killed them."

Another chill ran down her spine, but she couldn't help feeling the small surge of satisfaction in learning that her family's deaths had been avenged. Despite everything else, she was grateful to Erik for that.

"That night your family was killed," he continued, "I charged Michael with finding their killers—and he did. When we found Sedrick's body, he asked me to help him find his brother's killer. And I had every intention of finding him and turning him over to Michael—until I realized it was you."

She didn't have to ask him what Michael intended to do if he got his hands on her. "Thank you," she mumbled.

He shook his head. "Don't thank me yet, Kacie, because I'm not sure I made the right decision. You see, Sedrick wasn't just Erik's brother, he was my friend. *My friend,* Kacie. Can you understand that? These two men have been closer to me than my own brothers were when we were alive. Then you came home and in less than forty-eight hours, you've killed one and put me in the precarious position of possibly having to kill the other." He shook his head. "No, definitely don't thank me."

His eyes heated to a bright crimson and then he shook his head again. "I don't expect you to understand. Now, if you'll excuse me, I'm going to bed."

After Kacie left him, Erik locked both doors to his apartment. He was tired and wanted to rest, but when he finally had a chance to lie down, sleep eluded him.

So—in the end, it was a woman who came between us after all. Michael's words echoed in his head, dredging up a long-forgotten memory.

In the spring of his nineteenth year, when he'd had

everything in life to look forward to, he was in love. Her name was Alise and her smile was the sun that brightened his days; her voice was the song in his heart. There was nothing he wouldn't do for her. For weeks, they'd been sneaking around, hiding their love from family and friends.

On one fateful day, Erik had come to a momentous decision and, anxious to share the good news with Alise, had hurried out to the old oak tree where he hoped to find her sketching. Art was just one of the many interests they shared.

His heart racing in anticipation, he spied the tree up ahead and saw her sitting on the other side, her back to him. *Alise.* His mind whispered the word as he broke into a run. He was almost to her when he realized she wasn't alone.

"Your eyes are as blue as the clearest day," a familiar, deep voice said gently. "And your skin, as soft as a newborn lamb's wool. Let me make love to you, Alise."

She gave a soft giggle, but Erik was too focused on the man beside her to hear it. When he rounded the tree to face the couple, his pulse was pounding in his ears.

"Michael." He spit out the name as he drew his sword. "I'm going to skewer your traitorous heart."

"Erik? What the hell...?" Michael scrambled to his feet and out of reach of the sword's blade. "Do you mind?" he shouted in indignation. "I'm sharing a private moment with my future wife."

"What? How dare you." It was all Erik could do not to run him through right then and there. "She is mine. I was coming to propose just now."

"Well, you're too late."

Erik glanced at Alise, wanting to see her deny it. She seemed unfazed, saying nothing and watching with eyes wide with curiosity.

Erik used the blade of his sword to force Michael back. "I told you I was seeing someone."

Michael glared at him. "But you never told me her name."

"I was trying to protect her reputation."

"As was I," Michael growled.

Though he stood there defending Alise's honor, Erik knew things could never be the same. How could he ever be with her and *not* remember that she'd once been with Michael? "Draw your sword, Michael, and let us settle this. I will not fight an unarmed man."

He placed the tip of his blade beneath Michael's sword handle and flicked it up into the air where Michael snatched it.

"*En garde,*" Erik growled as soon as Michael faced him. "Win or lose, Michael, we are done. I will not be friends with a liar and a cheat."

"Nor I," Michael replied, raising his sword.

Erik swung his blade and the fight was on. The clashing blades echoed loudly on the hillside. Erik spared a quick glance at Alise and saw that she stood near the trunk of the tree, watching intently. The sight maddened Erik further and he renewed his efforts to beat Michael.

As they continued to fight, Erik became aware of a new presence. He shot a quick glance at Alise and saw that Sedrick had joined her.

"What do we have here?" Sedrick asked jovially, obviously unconcerned that his brother and friend were dueling. "Are we showing off for the sweet Alise?" He chuckled.

"Alise, my pet, are you impressed with the prowess these men demonstrate before you?"

"I'm afraid they might hurt each other," Alise said, her voice as dulcet as the sweetest songbird's.

"I doubt it," Sedrick replied. "They are both exceedingly stubborn and would not dare concede victory to the other and I'm afraid their skills are equal. They could be fighting well into the morrow."

"Indeed?" Alise asked.

"Go away, Sedrick," Michael growled as he blocked another of Erik's thrusts.

"Indeed, they could," Erik heard Sedrick reply. "Will you wait? Or perhaps you'd care to come with me? There is a nice spot by the beach that begs to be sketched. I'd love to show it to you."

Alise's reply was too soft to hear but when Erik glanced up, he saw her walking away with Sedrick, arm in arm. Sedrick bent his head close to hers and whispered in her ear. Alise's laughter floated back to them on a breeze. She never even looked back.

"Damn that brother of yours," Erik growled as he and Michael continued to clash swords.

"Sedrick has always been popular with the ladies," Michael replied, breathing hard. "You know that. They think he's charming."

"Charming, my ass." But Erik knew that Michael was right. And though his heart wanted to deny it, in his head he knew that if Alise had truly loved him, she would not have been out with Michael in the first place nor would she have walked off so readily with Sedrick.

So that left him where? Fighting with his best friend? Over a woman? He stepped away from Michael and lowered his sword. Michael had too much honor to keep fighting when it was obvious that Erik had stopped.

"What's this?" He gave Erik a curious look.

"What are we doing?" Erik asked him. "I don't want to kill you."

"Nor I, you," Michael replied.

Erik gestured after Sedrick and Alise. "We're fighting over a woman who has already forgotten us."

Michael gave him that devilish smile of his. "She's unworthy of our affections."

Erik sheathed his sword and though disappointed at the outcome, was glad not to have to kill his friend. He held out his hand to Michael. "I apologize, Michael. Forgive me?"

Michael sheathed his sword and grasped Erik's hand. "Never again will I let anything—or anyone—stand in the way of our friendship."

"Agreed."

Michael clapped him on the back. "Shall we go into town? I know a couple of wenches there whose charms are ample enough to satisfy any man and the ale never stops flowing. What do you say?"

That night, they'd drowned their sorrows in ale and found a measure of forgetfulness in the arms of loose women. In the course of the evening, something passed between them, forging a bond that would not be broken.

Six years later, Erik had been killed in a bizarre hunting accident by a creature later discovered to be a chupacabra. When he came back to life as a vampire, Michael showed the world that he'd taken his vow seriously by going in search of the chupacabra that had killed his friend. Sedrick, of course, couldn't allow his brother to go alone and went with him. Erik wasn't sure how Ty had come to be with them on that fateful night when they actually found the creature, but two nights later, all three were vampires.

For Erik and Michael, not even death, it seemed, had come between them. Their friendship had withstood the test of death, the test of time—and numerous other tests along the way. Sadly, it didn't look like it would survive Kacie.

Chapter 4

W ho the hell is she?" Michael demanded, pacing across the floor of his underground lair. The cavern would have been pitch black except for the battery-operated lanterns throwing out their dim light. Other than the fact that the room was underground, it looked much like the kind of great room found in almost any home. A huge tapestry hung behind the couch, which was old but functional. The two large side chairs looked like they'd been heavily used. There was an area rug laid across the floor and at the moment, Michael was well on his way to wearing it thin with his pacing. He was so mad that he wanted to put a fist through the wall, only these walls were made of solid rock and not even he could put a dent in them.

"I think that might have been young Kacie." In contrast to Michael's agitated pacing, Ty appeared relaxed, sitting sideways in one of the oversized chairs with his legs draped over one arm. "That was the name I heard him use."

Michael stopped and stared at him in shock. "No. It couldn't be. I thought she went off to college."

"She did, but that was several years ago. I'm sure she's finished by now."

"Has it been that long already?" Michael thought back, trying to figure out just how many years had passed. "You'd think Erik would have said something to us."

"Maybe he didn't know she was coming home."

It was possible, Michael silently conceded.

"She's certainly aged nicely," Ty went on with obvious male appreciation.

Michael glared at him. "I didn't happen to notice. I was a little preoccupied with the fact that my best friend was stopping me from avenging my brother's death," he snapped.

"He was my brother, too," Ty pointed out sullenly.

Half-brother. Michael had to bite his tongue to keep from saying the word out loud. The distinction wasn't important. He was just feeling testy because Ty seemed to be defending Erik.

He took a deep breath to calm himself and focused his thoughts. "If that was Kacie, then there's no hoping Erik will come to his senses."

"Because she's Gerard's daughter?"

Michael nodded. "That, but primarily because of the vow he made to Vince." He thought back to the moment of Erik's appearance and the look he'd given the woman. Had there been something more behind the fierce protectiveness? Something that would prevent Erik from avenging his friend's death—and destroy the friendship he and

Michael shared? Michael clenched his hand into a fist, anger surging through him.

"What are you going to do?" Ty asked softly from across the room.

Michael hated having Erik as an enemy and not just because he'd lost his best friend. Erik's cunning mind and fighting skills were not things he wanted to go up against. "I don't know." In that moment of loneliness, he saw Sedrick's face as it had appeared in life. There was really only one course of action. "I can't let her live and if Erik gets in the way again, then..." He hesitated, feeling more alone than he ever had before. "Then, I'll have to kill him, too."

Ty sighed. "I hate this. Maybe—"

He was interrupted by the sound of shouting and arguing from the antechamber of the cavern. Instantly, Ty jumped to his feet and the two raced out of the room.

When they reached the antechamber, they found the lair primes crowded around something that lay on the floor between them. Michael couldn't see what it was, but the stench of fresh blood hung heavy in the air.

"What's going on," he demanded of no one in particular.

Carrington, a relatively large but youthful vampire converted fifty years earlier, looked up from the center with a defiant expression plastered across his face. "You never told us how fantastic human blood could be."

"What?" Michael surged forward, tossing the primes closest to him out of the way so he could see the extent of the damage done. The rest of the primes moved back, leaving Carrington standing over the fresh corpse of a middle-aged farmer. Fury rose up in Michael as he glared around the room. "Who gave you permission to hunt humans?"

"Erik did, when he broke the pact," Carrington replied,

squaring off with Michael, his very stance challenging Michael's authority.

Michael wanted to know how Carrington knew about Erik, but now was not the time to ask. Moving quickly, he caught Carrington by the throat and heaved him across the room before the other vampire knew what was happening. The rest of the vampires cleared out of Michael's way as he stormed forward, hoisted Carrington up by the front of his shirt and backhanded him across the face with enough force that the man's head slammed into the wall.

Michael waited for the man to recover and then stepped back, inviting him with a gesture to attack him in return. To his delight, Carrington charged.

Michael's fists shot out in rapid succession, finding their mark. Carrington stumbled and Michael slammed him against the wall. Michael, being more experienced in combat, could have put a quick end to the fight, but he allowed it to continue for two reasons. First, he needed someone on whom to vent his anger and frustration and second, it was important that he make an example of Carrington to the others and the message he was sending shouldn't be rushed.

When Carrington recovered from the last blow to his head, he bent low and rushed Michael, catching him in the stomach. The impact forced the air from Michael's lungs; as he tried to catch his breath, Carrington drove him backward, into the wall. Pinned there, Michael clapped his hands over Carrington's ears. As the large vampire howled in pain, Michael brought his elbows down on either side of Carrington's neck, forcing him to his knees.

Michael grabbed Carrington's hair, pulled his head back and drove his fist into Carrington's face. The blow was hard enough to knock Carrington out and Michael watched the body slump to the floor. Then he turned to the others, glaring at each one in turn before addressing them as a group.

"*I* will tell you when the pact is broken, do you understand? *I* am the leader of this lair and if you live here, you live by my rules—or you die by my hand. Is that understood?" There was silence. "Is there anyone here who does *not* understand and wants me to explain it again?"

When the silence had stretched on long enough, he nodded. "The pact is still in effect until I tell you otherwise. This is my only warning. Next time I find someone has fed off a human, I won't be as lenient."

He walked back toward the doorway leading to the main living area and stopped just before he reached it. "Someone stake that human and dump the body in the ocean."

Ty followed him into the other room. "Do you think that was wise?" he asked quietly.

Michael went to the far wall and stood staring at the painting that hung there. Erik had given it to him years ago and while Michael wasn't a big fan of art, he used to like this particular piece. "You think I need to worry about Carrington?"

"Yes, I do," Ty answered. "I don't think he's someone you can beat into submission."

"What would you have done?"

"Killed him. By leaving him alive, you're giving him a chance to defy you again."

"That's your problem, Ty. You're always looking for the easy way out." He heard Ty's intake of breath and knew he'd insulted the boy. "I'm sorry. I guess I'm feeling a bit edgy."

There was a moment of silence as each retreated into his own thoughts. Then from across the room, Ty spoke. "What are you going to do about Erik?"

"He's got one more night to bring her to me."

"And when he doesn't?"

Michael stared at the painting of the big oak tree, its long branches almost blocking the sun as it set over the ocean off in the distance. He thought if he stared at it long and hard enough, he might be able to transport himself back to a happier place and time.

But he knew that wasn't possible. With a sigh, he turned and faced Ty. "Tomorrow, if Erik hasn't brought her to me, then they both must die."

Kacie woke up and saw from her dark windows that she'd slept through the day and night had fallen. She wasn't surprised. After everything that had happened the night before, she'd found it hard to relax enough to fall asleep right away. Every time she closed her eyes, she saw familiar nightmare images from the attack twenty years ago. She'd tried to recall the soothing tones of The Voice, but couldn't. And she'd refused to use the iPod simply because she didn't want anyone sneaking up on her again.

Getting out of bed, she left her room and went downstairs to the kitchen. To her surprise, Erik was sitting at the kitchen table. He seemed very relaxed, sitting bare-chested, wearing a pair of faded jeans and no shoes, reading a paper.

"What are you doing here?" she asked, feeling grumpy.

"What's the matter with you? Didn't you sleep well?" His voice held a touch of irritation.

"As a matter of fact, I didn't," she admitted, looking

around to see if by some stroke of luck he'd made a pot of tea. He hadn't.

"Welcome to my world," he replied, a definite smugness in his voice.

She ignored him while she searched the pantry for instant tea bags, slightly surprised when she actually found some. Next, she dug in the cupboard for a cup and filled it with water. Dropping in the bag, she placed the cup in the microwave and turned it on.

"So, you didn't answer my question," she said, turning to lean back against the counter. "What are you doing here?"

He waved a hand at two cans of soup and a box of crackers sitting on the counter. "You said last night that there wasn't any food in the house. I found these downstairs in my apartment."

She stared at the food, confused by the gesture. How could she tell him that she'd had her heart set on a big roast beef sandwich at Myrtle's or that two cans of soup might not fill her up? She didn't want to be rude. After all, the situation the night before with the two primes would have been much worse if he hadn't stepped in. "Thanks."

He shrugged. "No problem. I didn't want you to go hungry."

She didn't like the sound of that and stared at him suspiciously. "Because you think I wouldn't want to go back into town and eat at Myrtle's?"

"No, because you're not going into town tonight."

Arms folded, she faced him and cocked an eyebrow in mock surprise. She knew she should be used to Erik telling her what to do—he'd done it ever since he'd started teaching her fencing. "Is that right?"

Erik purposely set his paper down on the table. "That's right. Didn't you listen to anything I told you last night? Michael's going to have his followers out en masse looking for you."

"Good." She casually flipped a strand of hair over her shoulder. "Let them come. It will save me from having to go look for them."

Erik pushed away from the table and came to stand in front of her. His eyes shimmered with an angry glow though his voice was even. "Don't leave the castle tonight, do you understand?"

She felt an uncomfortable warmth spread over her at his nearness and though she tried to keep her eyes fixed on his, she couldn't seem to stop them from taking in the broad expanse of shoulders and muscled chest before her. The hair on his chest looked especially dark against the paleness of his skin.

Never in her wildest imagination had she thought Erik would look this good, and a different kind of hunger started burning inside her. Unable to resist, her gaze slipped to below his navel where the dark hairs trailed downward, disappearing beneath the waistband of his jeans.

His hand strayed to his waistband and he undid the first button. Mesmerized, she watched his fingers move to the second button. When he undid it, the fabric parted and she saw he wasn't wearing boxers or briefs. The dark trail of hair continued downward and if he undid one more button, he was going to be taking their relationship to a whole new level.

She waited with bated breath to see what he would do and when his fingers moved to undo the third button, she panicked.

"What are you doing?" She asked breathlessly, her eyes shooting to his face.

"Giving you a better look, since you can't do me the courtesy of looking me in the face."

She was mortified. "I'm sorry. I didn't mean to stare." What was she thinking? She was looking at him like he was Matthew McConaughey. Not a bloodsucking killer. "Wh-what were you saying?"

"I don't want you leaving the castle tonight. It's too dangerous."

"What about you?" she said, pleased that her voice sounded normal again. "After last night, you're probably on their hit list as well."

"I can take care of myself," he said, buttoning his pants.

"So can I," she shot back.

"Michael's not the only threat out there, Kacie. Things aren't like they were when you were growing up. They've gotten worse."

That took her by surprise. "How much worse?"

At first, she wasn't sure he'd answer her, but she had to give him credit. He never looked away. "Last month, I killed twenty vampires."

Kacie was glad she was leaning against the counter because she suddenly felt weak. "Twenty?" The number was nearly incomprehensible. There'd never been more than two or three a week. "That's unreal. Were all the victims from Hocksley?" The town wasn't large enough that so many could disappear without alarming the authorities.

"No. Most were from outside the area."

There were enough little towns and villages around that it was possible, but why bring them back here? Unless . . . the lair was here. "It sounds like Michael's already broken the pact," she said.

This time, he did look away. "Maybe. Or maybe one of the other lairs is getting larger and has expanded their hunting ground. In any case, I'm looking into it." He held up his hand to stop her when she opened her mouth to speak. "The point is, it's not safe for you to be out roaming about town by yourself."

An idea had come to her while he'd been talking. "If they broke the pact first, then the situation here has changed. Not only are we both targets, but now the townspeople are in danger." She paused to let her point sink in. "Erik, we have to stop them before it's too late." His gaze left her face once more to stare off into the distance, but she knew he was still listening, so she hurried on. "Tell me where the lair is and tomorrow, after the sun comes up, I'll end this."

She waited as he seemed to consider her suggestion. When he turned back to look at her, his expression was hard.

"You know, I believe you'd do it. Go in and kill them, without conscience or regret. Some of them deserve it, I admit—but do you know which ones? Do you know which vampire is the escaped convict and which is the man who died because he was working three jobs to feed his family and had the bad luck to fall asleep in the wrong place at the wrong time? Do you know which one used to beat his wife every night because he enjoyed inflicting pain and which one is the returned World War II hero who, in trying to build a new life for his wife and unborn child, had the misfortune of being out after dark on the wrong night?

I could go on but I think you understand my point. So no, I won't tell you where the lair is."

He shook his head and glared at her, making her feel small and insignificant. "Do me a favor," he continued. "Give me your word that you'll stay in tonight so I won't have to lock you away somewhere."

His words shocked her. "I'll stay inside," she agreed because she had a feeling he was serious. She refused to look away when he held her gaze.

Finally, he nodded and walked off, presumably heading back down to his apartment, though she didn't follow him.

Instead, she fumed. Where did his loyalties really lie? It was vampire nature to want to feed off humans and yet, for as long as she'd known him, he'd never fed off one— and he'd killed probably a hundred or more of his own kind. Yet he claimed these few vampires were his closest friends and for years now, had had some type of pact with them. She wondered if Gerard was aware of such a pact and guessed he wasn't, or he would have told her and Jess about it. So, how far could she trust Erik? Would there come a time—in the very near future—when she would have to kill him?

The thought left her depressed.

Taking her cup from the microwave, she discarded the bag and took a sip. The hot liquid slid down her throat and warmed her from the inside out. Carrying her cup with her, she left Erik's apartment and went through the main part of the castle to the family room where she sat in the old recliner to think about the conversation she'd just had with him. Several parts of it bothered her, not the least of which was the number of vampires Erik had recently killed.

There were only two ways to produce vampires—either by vampires killing people or chupacabras killing people. That meant that someone wasn't sticking to the no-feed pact or there was a chupacabra colony nearby. For years it had been assumed the colony had died out.

Erik hadn't told her whether the vampires he'd killed had been progeny or primes, so she didn't know which scenario she was dealing with.

She sighed. This trip was supposed to have been relatively simple. Come home, maybe try to patch things up with Gerard, pack the last of her belongings, and say goodbye. Now it looked like she'd have to save the patching-things-up part until some other time. Finishing the last of her tea, she carried her empty cup into the kitchen to rinse it.

The house seemed empty without Jess and Gerard around and she found herself strolling into Gerard's study, off the main room.

Immediately, she was surrounded by the stale smoky aroma of Gerard's favorite cigars. It had bothered her as a child, but now the familiar scent was comforting. She walked around the room, gazing at the swords hanging on the walls in between the filled floor-to-ceiling bookcases. Everything here was just as she remembered it.

Going over to Gerard's desk, she sat down in the chair. It creaked under her weight, just as it always had when Gerard sat in it. Closing her eyes, she imagined him sitting there. He'd look up and smile when she entered the room. Then he'd put whatever he was working on to the side so he could give her his full attention.

She missed those days.

Opening her eyes, she let her gaze scan the surface of

the ancient desk. So much history behind this desk. She wondered if it had been in the family as far back as Erik's time. Had he or any of his three brothers sat at it, writing letters or balancing ledgers?

She trailed a finger along the wood, feeling the texture of the grain. In doing so, she noticed a stack of letters, rubber-banded together and sitting off to the side. Curious, she picked them up and looked at the return name and address. They were correspondences from Gerard's cousin Charles, over in the States.

Charles Winslow was an Admiral in the Navy, retired now that he was working and living with the two Night Slayers.

Curious, she flipped through the letters and saw they were in order, going back almost three years.

She opened the first couple and read them. They predated the finding of the chupacabras and weren't all that interesting. The fourth one she opened was dated about two years ago. She scanned it quickly.

...found two unidentifiable creatures in the Amazon. One is adult and the other is much younger. I can't go myself, but I've talked my friend Clinton Weber into going. You remember him. He will be cautious and let me know if they are, in fact, chupacabras...

She folded the letter, replaced it and pulled another out, dated several months later, after one of the vampires created by the adult chupacabra had tried to assassinate the President. Kacie had heard bits and pieces of the story.

...it was most peculiar. Mac swears that when he got back to the hotel room, Lanie was dead. Thank God he didn't stake her there and then. I'm not sure exactly how it happened, but the baby chupacabra, which had been in

*their room, broke free and bit Lanie, injecting her with its
venom. Instead of turning her into a vampire or a changeling, it miraculously restored her to life. She made a full
recovery. Whether Lanie was really dead or not, we can't
be certain, but there is something about the young chupacabra's venom that is different from the adult's. I wish
Clinton were here to study it but he has disappeared. I
guess he thought that being a vampire, it was too great a
threat to his daughter and others...*

She read the rest quickly, then put it away. The next
letter spoke of the new assistant Charles had hired. Judging from his tone, he was fond of this woman. Kacie continued to read, ignoring the guilt brought on by invading
Gerard's privacy. Despite the façade of indifference she
wore, she'd missed her family and eagerly devoured all
the news of the things that had taken place while she was
away at university.

Two hours later, Kacie had read all but the last letter
and was finally growing bored. She studied the postmark
of the last one and saw that it had been received just last
week. It was from Jessica, and Kacie opened it wondering
if there was anything in it she didn't already know from
talking to her sister a couple of weeks ago.

She scanned the lines quickly.

*...an entire chupacabra colony living in the cemetery
behind the old Winslow Manor...helped deliver a baby
chupacabra...so exciting...tracked the serial killer vampire to his lair in the cemetery...he got away...John and
his vampire friend Harris set a trap...destroyed him...*

Jess had already shared with Kacie most of the story
of her adventures with the serial killer turned vampire,
so there was nothing new. She folded the letter and was

just putting it away when a flicker of light outside the window caught her attention. She quickly turned off the desk lamp and hurried over to the window to look out. The full moon was out and its light glinted off Erik's white shirt as he walked across the lawn toward the wooded path that led to Hocksley.

Where was he going, she wondered? He shouldn't be outside any more than she should. About to shrug it off, another thought occurred to her. Maybe he was going to the lair to meet his friends. But Hocksley lay at the other end of the path and it was doubtful the lair was in town. That meant the lair had to be someplace near the town so that it was faster to take the path to get to it than to go the opposite way along the road through the countryside.

The path to town ran closer to the cliff's edge and so, in a way, that made more sense. There were caves all through the area, she had no doubt. And there was the cemetery.

Her thoughts ground to a halt. That was it. The lair had to be in the cemetery. Hadn't Jess told her that when they finally found the killer, he'd made his lair in the cemetery? It was perfect.

Kacie decided that's where she needed to focus her attention—but not tonight. She'd go tomorrow, when it was daylight.

Feeling better now that she had a plan of action, Kacie turned to the books in Gerard's study. He wasn't one for popular fiction, so her choices for reading material were limited to wartime history or local history. She chose the latter and settled in for a long evening of reading and soup.

The evening passed quietly and Kacie didn't see Erik again before sunrise. Her alarm went off too early in the

morning and after a few false starts, she finally dragged
herself from bed only to discover it pouring down rain
outside. She was anxious to search the cemetery for the
vampires' lair, but resigned herself to waiting and fell
back asleep.

When she woke up later, the rain had stopped. A
glance at the clock showed that it was almost noon. That
was later than she'd wanted to begin her search, but there
were still a good six hours before dark. It was enough to
get started, she decided.

Getting dressed, she went downstairs to the mud room
where the family kept a bin of wooden stakes. She was
torn between taking enough to stake every vampire she
might find versus having her movements hampered by the
weight of hauling around too many. She ended up filling
a small backpack with twenty stakes. If there were more
vampires than that, she would have to improvise.

There wasn't time to go into town to eat so she broke
her fast with crackers and water. Packing a bottle of
water, she made sure she had enough money on her to buy
a decent meal in town after she finished. With luck, she'd
have much to celebrate.

Outside, she crossed the lawn, barely noticing the wet
grass or the cool chill of the afternoon air. Her attention
was focused on getting to the cemetery by the most direct
route.

She hurried along the path through the woods and
when she reached town, headed left. As soon as she could,
she ducked behind a row of houses to cut over to the dirt
road that would take her north to the ancient cemetery.

Few traveled this road anymore since the old cemetery
had run out of space and a newer, larger cemetery had been

built south of town. Only those with long-established families ever came to it, and it was here that the Winslow family mausoleum was located.

Kacie thought some of the larger mausoleums or vaults might be great places for the vampires to sleep during the day—they'd be roomy, dry, and dark.

Reaching the cemetery, she surveyed the area. The place was open on three sides, but the back of the cemetery butted up against the back of the cliff. The trees had grown so large that their limbs formed a rough canopy overhead that cast the grounds below into perpetual shadow. Roots bulged out of the ground, cracking the paved walkways that once ran smoothly throughout. Years of fallen limbs and leaves had been swept into erratic piles by the constant wind.

An overwhelming silence enveloped the place so that Kacie became acutely aware of the sound of her own breathing. She approached the old gate slowly, with reverence, not fear. There was so much history here, the place never failed to impress her.

The gate opened with little protest and she stepped inside. There were all manner of burial sites within and most of the in-ground sites had become overgrown with grass and shrubs until it was hard to tell where one site ended and another began. The headstones ranged from humble markers to huge stone monuments. Her feet, seemingly of their own volition, maneuvered the familiar broken path that led to the far corner where a large mausoleum stood. She stopped before the ornate iron door and looked at the name inscribed across the doorway: WINSLOW.

Sliding back the bolt, she pushed on the door. It opened

on well-oiled hinges and she went inside. The murky darkness swallowed her and if she'd been more prone to fantastical imaginings, she might have been frightened, but life had taught her to be realistic.

She stared into the shadows, barely able to see the outlines of the various burial chambers along each side wall. She'd been here numerous times before and turned now to the shelf just inside the door where she found the battery-operated lantern.

Turning it on, she looked around. The chamber appeared as it always had. Plaques with the names of the deceased marked the front of each chamber and she walked past each one, not so much reading the names as reciting them from memory. Marcus and Elizabeth Winslow, parents of what the family referred to as the original four: Angus, Sean, Ewan, and Erik. Until Erik had been attacked by the chupacabra, no one in the family had realized chupacabras or vampires existed. Then Angus survived his chupacabra attack and had become both a changeling and the first Night Slayer—thus starting the family tradition of hunting vampires. Plaques for all four brothers, including Erik, followed their parents'.

Kacie quickly scanned the rest of the names until she reached the most recent—Lily Winslow. Beside hers, there were three more plaques. Kacie lovingly traced the names etched on them: Vince Renault, Sarah Renault, and Robbie Renault.

Dropping her hand to her side, Kacie turned around and studied the four walls with a critical eye. The building was free-standing and there was nothing on the inside that would lend itself to being a secret entrance to an underground vampire lair. She didn't think the lair was likely to be in the Winslow family vault anyway. If it had been, one of the Winslow slayers would have found it and destroyed it years ago.

She walked toward the door and started to replace the lantern, then changed her mind. The other mausoleums and burial vaults were bound to be dark inside. It would be good to have a source of light with her.

Closing the iron door behind her when she stepped out, Kacie checked her watch. It was almost 2:00 p.m., which meant she still had a couple of hours to look around. Whether she'd have time to stake the vampires before they awoke depended on how long it took her to find them.

Looking about, she saw that there were only two other buildings large enough to hide a secret entrance. She walked over to the first one and looked at the name above the door: BARROWS. The name on the other building was ELLINGTON. The name sounded familiar to her and she tried to remember why. Then it hit her. According to the family legend, Ellington was the last name of the brothers who had followed Erik into death by hunting down the chupacabra that killed him.

She stared at the large stone structure with fascination. Could this be Michael's family vault? If so, then wouldn't it be the perfect place to hide an entrance to their lair?

With a sense of excitement, she tried to slide back the bolt. It wouldn't budge. Holding the lantern close to give herself better light, she examined it for signs that it was rusted closed. Seeing none, she stood to the side and then tried to kick the bolt with the bottom of her foot. It worked surprisingly well and the bolt shot back, but when she tried to push open the door, it held fast.

Confused, she thought it was locked, but then realized

it was simply stuck. That put a chink in her theory. If the vampires used it all the time, wouldn't the door be easier to open?

Unwilling to give up, she threw all her weight against the door, ramming it with the side of her arm until her shoulder ached from the impact. About to give up, she gave it one last shot. Heaving herself against the door, it suddenly swung open. Thrown off balance, Kacie stumbled forward. She might have regained her footing had it not been for the short set of steps just inside. As she fell, she caught sight of a dark form lurking just inside the doorway.

Fear for her life had her twisting in midair, wanting to face her attacker. She landed on her shoulder and pain shot through her body. Tears sprang to her eyes and she blinked rapidly, trying to clear them as she reached for a weapon. Only her arm was numb and wouldn't obey her command.

With a feeling of desperation, she looked at the figure standing just to the side of the doorway, deep in the shadows. With her heart in her throat, Kacie tried to make out the features of her attacker. His face, what she could see of it, was twisted into a feral snarl. With a start, she realized this was no vampire. It was a chupacabra. Terror washed over her as she lay there helpless, her eyes locked on the long fangs prominently exposed and ready to rip out her throat.

Chapter
5

Kacie braced for the attack, certain that death was only seconds away. Nothing happened. The chupacabra didn't move. Curiosity slowly replaced fear and with it came her ability to think again. Then she felt like a fool. It wasn't night yet, so the chupacabra was still in its stone phase.

Feeling really foolish now for being so afraid, she tried to push herself to her feet. Pain shot through her injured shoulder and the arm collapsed beneath her weight.

Great, she thought. The last thing she needed at the moment was to have an injured sword arm. Fortunately, she knew how to fight with her left hand, but it wasn't the same.

Rolling onto her hands and knees, Kacie got to her feet. Now that she was standing, the chupacabra didn't seem nearly as intimidating. Going up to it, she hesitantly reached out and touched it. Its rough, stone-like surface felt cool and damp. Retrieving the lantern from where it had fallen, she turned it on and held it close to the chupacabra. Now that she had the light to help her see, Kacie was no longer sure this was even a day-phase chupacabra. It might simply be a statue erected to memorialize how the brothers—Michael and Sedrick—were killed.

Turning away from it, she looked around the inside of the mausoleum. This was set up differently from the Winslow one. There were four ossuaries standing side by side. Behind them was a small stone altar with a standing cross in the center. A short distance behind the altar, the family coat of arms had been carved into the wall.

Kacie moved forward. This mausoleum offered so many more possibilities for secret entrances. She walked up to the ossuaries and read the names on each: Viscount Richard Ellington, Lady Vanessa Ellington, Lord Sedrick Ellington, and Lord Michael Ellington.

Kacie's excitement grew. The last two ossuaries would be empty.

She remembered seeing a movie once where the stairs to an underground chamber had been hidden inside an ossuary. She stood beside Michael's and shoved at the stone top. Pain shot up her arm and the stone cover didn't move.

Gingerly, she ran her fingertips along the edge, searching for a secret mechanism that would open it, but the edge was smooth. She turned her attention to Sedrick's ossuary and searched it—with the same results. There was no way she was strong enough to move them on her own—they were too heavy.

Frustrated, Kacie glanced at the time. It was getting late and she didn't want to be in the cemetery when night fell. Besides, she was starving.

Deciding to call it a day, she vowed to come back again tomorrow to finish exploring. With a last wary glance at the chupacabra statue, she left the Ellington mausoleum and pulled the door closed behind her.

Minutes later, she'd returned the lantern to the Winslow mausoleum and left the cemetery. Glancing at her clothes, she saw they were covered in dust. She should probably go back to the castle and change, but she was tired, hungry, and her arm hurt, so she brushed herself off as best she could and continued on toward town.

Myrtle's was already busy by the time she arrived and was shown to a table. She placed her order and then ran to the restroom to wash some of the dirt from her face and hands. By the time she sat back down, her food was waiting for her.

Though she was hungry enough to inhale her food, Kacie forced herself to eat slowly. She let her gaze travel around the room, savoring the familiarity of Myrtle's wooden tables and floors, worn with age. On the far wall was a stone fireplace and during the cold winter months, patrons could warm themselves in front of a blazing fire. The gaming tables were off to one side and there was a bar along the side wall where those just wanting a drink could sit.

The bar and grill represented one half of the inn. The adjoining room served as the lobby for the hotel side and a set of stairs led to the upper floors where the guest rooms were located.

Kacie casually studied the people around her without really seeing any of them. Her thoughts were on Gerard. She hadn't seen him in three years. Once she moved to the States, it would be a lot longer than that before she saw him again, if ever. Despite her anger toward him, she grudgingly admitted to herself that she would miss him.

But she would have Ben to keep her company. Lean and wiry, he was the consummate martial arts instructor. She'd hired him to train her because she wanted to keep her fighting skills well honed. They'd become friends instantly and started spending much of their free time together. When he'd invited her home to spend Christmas with his family that first time, they'd welcomed her with open arms. His family was huge and everyone seemed to get along so well that Kacie had taken to them right away. In fact, she often joked that she'd fallen in love with Ben's family long before she fell in love with him.

Being in love wasn't anything like she'd imagined it, though. It wasn't the heart-pounding, can't-live-without-him feeling one read about in storybooks. Unless what she felt for Ben wasn't the "real" thing. But if it wasn't, then what the hell was she doing moving overseas with him?

Normal life, she reminded herself. Even if she went with Ben and they both decided that friends was all they'd ever be, at least she'd have a new, normal life—as far from Hocksley as she could get.

The waitress came and laid the bill on the table, snapping Kacie out of her mental ramblings. When she reached into her pocket for money, her arm—which had grown stiff while sitting there—ached in protest, reminding her it would be a while before she could lift her sword again.

All the more reason to hurry home before nightfall.

Laying enough money down to pay for her meal, Kacie stood to leave. Her glance fell on the window and with a start, she saw that it was already dark outside. She'd lost track of time.

Just then, the door opened and a figure walked in. Kacie abruptly sat back down, making herself as inconspicuous as possible, her gaze following Erik as he walked past the dining area and headed straight for the lobby. He never looked around, but headed directly for the stairs and went up.

Kacie sat there, stunned. What was he doing here?

She looked around, wondering at the reaction of those around her. A vampire had just walked past them and none of them seemed the least disturbed. Of course, they didn't know he was a vampire, did they?

Kacie settled back down to wait.

"I changed my mind," she told the waitress, when she gave Kacie a bewildered look.

"You want a drink?"

"Whiskey sour, thanks." Kacie's arm was still aching and she hoped the alcohol might ease the pain.

Two hours and three drinks later, Kacie was still sitting at the table waiting for Erik to reappear. The demographics of the bar crowd had shifted from families eating dinner to individuals wanting to drink and have fun. Kacie was beginning to wonder if Erik had left by some back way when she felt someone watching her. Looking around, she saw a young man, built like a college football player, sitting at the next table. When their eyes met, he smiled.

There was something about him that made her uneasy, so she ignored him and continued to look around the room, stopping when she spotted a couple coming down the stairs.

When they reached the bottom, they turned and Kacie felt her heart slam against her chest. Erik was standing with a stunningly beautiful woman with short blond hair. Her hand was resting on his arm and their heads were bent close together as she said something that caused him to smile.

Kacie forgot the drink held halfway to her lips as she watched, confused. What, exactly, had he been doing up there? And who was that woman hanging all over him?

Then, to her utter shock, Erik leaned down and kissed the woman. A gentle touching of the lips that left Kacie so shaken, she lost her grip on her glass. It slipped from her fingers, bounced off the edge of the table, and shattered against the floor.

She cast a quick glance at Erik to see if he'd noticed, but his attention seemed focused solely on the woman by his side. Mortified, Kacie bent to pick up the pieces of glass and felt the sharp bite of pain.

"Ye must be more careful, lass," the young man who'd been watching her earlier said in a soft Scottish lilt as he knelt beside her. "Ye've cut yourself."

She looked down at her finger and saw blood. She reached for the paper napkin on the table, but he grabbed it first.

"Here now, let me." The young man took her hand and gently wrapped the napkin around her finger, applying pressure. After a second, he took the napkin away. The bleeding had slowed considerably, although even as she watched, a small bead formed at the edge of the cut.

She tried to pull her hand away, but the young man wouldn't release her. Wondering how she could free herself without being rude, she watched with a growing sense of horror and disgust as the young man lifted her finger to his mouth. He wrapped his lips around it and gently sucked the blood from it.

Alarm shot through her as she gazed into eyes that shone a little too brightly to be human. Afraid that if she jumped up and pulled her sword, innocent people would be hurt, she searched for a way out of her predicament. Hoping he would think her reaction was from shock—and not because she knew what he was—she mumbled something under her breath, pulled her hand free and hurried for the door.

Outside, the noise of the bar receded and she took a deep breath, stopping to collect herself. She looked around, wondering how she could possibly lure the vampire outside when suddenly he was there, standing behind her.

"Here now, don't be rushing off."

She whirled around and pulled her sword in one smooth action. "Oh, I'm not going anywhere," she assured him.

He raised his eyebrows, but looked amused rather than worried. "And what do you think you'll be doing with that?"

She kept the sword between them. "I'm going to kill you."

He laughed. "Is that right? Be a good girl and put the sword away."

"I have a better idea," she countered. "Come and get it."

When the vampire lunged at her, she swung her sword. It was a fast, smooth arc, until something that felt like a bulldozer hit her sore arm. The pain was blinding and she couldn't hold on to her sword. It went sailing across the street.

She stared after it, horrified, as the vampire grabbed

her and jerked her forward. She felt the warm trickle of blood and knew her stitches had torn open.

She turned to glare at the vampire, praying he wouldn't notice the scent of more blood. "That was a mistake," she warned him.

"Oh, you have me quaking, pet," he replied, no longer sounding in the least bit Scottish. His smile told her that long before he was done with her, she'd wish she were dead. "Now, why don't you—"

She slammed the heel of her free hand into his nose as hard as she could, taking him by surprise. As hoped, he loosened his grip on her arm and she jerked free.

When she turned to run, two more vampires appeared. Seeing them, she made a dive for her sword. As soon as her fingers wrapped around it, she rolled to her feet. The strain to hold her sword was intense and she tried to ignore it as she faced her attackers.

"Carrington, you all right, mate?" One of the vampires asked the fake Scot, keeping his eyes trained on Kacie. "Hey, isn't that the one Michael's looking for?"

"Yes," Carrington said. "And we're going to take her to him, just as soon as we've had our fun. Bring her to me."

The other two vampires smiled as they stalked forward. They seemed unconcerned that she was armed, which was their mistake. Kacie sliced the air in a figure-eight pattern before leveling the blade, once more, in their direction. The vampires hesitated.

"What are you afraid of," Carrington goaded them. "Get her." They rushed her, but Kacie held her ground. When they were within range, she swung her sword as Erik had taught her. It should have been easy. She was armed and they were not, but she was slowed by her injury and they, being vampires, moved faster.

Afraid she might not last much longer, she searched for an opening and found it. With a quick forward drive, she sank her blade deep into the chest of the nearest vampire. As he dropped to the ground, his companion closed in. Instinctively, her fist shot out, catching him in the jaw, knocking him back.

"Idiots," Carrington swore, coming for her himself. She tried to pull her sword from the fallen vampire's chest, but before she could, Carrington tackled her to the ground.

She fought with all her strength, beating at whatever she could reach with her fists, twisting her body in an effort to throw off her attacker. When she felt his fangs sink into her throat, blind panic hit her.

She screamed over and over until the constriction of her throat cut off the sound. With it went her air, but not her will to survive. Kicking and struggling, she continued to fight until consciousness slipped away.

"Kacie."

Arms tried to lift her but she fought against them, crazed with the need for self-preservation.

"Kacie, it's Erik. Look at me." Gentle hands held her face and slowly she realized she was no longer pinned to the ground. A distorted image swam before her eyes and she blinked away the tears until Erik's face came into focus.

"Erik?"

"Yes. You're safe now."

She clutched his arm and looked around. There was a

body lying nearby and it took her a second to realize that it wasn't her father's. She wasn't five years old. She was an adult and had fought enough vampires that she shouldn't be this terrified.

The five-year-old voice in her head said differently, but she hushed it and forced herself to take another look at the body. It was the vampire she'd killed. Another lay nearby. Only Carrington was missing and she guessed he'd gotten away.

"You're safe now," Erik assured her while searching her face. "Do you think you can stand?"

She trembled with delayed reaction and the thought of standing seemed beyond her capabilities.

"Put your arms around my neck," he said, still squatting before her.

As soon as she complied, he placed his hands about her waist and stood, lifting her with him. A wave of dizziness washed over her and she fell against him.

"You've lost some blood," he told her, holding her close. "Let's stand here a moment and let the dizziness pass."

Too weak to argue with him, she laid her head against his chest. She thought she should probably feel self-conscious or angry or maybe even embarrassed. Instead, she felt safe. Wrapping her arms around his waist, she pressed herself against his solid warmth.

She heard his quick intake of breath but ignored it as she fought to pull herself together. As if he understood, Erik simply held her.

"We should get back to the castle before the one who got away comes back with reinforcements," he finally said, breaking the silence. "Do you think you can walk?"

She nodded and he slowly loosened his arms around her until she was standing on her own. Moving over to the body of the vampire she'd killed, he retrieved her sword. He wiped the blade and sheathed it for her and then, taking her by the hand, led her from the scene.

Kacie was tired. It took almost all her energy just to keep putting one foot in front of the other. Unfortunately, walking didn't command all of her attention—the man holding her hand did.

She never would have thought him capable of such tenderness—especially to her. It was no secret to anyone that she despised him. He was a vampire. And yet...

Sneaking a glance at him from the corner of her eye, she saw his attention was focused on their surroundings. Worried that vampires might, even now, be sneaking up on them, she snapped to attention, suddenly aware of where they were.

Instead of heading for the wooded path back to the castle, they were walking along an alley. Halfway down, Erik stopped in front of a garage door. Letting go of her hand, he reached into his pocket and pulled out a key that he fit into the lock.

Kacie gaped at him in surprise. When he saw her face, he actually smiled.

He lifted the door and Kacie looked past him. Inside, she saw a black BMW 325i. It looked virtually new. "Is this yours?" She asked, astonished.

He shot her an amused look. "No, I just go around taking whatever I want." She didn't say anything and he rolled his eyes at her. "Of course it's mine. I loaned it to the man who owns the shop in front—or rather, Gerard loaned it to him on my behalf. His mother lives in the next town. She's getting on in years, so he likes to check on her every now and then. His car is old and does fine around town, but it's not so great for the longer trips, so I keep mine here and let him use it when he needs to."

She stared at him, stunned at his generosity. "That's really nice of you."

He frowned. "It's not like I'm a monster. Besides, I don't need it. I still have my other cars back at the castle."

He walked her to the passenger side and opened the door. Once she was seated, he closed the door. There was something on the floorboard and she tried to nudge it aside with her foot.

"What do you have down there?" She asked as he climbed behind the wheel.

He leaned over and took a look. "Oh. I forgot I'd put that there."

"What is it?"

"About a hundred meters of steel cable," he said, popping open the glove box. Kacie could just make out the key, lying inside, before Erik took it out and inserted it into the ignition.

She looked down again, but couldn't see much in the dark. "Why is it here?"

He turned the key and started the engine. "It's for my Hummer, if you must know. I just had a winch installed on the front and this is the cable for it."

"A Hummer?" She was surprised because in the past, his tastes had always run to sports cars.

He gave her another look before steering the car out of the garage and stopping. "Yes. A Hummer."

He got out long enough to close the garage door and then they were driving through the streets of Hocksley until they reached the long winding road that would eventually take them to the castle.

"Why are you smiling?" he asked after a few minutes, reminding her that he had no trouble seeing in the dark.

"I never thought of you as the Hummer type."

"Really? I know I shouldn't ask, but exactly what type did you see me as?"

She hesitated. "After tonight, the type who rides a white steed," she said softly.

Too embarrassed to see what his reaction might be, she looked out the dark window. Neither spoke again during the ride to the castle and, thirty minutes later, they pulled into the drive.

The old stables had been converted into a garage years ago, but rather than park there, Erik drove around to the door that led into the back of his apartment. After he shut off the engine he sat there quietly, and Kacie knew he was listening for the sounds of vampires. Just the thought that there might be some lurking in the dark, waiting for them, had her looking about nervously.

"Let's go," he said after a moment. She quickly got out of the car and followed him into his apartment.

She didn't breathe easier until the door was closed and locked behind them. She stared at it as Erik walked off, knowing it was the only thing between her and the vampires outside. She wondered if it would hold under attack and, tentatively, placed her palm against it. It felt solid enough. Satisfied, she turned around.

Erik was nowhere to be seen. Logic told her he was there somewhere, but after her recent scare, logic wasn't playing a big part in her thought processes. As fear threatened to pull her back into its grip, she hurried through his apartment, looking into each room she passed.

She finally found him in his bedroom.

"Oh, I'm sorry," she mumbled, stopping in the open doorway just as he was taking off his shirt.

His back was to her, but at the sound of her voice, he turned. She gasped out loud and hurried forward. "Oh my God. You're hurt. Why didn't you tell me?"

"They're just scratches."

"You're a bloody mess. They should be cleaned before they get infected. Let me help you." She held the edges of his shirt away from his skin as he finished taking it off.

"Thanks." He sounded surprised that she would help him and that made her feel bad.

"The first aid kit is in the kitchen, right?"

"Yes—in the cupboard."

"All right." She started for the door and then noticed that he wasn't following her. "Are you coming?"

Bare-chested, he followed her to the kitchen and showed her where the kit was located. She batted aside his hand when he started to reach for it and took it down herself.

Setting it on the counter, she opened it and found everything she needed. Taking out a cotton ball and antiseptic, she studied his scratches, considering how best to clean them. His heavy breathing caused her to glance at his face, which was unusually pale. "You look like you're about to pass out."

"I am *not* about to pass out," he growled at her.

She put her hands on her hips. "Then why are you as pale as a ghost?"

He looked like he was going to refuse to answer her,

but then he heaved a labored sigh, clearly not wanting to tell her what was bothering him. "If you must know, I haven't fed tonight and standing this close to you when you're covered in blood isn't easy."

"What?" Alarmed, she put a hand to her neck, shocked that she could have forgotten her own injuries. "Why aren't I dead?"

"It takes a long time to kill a human by drinking their blood," Erik told her, his eyes burning bright. "He didn't get more than a taste before I..." He trailed off and she didn't press him for details of the fight. She didn't want to know.

"Thank you," she said softly.

"You're not drinking the tea," he said accusingly. "If you had, I wouldn't have had to save you."

"The tea?" She glanced at the cotton ball in her hand, not wanting to see the disapproval on his face.

She'd forgotten about the tea. As children, they hadn't been allowed to drink the special Winslow family brew and she'd moved away from home at about the age she would have started. "I forgot about it."

"You really should start drinking it, just in case."

She nodded, glad he wasn't going to lecture her about it. She already felt stupid for not remembering.

The "tea" was made up of the crushed, dried flowers and leaves of a hybrid plant developed centuries ago by the Winslow family. They called it *le fleur de vivre*. When consumed by a human, enzymes from the tea filtered into the bloodstream, making the blood toxic to vampires. A vampire who drank the blood of a human who'd had the tea within the last twenty-four hours usually died after a couple of swallows.

For the humans who drank the tea, there was an interesting side effect, which the family went to great lengths to keep secret. For reasons no one had, as yet, discovered, consuming the tea significantly slowed the aging process. For this reason, children were given the tea only under extreme conditions.

Kacie brought her thoughts back to their current situation. "Don't you have bags of blood around here or something? I don't want you to lose control and eat me."

His gaze snapped to hers, darkly intense, and she felt herself blush at her poor choice of words, but she refused to look away. She half expected him to come back with some inane quip like he'd be happy to eat her, but he simply said, "I'll take care of it later, thanks."

"Fine." She pointed to a chair. "At least sit down."

It was a sign of how weak he really was that he didn't even try to argue with her, but lowered himself into the nearest chair while she gathered the supplies and brought them over to the table.

Wetting the cotton with antiseptic, she bent over and did her best to reach the scratches on his chest, but it was nearly impossible to do while standing over him. Frustrated, she knelt by his side and was able to clean a couple of them, but to get to the rest of his chest, she had to practically lie across his lap, which was more than a little embarrassing.

Finally, seeing no other option, she tapped him on the inside of each knee until he spread them apart. When she risked looking at him to see his reaction, he raised an eyebrow at her, making her blush. "I can't see what I'm doing, do you mind?"

"Not in the least," he said, opening his legs wider so

she could move between them. Once there, she dabbed at one of the scratches and Erik hissed. "Ouch, that hurts."

She thought about blowing on it to ease the pain and then decided he was already enjoying the situation too much. "Don't be such a baby."

To her surprise, he laughed. "Nice bedside manner. Ow." He flinched and leaned back to get away from the cotton ball she held in her hand. "You did that on purpose."

"I did not. Now hold still. I have to clean these." She reached out to treat another deep scratch, but he leaned to the side and grabbed her hand instead.

"That's good enough."

She frowned at him. "No, it's not. If I don't clean them, they'll get infected."

"So?"

"So?" she said in disbelief. "You could d—" She stopped talking, embarrassed.

"I could die? Been there, done that."

It was a harsh truth and she pushed it aside for the moment. "Take your hand away, please," she said in her firmest voice. "I'm going to clean these because if they get infected, they could leave nasty scars." *And that would be a real shame.*

"Fine." Surprisingly, he sat quietly while she finished treating each scratch. On one of the deeper gashes, he winced despite her effort to be gentle. It reminded her so much of the night before—of how she'd felt while he was stitching her arm. It made him seem more vulnerable to her; more human.

With a start, it occurred to her that he had been human— once. "What was it like?" she asked hesitantly. "Dying."

He watched her work, silent for so long that she was afraid he might not answer.

"It was different," he finally said with a slight smile. "No angels singing. No white light to lead me to Heaven. Just a demon from Hell, ripping out my throat. One minute, I was praying for death and the next, I was waking up with this terrible, gnawing hunger for blood."

"I'm sorry," she said sympathetically. "I can't even imagine what it must have been like."

"Worse than the hunger was the guilt afterward," he went on. "You see, when you first wake up, the hunger is everything. It's not until the hunger is sated that rational thought returns. We—Michael, Sedrick, Ty, and I—have ways of helping a newly created vampire to ease them through that transition—using animal blood—but back then, well..."

Kacie had a mental image of Erik rising for the first time. "You're talking about the people who died?" She asked gently, remembering the stories she'd heard.

"Not *people,* Kacie. Family and friends. They came to mourn my passing. I repaid them by killing them and turning them into vampires; progeny destined to be monsters until someone could destroy them, permanently."

He fell silent and she watched the emotions play across his face.

"Close family and friends?" she asked.

He stared at her. "Does it matter?"

"No, I'm sorry," she apologized because he was right. It didn't matter if the people he'd killed had been close or not.

He heaved a sigh. "That's where a lot of the guilt comes from," he admitted. "Because it shouldn't matter, but in a small recess of my mind, it does. I can't begin to explain the depth of my regret for killing anyone, but there's a part of me that's relieved I killed distant cousins and townsfolk instead of my brothers or close friends. That's the guilt that's hard to live with."

She knew him well enough to realize how the weight of that guilt must seem crushing at times. Wanting only to comfort him, she laid a hand across his cheek. "I'm so sorry." At the rough feel of his whiskered jaw, awareness shot through her.

Needing something to distract herself, she pulled away and picked up another cotton ball to finish cleaning the scratches. As she did, she was very conscious of Erik—the man—and couldn't help but notice the contours of his chest. He was by far in better physical shape than any man she'd ever known—even Ben. In fact, if she let herself forget that he was a vampire, he was pure sex appeal. Embarrassed at the direction of her thoughts, she glanced up and found Erik watching her. The intensity of his gaze took her breath away.

Mentally shaking herself, she cleared her throat and stood up, needing both the physical and emotional distance. "How old were you when it happened?" She asked, trying to distract herself. "The attack."

"I was twenty-five." His voice sounded huskier than normal and it teased her senses, making her want to crawl back between his legs again and tempt fate.

"My age."

He smiled. "Back in the mid-1600s, you were lucky if you lived long enough to see thirty-five, so twenty-five was considered old. My brothers and I were basically past our primes." He smiled. "These days, when you're twenty-five, you're just starting your life."

"What about your parents? Were they alive when...it happened?"

"My father was, but not my mother." His eyes took on that haunted look again. "She'd died a couple of years before."

"I'm sorry," she said, filled with empathy.

He glanced up at her and gave her a sad smile. "I haven't thought about my family in a long time."

She squeezed a small amount of ointment on her finger and applied it to each of his scratches. "What's the story with Michael? You say he was your best friend, but I don't ever remember seeing him around."

"No, you wouldn't have. I wouldn't let any of them near you and Jess when you were younger—but he was around. We grew up together. His father was Viscount Ellington. He owned the property adjacent to the Winslow estate, which was much larger at the time."

"How did he die? Michael, that is. I mean, I know a chupacabra killed him, but not the circumstances."

Erik's eyes took on a faraway look. "He thought the idea of staying young forever sounded good, so he decided to become a prime as well."

"What?" Kacie couldn't believe anyone would voluntarily do that.

"Sounds crazy, doesn't it?" he agreed. "Sedrick and Michael were like that. They had a zest for living and the idea of living forever was too good for them to pass up, so they went out every night, hoping to run into the chupacabra that killed me. It didn't take long before they got lucky. Ty, their younger brother, was with them that night and died as well. He was seventeen."

Kacie thought of the poor boy who would be trapped forever in his teenage body. "Did you know what they were going to do?"

He gave her a sharp look. "Of course not. If I'd known, I would have tried to stop them. By the time I figured out what was going on, it was too late."

"I'm sorry," she said, not sure what she was apologizing for exactly. "I guess I'm done here," she said, throwing away the soiled cotton balls she'd used and placing the antibiotic back in the box.

"What are you doing?" he asked her.

She gave him a curious look. "Putting the supplies away?"

He stood up and moved close enough to slide the first aid box toward him. "There's still your neck to see to."

She raised her hand to touch her neck, but he gently pushed it aside. She'd done her best to pretend the attack had never happened. She'd hoped to make it back to her room before having to look at the damage—and face her fears.

"It's over," Erik said as if he'd read her mind. "Let me clean off the dried blood, all right?"

She nodded and stood still while he moistened a cotton ball and stroked it over her skin, slowly loosening and wiping off the blood. The long rhythmic strokes of the soothing cool cotton over her heated skin lulled her into a dreamy state until she could no longer keep her eyes open and let her lids close. She felt the weight of his hand resting against the base of her neck right before his fingers sifted through the length of her hair, lifting it away from her neck; away from the wound. She caught herself just before she rubbed her head against his palm.

She could just imagine how shocked he'd be if she'd done that. It was a reaction to the trauma of being attacked, but still wrong on so many levels.

Opening her eyes, she saw him regarding her intently. "Thank you for everything," she said formally, stepping away. "I'm glad you got there when you did."

He gave her an odd look, but nodded. "Me, too."

Suddenly exhausted, she headed for the door that would take her to the rest of the castle.

"Hold it; where do you think you're going?"

Surprised, she turned back to face him. "My room. My neck hurts, my arm hurts, and I've been up all night. I just want to take a shower and go to bed."

"No."

Surprised, she cocked her eyebrows and stared at him. "I'm sorry?"

His expression was grim. "I need you to sleep down here tonight."

"Yeah, I don't think so," she assured him smartly. She wasn't sure if he was suggesting she sleep with him or just in his apartment, but both ideas sent her pulse racing— and she was afraid it might be for the wrong reason.

He gave her a dour look. "Those vampires who attacked you were members of Michael's lair. He's not going to stop coming after you just because it's daylight."

She struggled to find her former bravado. "I'd like to see Michael try to attack me during the day—the sun would turn him to stone before he got too far."

"Michael won't come for you himself. He'll hire human help."

"Well—"

He held up his hand. "No more arguments. You killed his brother. Trust me—he will find a way to hunt you down."

You killed his brother. Erik's words echoed in her head—as did his words from the night before. *He was my friend.* Was this an attempt to keep her close so he could exact his own revenge?

"I can take care of myself."

He eyed her. "Like you did tonight?"

It was a low blow that hit its mark. She glared at him with raw anger. "Aren't you afraid I'll stake you while you sleep?"

That she'd struck a nerve was evident in the way his eyes took on a bright red glow. "You want to stake me?" He growled. "Be my guest—you'd be doing me a favor. I've already lived longer than any man should." He stormed up to her, stopping just centimeters away. "Hell, I'll make it easy." He reached behind his back and pulled out his sword. Grabbing her wrist, he slapped the hilt of it into her palm, making sure her fingers curled around it. Then he placed the tip of the blade against his chest, over his heart. "I'll even stand still. All you have to do is push."

She stared at him defiantly. "You should know better than to challenge me."

"Come on, love," he goaded. "Don't make me do all the work. I know you can do it; you've done it before."

Angered beyond words, she pressed the blade into his chest until blood welled beneath the tip.

Erik never made a sound, but she felt his eyes boring into her. Tears of anger filled her eyes and she watched, horrified, as a thin stream of blood traveled down his chest, seeping into the scratches she'd worked so diligently to clean. All she had to do was push and Erik would be dead. Permanently dead.

She couldn't do it. Didn't want to do it. She blinked, sending a single tear slipping down her cheek. In that moment, he knocked the sword from her hand, snaked a powerful arm around her waist and hauled her against him.

Then his lips captured hers in a searing kiss.

Chapter
6

For a second, Kacie was too stunned to respond. Then white-hot need shot through her and she returned his kiss with unabashed passion, everything else forgotten.

"Kacie," Erik breathed against her mouth, freeing her lips only long enough for them both to catch their breath. Then he was kissing her again, as demanding as he was masterful, and she gave herself over to him willingly.

Everything in her world narrowed to what Erik was making her feel and she couldn't get enough of it. Running her hands up his arms and along his broad shoulders, she savored the hard muscled strength of him.

The arm around her waist dropped and he grabbed her butt with both hands. He pulled her to him, thrusting his own hips forward, leaving no question in her mind that he was as aroused as she was. He held her there while one hand caressed a path up along her waist, then farther, skimming the side of her breast once, then again.

Unashamedly, she leaned away from him, giving him

better access. She caught her breath when he took the invitation. She nearly moaned aloud as he massaged her through the fabric of her shirt and she gripped his shoulder tighter.

In a distant part of her mind, she knew she should be embarrassed, but it felt so good. *He* felt so good.

He snaked a hand beneath her shirt and found the clasp of her bra, which he undid. When she felt the rough texture of his palm against her bare breast, she moaned out loud. Encouraged, he flicked her nipple with his thumb until it was hard and distended. Her breasts swelled under the stimulation and the pressure deep inside her started to build.

Peering into his eyes, she saw they were glowing; hot coals of desire. She knew a brief moment of fear, wondering if she had allowed things to go too far, and then Erik grabbed the front of her shirt and ripped it down the center. Before she could react, he lowered his head to lave her nipple with his tongue before pulling it into his mouth with a gentle suction.

She held his head there, little whimpering noises escaping her throat. The sweet spot between her legs tingled, making her squirm and rub against him in an effort to ease the ache building inside of her. She needed him to address that ache, but he wasn't through teasing her.

Sliding her hand between their bodies, she cupped him, letting his fullness overflow her hand. She squeezed and heard his muttered "sweet Jesus," as he lifted his head to trail kisses along the side of her neck, sending delicious chills down her spine.

Needing to feel his flesh against hers, she reached for his waistband and fumbled with the buttons.

"No, Kacie," his voice rasped in her ear as he caught her hand in his. "We have to stop."

"No," she whispered back insistently.

He rested his forehead against hers, breathing heavily, She waited. When she finally got the courage to look into his eyes, he was watching her with such an expression of regret, she felt that a vise was squeezing the life from her heart.

He opened his mouth and she knew if he apologized, she'd lose her composure. "Please don't say anything," she said, stepping away from him, clutching the front of her shirt closed. A sick, horrifying feeling was starting to settle in the pit of her stomach, making her sick. "It was..." *Great. Fantastic. A mistake.* "Adrenaline." What else could it be? "It didn't mean anything."

"You should stay in the guest bedroom tonight."

"What?" It was the last thing she expected him to say.

"It's not safe for you to stay upstairs during the day when I can't protect you."

"All right," she agreed, too tired and sick to argue. "Let me just run up and get my things."

"It would be better if you didn't." He moved toward the door and she tried not to notice the way his pants continued to bulge in front.

"But—"

"The thing is," he interrupted, "I don't want you wandering around the castle by yourself and since the sun came up about ten minutes ago, I can't go upstairs with you. The light's not good for my...complexion."

Surprised, Kacie glanced at her watch, then at Erik in shock. "You're still alive." She felt her face heat with embarrassment. "What I mean is—shouldn't you be in some sort of death-like coma, or something?"

He actually smiled. "Contrary to popular belief, we don't fall into a near-dead stupor as soon as the sun comes up. Like the chupacabras, my metabolism slows down dramatically and I get very tired, but after four hundred years, I've learned how to handle the fatigue. Just because I'm awake doesn't mean I'd be much good if someone was to attack right now, though, and considering that Michael is one of the most cunning bastards I know, it's better if we don't risk it."

"All right." Another layer of illness settled in the pit of her stomach. She hadn't known vampires could stay awake during the day and shuddered at the thought of how badly her trip to the cemetery could have turned out if she'd actually found the lair.

Fortunately, Erik was unaware of her thoughts and he gestured for her to follow him to the guest room. "I'll get you a T-shirt to sleep in," Erik offered. "I'm afraid I don't have any extra women's clothing."

"The T-shirt will be fine," she assured him as he walked off. She waited in the guest room, finding it oddly comforting. The antique four-poster bed of dark walnut was the central focus of the room and bore a faded moss green and white bed cover that Kacie found soothing to the senses. The dresser and mirror matched the bed. The only other door in the room was to the closet. It was a small but comfortable room.

Erik came back carrying a folded shirt which he held out to her. When she reached for it, however, he didn't let go. Curious, her gaze snapped up to his and she found him watching her intently. "If there's anything you need..."

His voice sounded husky and he didn't bother to finish the sentence.

An awkward silence settled between them and it was everything she could do not to look away, embarrassed. With iron determination, she looked him in the eyes and found her voice. "Thank you. I'll be fine."

"In that case, I'll say good night." He walked to the door and stopped. "At some point, we'll have to talk about what happened."

"Not tonight, Erik. Please." She didn't think she could do it.

He nodded solemnly and then walked out, closing the door after him.

When she could finally move again, it was to sink onto the bed. She was sick and confused. Stripping out of her clothes, she pulled his shirt over her head and crawled under the covers of the bed. As she lay there, she tried to ignore the tingling that persisted between her legs and the ache in her breasts that matched the ache in her heart. The way he'd held her; the way he looked at her. It left her excited, breathless, and a little frightened because she'd never felt that way with any man. Not even Ben. And Erik wasn't even a man.

Inside his room, Erik was in pain and it had nothing to do with the scratches across his chest. He shifted his erection, trying to find some small measure of comfort from pants that were too tight.

He'd kissed her. He'd held Kacie in his arms and kissed her.

Even now, he remembered the feel of her slender waist beneath his hands, the crush of full breasts against his chest. He could still taste her on his lips. Still smell her powdery scent every time he inhaled. He shifted again.

What the hell was he thinking?

He'd made a promise to Vince to protect her—not ravage her. And what about Sedrick? How could he have forgotten that she'd killed his friend? Then there was the little problem of her hating vampires. He didn't believe for one second that he was exempt. Hadn't he, for years, believed she'd stake him if given half a chance?

Well, she'd had her chance tonight. He didn't know if he was more surprised that she'd drawn blood or that she'd stopped.

A small voice in his head pointed out that she *had* stopped. And the single tear she shed—had it been because she regretted her actions? Or because she regretted her lack of courage?

It bothered him that he didn't know the answer. He just knew in that moment, he'd looked into her confused face and known that he'd wanted her. It had been a mistake. He knew that now. He should never have crossed that line with her. It changed the dynamics of their relationship in ways he couldn't even anticipate. He had no doubt that she would hate him more than ever now, which shouldn't be anything new, except now he found that he cared. A lot.

Reaching for the deadbolt, he slid the lock noiselessly into place. A precaution, he told himself, because while death didn't bother him, he wanted a chance to face it head on, not have it sneak up and stab him in the chest while he slept.

Letting fatigue catch up to him, he stripped out of his clothes. About to climb into bed nude, he thought better of it and put on a clean pair of boxers. When he finally lay down, he was so tired, it took only seconds before he fell asleep.

It seemed only moments later that he was jerked awake by the sound of Kacie's screams.

In one fluid movement, Erik threw back the covers and leaped out of bed. He grabbed his sword and raced out of his room. When he reached her door, he threw it open and did a quick scan of the room's interior, searching for the threat.

He saw no intruders. Stepping inside, his gaze was drawn immediately to the bed where Kacie thrashed about under the covers, whimpering. She screamed again and he realized the demons she fought were in her dreams.

Going to her side, he leaned his sword against the wall as he sat beside her and brushed an errant strand of hair from her damp forehead.

"Kacie, it's okay. It's just a dream." The moment he touched her, she shrank away. "Kacie!" he said more forcefully, trying to waken her.

Her eyes shot open. "Erik? What are you doing in here?" Some of the panic faded from her expression as she focused on his face.

"I heard you scream."

She took a bracing breath and reached for the bedside lamp. "I'm sorry I woke you."

He turned the lamp on for her and light flooded the room, chasing away the shadows. "Want to tell me about the nightmare?" When she looked at him in surprise, he shrugged. "Sometimes it helps."

She looked doubtful, so he was surprised when she spoke again. "It's always the same. I can't see anything, but I know something's out there. A monster. It's coming after me and I try to run, but my legs won't work. I try to put my hands up, but I can't seem to raise them." He could tell she was getting upset, but he didn't want to stop her. "Then the monster grabs me and all I can feel is pain. I know I'm going to die. That's when I usually wake up."

Erik felt her fear as a physical pain and it was all he could do not to gather her into his arms and hold her. Instead, he brushed the hair back from her face. "It's my fault," he said. "I should have gotten there sooner. Maybe if I had..."

"What are you talking about?"

He studied her face. "How much do you remember of the attack twenty years ago?"

Her eyes took on a distant light. "Not much. I ran outside with everyone else to see what was happening. The vampires had my brother." She paused, taking a breath. "I saw them kill him." She swallowed and made a helpless gesture with her hand. "I don't remember anything after that."

He took a deep breath. "Your conscious mind doesn't remember the rest of it, but obviously your subconscious mind does. That night, you almost died. By the time I got there, one of the vampires had you pinned to the ground, had his fangs in your neck." He clenched his fist as he remembered the rage that had filled him when he'd gotten there and seen the massacre, seen the vampire as he fed off Kacie. She'd fought him just as she'd fought the vampire earlier that night, kicking and thrashing without even realizing she was doing it.

"Wh-what happened?" Her voice was quiet, barely intruding on his thoughts.

"I went berserk," he admitted, recalling his actions. He'd shoved his hand into the vampire's back with such force that he'd been able to grab the heart and pull it free, but that wasn't something he wanted to share with her. "It doesn't matter how I killed him; he was dead before he hit the ground. By then, the other vampires had run off. Gerard was beside himself with grief. He'd lost his wife, your parents, and young Robbie. On top of that, Jess was as traumatized as you were. Gerard did everything he could, but he couldn't do it all alone."

"So you helped."

He nodded. "You let me carry you back into the house, but when I tried to put you down to leave, you wouldn't let go of my neck. When the nightmares started, I seemed to be the only one who could ease your mind. So I would sit with you night after night, just so you could sleep."

She stared at him with a look of surprise on her face. "I remember a voice telling me everything would be all right. That I was safe. That was you?"

He nodded, remembering those long nights so vividly. For months after the attack, he'd sat with her while she slept, keeping the nightmares away. Eventually, her young mind couldn't deal with the trauma and wiped away the worst of the memories—and with them, Erik's role in helping her. It was then that he'd disappeared from her life, hiding out in the basement until she was old enough to handle the truth.

"Sometimes, when I feel the nightmare coming, I remember your voice and it makes me feel safe," she said softly.

The admission surprised him. He was searching for something to say when she surprised him again by reaching for his hand where it lay beside her on the bed. "You shouldn't blame yourself for what happened that night, Erik. It wasn't your fault." Her features hardened slightly. "It was Gerard's."

The accusation was so unexpected that he didn't know how to react. "What makes you say that?"

"Because he knew about vampires and never told my family. Maybe if they'd known, they could have defended themselves—or moved away. Then, at least, they'd still be alive."

Her voice shook with emotion and Erik felt so sorry for her that he hated to tell her the truth. But he couldn't let her keep on believing Gerard was to blame. "Your folks knew."

Her eyes opened wide. "What? No, they didn't. Gerard told me himself, when I was seventeen, that he'd kept the secret from them."

"Out of respect for your parents, he allowed you to blame him because he was afraid that if you learned the truth, you might blame them instead. Vince Renault was his closest friend and Gerard didn't want his friend's only daughter hating the memory of her father."

"What?"

He saw the shock on her face. "The Renaults have worked for, and lived with, the Winslows for generations. Of course they knew about vampires. Not only was your father Gerard's closest friend, he was mine. We often went hunting together."

"But if Gerard and my father were Night Slayers, then why . . . ?" Too much emotion forced her to leave the sentence unfinished.

"Gerard and your father were vampire hunters, not Night Slayers. Only changelings can be Night Slayers because they are half-vampire themselves, with enhanced strength and ability. Vince and Gerard didn't have a chance against that many vampires. I should never have left them alone."

"Did you know the vampires were going to attack?" She asked quietly.

He was stunned by the question. "What?"

"I asked if you knew that the vampires were going to attack us. Did you do something to cause them to attack?"

"No, of course not." He was trying hard not to be insulted by her questions.

"Then how would you have prevented it? How do you prevent something from happening when you don't even know it's going to happen?"

"Wow," he muttered, feeling truly amazed. "I can't believe what I'm hearing."

"What?"

"You're actually trying to ease my guilt." He was touched more than he wanted her to know. "Thank you," he said in a quiet voice.

"You sound surprised."

"It's just that I know how much you hate us."

"Us?"

"Vampires." He waited with bated breath for her to deny it.

"I do hate vampires," she said solemnly. Then in a voice almost too quiet to hear without a vampire's exceptional hearing, she added, "but I don't hate you."

The admission shot through him and he worked hard not to react.

She struggled to sit up and he moved over to give her room. When he looked up, he found her studying his face, her expression troubled. "I'm sorry," she said finally. "I'm sorry that I killed Sedrick. I didn't know he was your friend."

Erik felt himself stiffen. "I don't want to talk about this, okay? You should try to get some sleep," he suggested, rising from the bed and starting for the door.

He stopped when he reached it and looked back at her. She lay stiffly in the bed, watching him. He didn't think she even knew how tightly she clutched the bedcovers. She was exhausted and despite being one hell of a vampire hunter, she couldn't fight her own inner demons.

It tore at his heart to see her like that, and before he'd even thought through what he was doing, he'd turned around and went back to her bed. "Do you trust me?" he asked.

"Yes," she replied without hesitation. His heart leaped for a second time that night.

"Then move over," he said to her.

He saw her look of surprise, but noticed that she was already obeying even as she questioned him. "Why?"

"I'm going to sit with you until you fall asleep." There was no chair and while he could have gone into the other room to find one, he didn't want to. Sitting down, he turned so he could lean against the headboard and stretched his legs out in front of him on the bed.

"What about you? Aren't you tired? I mean, the sun is up. I would think you'd be exhausted."

"I'll be fine," he said simply. "You go to sleep now."

"All right, but as soon as I'm asleep, you should go back to your room. You need your sleep, too." She shifted her body, getting comfortable. He saw her eyes close. A couple of minutes passed but he still felt the tension radiating from her.

"Relax, Kacie." He reached out and gently started combing his fingers through her hair. After a minute, her breathing slowed.

"Erik?" she asked in a drowsy voice.

"Yes?"

"Why didn't you turn me over to Michael?"

Erik's heart tightened. "Because when I found your father that night of the attack, he was still alive. With his dying breath, he asked me to protect you and I promised him I always would."

"Oh." He could tell his answer wasn't one she'd expected.

"Now, go to sleep, little one. I'll watch over you," he intoned softly.

As he listened to the rhythm of her breathing even out, he indulged himself in the fantasy that he wasn't a vampire, she hadn't killed his best friend, and any time they wanted, they could finish what they'd started earlier than night. Tomorrow, that fantasy would have to end because he was sending her back to York.

Kacie woke up alone, feeling sore but surprisingly rested. She didn't know what time Erik had left and the thought of seeing him again—after almost running him through with her sword, then almost having sex with him, and then freaking out on him—had her dreading even stepping out of the room.

Still, she was in desperate need of a shower and a change of clothes. The ones she'd worn yesterday were covered in blood.

Deciding to risk at least a shower, she eased open her door and looked down the hall. Erik's bedroom door was still closed, so thinking it safe, she hurried to the bathroom.

She was reaching for the doorknob when the door suddenly opened. Erik stood there, stark naked except for the towel wrapped around his waist, his skin glistening with moisture and his wet hair combed back from his face.

Immediately, her gaze flew from his broad chest to his defined abs and then lower still. At the sight of the bulge in his towel, her mind leaped right back to the night before. The slight humming of her nerves burst into a hallelujah chorus and heat flooded her face. She still wanted him.

"I didn't realize you were up," he said, sounding so calm and undisturbed that she actually felt disappointed.

"Yes, I...I just woke up a little while ago." She was too self-conscious to hold his gaze and had to look away. "I was going to take a shower, but I can wait."

"No need. I'm done." He moved to one side to let her by as he stepped out, bringing them into exceptionally close contact as they passed each other.

Feeling horribly self-conscious in nothing but his shirt, Kacie did whatever she could to avoid touching him and didn't breathe easy until the door was closed behind her.

"Brilliant," she muttered to herself. "Now he thinks you're a loon on top of everything else."

She went over to the tub, pushed aside the shower curtain, and reached in to turn on the water. There was a decidedly cool feel to the tub, and the bathroom, in general, lacked the moisture in the air or condensation on the mirror that would have been there if he'd taken a hot shower. She shook her head, wondering why anyone would want to take a cold shower. One possible reason came to mind, but she quickly discounted it because the idea of Erik being attracted to her was a complication she didn't need. She had enough problems already.

Turning on the water, she let it run until it was warm and then pulled up the lever that diverted the water to the shower. While the running water warmed the bottom of the tub, she stood up and pulled off her shirt. She was about to step into the shower when she noticed her reflection in the mirror. She studied it, trying to see it with an impartial eye. Would Erik find her attractive, she wondered?

Her breasts were full, but not huge. Her waist wasn't as narrow as current fashion said it should be and neither were her hips. Her stomach, which had never been flat, had a slight swell to it. Her legs, however, were long and toned, but probably wouldn't stay that way if she didn't get back to running every day.

She turned around to see her back and smoothed her hands down either side of her butt. She supposed that it had a decent enough shape. Turning back around, she sighed. Erik had probably seen hundreds or thousands of naked women before. She was nothing special.

Besides, what Erik thought of her didn't matter. She had a life to return to that did not include vampires or Erik, though the prospect of returning to Ben and a life of accounting wasn't nearly as appealing as it had once been. Vampire slaying made her feel alive, and Erik...she didn't want to even think about how Erik was making her feel.

No. The sooner she returned to her "normal" life, the better for everyone.

Listening to the sound of the shower, Erik had a hard time thinking of anything other than Kacie standing nude beneath a spray of water, one room away. Unbidden, the thought of her fiancé rose up and he almost growled. Just thinking about Kacie lying in bed with another man as she had with him hours ago had him clenching his fists. It wasn't any of his business, he told himself, leaving the study to head back into the living room. When he heard the bathroom door open, he turned in time to see Kacie step out.

She was a vision with her damp hair hanging about her head, and he had to force himself to look away. "I don't have much in the way of food to offer," he said. "But I do have a little. Can I get you something?"

She gave a casual gesture. "I'll have whatever you're having."

He smiled at that. "I don't think you want what I had—how about toast instead?"

She blushed and smiled. "Yes, thanks."

He wanted to stand there, devouring her with his eyes, but instead he walked into the kitchen.

"Do you do a lot of cooking?" she asked, following him.

"More than you'd think," he said, popping two pieces of bread into the toaster. "Not for myself, but for Gerard. While you and Jess were away at school, he got lonely and started coming down here. One thing led to another and we fell into the habit of dining together."

At that moment, the phone rang. Erik exchanged a quick questioning look with Kacie as he crossed the room to answer it. "Hello?"

"Erik—it's Gerard," the familiar voice said on the other end.

Erik took a deep breath and tried to sound as normal as he could. "Gerard—how's the armory convention?"

"It's great. You wouldn't believe the reaction I've been

getting to my swords. I've received several lucrative offers for commissioned work."

"Really? That's great. It's good to know your work is being appreciated."

Feeling Kacie's gaze on him, he looked up and saw her point to herself and then shake her head. She didn't want Gerard to know she was there and he had to agree with her decision. If Gerard knew, he would come rushing home and, in doing so, put himself in danger.

"Things are quiet here," he lied.

"Are you sure?" Gerard asked. "Because I'd like to stay a bit longer. Several galleries have asked me to display my swords in their showrooms and I want to work out the details. And I've been asked to stop at another gallery in London to discuss a showing, which will take another day or so."

"That's great," Erik said. "Stay as long as you need to."

"All right, then. I'll ring you in a couple of days."

They said their good-byes just as the toaster popped. Setting down the phone, Erik went to get the toast. "Butter?"

"Yes, please." She nodded to the phone. "How is he?"

"He's good. His sword designs are receiving high praise from the sound of it."

"That's good." She watched as he set the buttered toast in front of her. He wanted to talk to her about Gerard, but wasn't sure how to broach the subject. Then a ripple in the psychic link chased all thoughts of Gerard from his mind.

"Do me a favor," he said to her. "Get your sword and go into the bedroom. Lock the door. There's someone outside."

Kacie took one look at his face and didn't argue. "I don't suppose you have a pair of sweats I could borrow? If worse comes to worst, I'd just as soon not fight wearing only a T-shirt."

"My bedroom, bottom drawer of the chest. Take your toast with you," he told her. "My sword's already in there."

She nodded, picked up her toast and went to his room. When Erik was sure she was safe, he pulled a knife from the kitchen drawer and went to open the door.

Ty stood on the other side, completely alone.

"I'm just here to talk," he said, not moving a muscle.

Erik studied the young man briefly, considering the wisdom of letting him into his apartment. Then he nodded and stepped aside. "How are you?" he asked, concerned about his friend despite their problems.

"Worried—about you and Michael. He's mad, Erik," Ty said. "He's mad and hurt and can't believe that his best friend would defend the murderer of *our* brother and *your* friend."

Erik heaved a frustrated sigh. "I understand, but I won't turn Kacie over to him."

"I don't understand," Ty said, sounding frustrated as well. "What's so special about this one?"

"Does it matter what my reasons are?"

"No, I guess not," Ty admitted.

"I don't suppose you can tell me what Michael plans to do?"

"It's not good, Erik."

"Knowing Michael, I wouldn't expect it to be. I…" He paused, thinking he'd heard a noise. "I'll be right back," he said to Ty before walking back to his bedroom door.

"I thought I told you to keep this closed and locked," he growled, pulling the door closed. "Now, lock it."

He waited until he heard the sound of the lock bolt sliding into place before walking back to the living room. He knew Kacie wasn't happy, but frankly, he'd rather have her pissed off and alive than dead because he'd misjudged his friend's intentions for being there.

"Okay, go ahead," he said to Ty, who was staring at him with a shocked expression on his face.

"She's here? In your bedroom? Are you sleeping with her?"

"I don't think that's any of your business, Ty." Erik gave him a look that he hoped would dissuade Ty from asking any more personal questions, but he should have known better.

"I thought you were protecting her because she's a Winslow. I didn't realize you were sleeping with her."

"Leave it alone, Ty, and tell me what Michael's up to."

Ty looked like he wanted to ask more questions, but another look at Erik's face must have changed his mind. "Okay. Michael's planning to launch an all-out attack."

"When?"

Ty shook his head. "I don't know. Soon, though."

Erik thought for a few minutes. With Kacie fighting by his side, maybe they could defeat the primes in Michael's colony. As if reading his thoughts, Ty shook his head. "It's worse than you think."

"What do you mean?" Erik asked.

"Michael has at least fifty primes."

"What?" Erik couldn't hide his shock. "How is that possible?"

"It's been a gradual thing over the years, but we've gotten

several from other lairs and then we still get one or two each year as a result of The Dare."

"The Dare? My God, they're not still doing that, are they?" About two hundred years after he died, the tale behind his death rose to cult status. Soon, spending a night in the Winslow mausoleum became a popular test of courage. Unfortunately, the chupacabras in their area weren't extinct—as Erik had led Jess and Kacie to believe years ago—and they tended to roam the cemetery at night. Some of the young men who took The Dare never made it home again.

Erik digested the news. "Anything else?"

"I can't say for sure, but I think he's been allowing the primes to feed on humans, so not only are they stronger, but he's also got a small army of progeny at his command as well."

"All right." That was definitely not good news. "Is that it?"

"Bloody hell, Erik, isn't that bad enough?" Ty glanced at his watch. "I've got to go. Michael will wonder where I've gone and I can only block him from the psychic link for so long before he gets suspicious."

Erik walked him to the door and they shook hands. "Thanks, Ty. I appreciate the information."

"Listen, mate, I don't want to tell you what to do, but maybe you should think about turning the girl over. I could make sure she doesn't suffer—and then Michael would be appeased."

Erik stifled the sudden anger that welled up inside him. "I meant what I said, Ty. If Michael—or *anyone*—wants Kacie, they'll have to kill me first."

"You can't hold Michael off forever."

Erik knew he was right. "Not forever, Ty. Just one more night. Tomorrow I'm sending her back to York."

The news seemed to surprise Ty, but he quickly nodded. "Okay. Good idea. I'll try to keep Michael busy and give you that time, but no guarantees."

The two men shook hands. "Thanks, Ty, I appreciate it. Anything you can do to help is appreciated."

He opened the door so Ty could leave. "I'll contact you if there's a problem," Ty promised.

"Thanks, but not across the link. Use the cell phone, okay?"

Ty nodded and then left. Erik closed and locked the door after him and then headed down the hallway to his bedroom. It was time to make arrangements for Kacie to leave, and despite everything, he wasn't looking forward to it.

Chapter
7

K acie stood in the middle of Erik's bedroom holding the sword loosely in her hand, straining to hear what was being said in the other room. She was so focused that when the sound of knocking came, it startled her.

"Kacie, it's Erik."

She threw back the deadbolt and pulled open the door, irritated with herself for not having heard him coming. As soon as he walked in, she automatically ran her gaze over him to make sure he was okay. He seemed fine. "What was that all about? Who was that?"

He didn't seem to mind her questions. "That was Ty wanting to see if I'd changed my mind about turning you over to Michael."

She searched his face. "And . . . ?"

He looked irritated that she would even ask. "No. I haven't changed my mind." She nodded, but before she could say anything, he went on. "What I *have* changed my mind about is you staying here. It's not safe, and so . . ." He paused and took a breath. "I think you should leave. Go back to the university."

For some inexplicable reason, his words hurt. "You do?"

He nodded. "Michael isn't going to stop until you're dead, but he won't follow you to York. You'll be even safer when you move to the States."

She nodded absently, wondering why she suddenly felt like crying.

He heaved a sigh. "I'll call the train station in Newcastle and make a reservation for you. Tomorrow morning, we'll call a cab to take you to the station."

Finally, she snapped out of her daze. "What about you? Michael won't be happy to know you helped me escape."

"I can handle Michael," he said, though he didn't sound particularly happy. "I'll go upstairs with you while you pack and then we'll come back down here for the rest of the night."

She nodded. "Fine."

They left his apartment and went up the two flights of stairs that would take them to the second floor. Erik followed her into her room and Kacie couldn't help remembering the last time he'd been there. She felt her face heat up and carefully avoided looking at him as she pulled her suitcase out of the closet and started to pack her clothes.

"Your fiancé will be glad to have you back," Erik said quietly from where he stood in the corner, watching her.

"Maybe," she said, not bothering to hide her doubt.

"About what happened last night," he started, misunderstanding her. "No one else ever has to know."

She paused in the middle of dropping clothes in her suitcase and glanced at him.

"And it's not something you should feel guilty about," he hurried on. "It just happened."

She knew what he was trying to do. He was trying to ease her guilt for cheating on Ben because he still thought she was engaged. Now was not the time to set the record straight.

She finished packing, except for the set of clothes she was going to change into, and closed the lid of the suitcase. She took a look around the room. "I think that's everything."

"All right. I'll carry this downstairs and put it by the front door. You change and come downstairs. Maybe we'll get lucky and there'll be a movie or something on we can watch."

She watched him carry her suitcase out of the room with a heavy heart. Her emotions were a tangled mess. It was impossible for her to pretend that nothing had happened between them and yet she wasn't sure how to feel about it. She'd killed his friend and he hated her, but by his own admission, he felt honor-bound to protect her—so had last night been about dominance and control? Not any sense of affection? The thought that she'd been manipulated didn't set well.

Picking up her clothes, she carried them into her bathroom and changed. The first time she'd left home, she'd wanted to leave. Now she found herself longing to stay. She didn't like running away, but that's what she'd do— if only to help Erik. She'd already caused him enough trouble.

Folding Erik's shirt, she placed it on the bed for him to get later. Then, grabbing her purse, she walked out the door. She only made it two or three steps before she changed her mind and went back into her room. She stared at the shirt and hesitated only a second longer before picking it up. Folding it into an even smaller bundle, she stuffed it into her purse, trying not to think about why she wanted it, and went to join Erik.

For the rest of the evening, they sat watching television and playing chess. Kacie, who had grown up playing the game with Gerard, found Erik to be a cunning strategist and impossible to beat.

"Don't be too hard on yourself," he told her after a particularly difficult and drawn-out game. "I've been playing a lot longer than you have." Then he winked at her.

As the night finally drew to a close and dawn approached, Kacie looked back on the night and knew she would remember it as being one of the best nights of her life. That it had been spent in the company of a vampire never even occurred to her.

As the time of her departure drew closer, Erik became quieter until it seemed he was hardly talking at all. She supposed it must be because the sun was up and he was tired.

"Take care of yourself," he said, his voice sounding a little rougher than usual when they finally stood at the door to his apartment. Her cab was due to pull into the drive at any minute. She searched his face for some indication of how he felt, but he was a blank mask.

"I'd walk you upstairs, but . . ."

She nodded. "I understand. Please tell Gerard—Dad—that I'll call him."

"I will."

She felt like there were other things that needed to be said, but had no idea where to start. A part of her felt like throwing her arms around him, but she could imagine the shock and alarm that might elicit. "I guess it's time," she said at last.

"Oh. I almost forgot. I have something for you." He went into the back room and appeared a minute later with a large, rectangular wrapped package in his hand. "I want you to have this." He held it out to her and she immediately glanced at the wall where the McLaughlin picture had been hanging. It was missing. "Oh," she breathed. "I can't accept this."

"Why not? I thought you liked it," he said, his eyebrows furrowed.

"I do. I love it, but it's an original, isn't it?" He nodded and she hurried on. "It's too expensive."

She tried to hand it back, but he wouldn't take it from her.

"I want you to have it," he insisted. "To remind you of . . . home."

Her vision blurred and she blinked to clear it. "Thank you."

He moved past her to the door and opened it. Clearing his throat, he said, "You'd better go."

There seemed to be nothing more to say, so with the McLaughlin in hand, she walked out. The door to Erik's apartment closed behind her with a finality she felt all the way to her very soul. She took a deep breath and continued down the hallway to the stairs and had just started up when she heard a loud crashing noise from Erik's apartment. It sounded suspiciously like he might have put his fist through a wall or a door. Briefly, she considered going back to check on him, but knew he wouldn't appreciate it.

When she reached the ground level and looked out the

front door, the cab was just turning into the driveway. She waited for it to reach the castle before grabbing her suitcase and purse and going outside.

"Morning, Miss," the cabbie said, climbing out of the car and hurrying to take her suitcase from her.

"Good morning," she mumbled, her thoughts still down in the castle dungeon apartment. She closed the front door to the castle and listened for the modern automatic lock to set. Then, she walked to the cab, climbed into the back seat, and waited for the driver to finish stowing her suitcase in the trunk.

"Where to, Miss?" He asked, once he was back behind the wheel.

"To the train station in Newcastle," she instructed him.

She gazed out the window, barely paying attention to the scenery. Her mind felt too numb to think.

After a long time, she took a breath and forced herself to think about her return to York. Maybe she'd see things differently once she was back. Maybe that normal life she'd wanted would still be worth pursuing, even if it wasn't as exciting as slaying. There was definitely an adrenaline rush that came with risking one's life that couldn't be found in spreadsheets or balance sheets. But if she ever went vampire hunting again, she would no longer kill indiscriminately. It was her concession to Erik—not that he'd ever know.

She wondered if she'd ever see him again. How long would she have to wait until she could go back to Hocksley again? What if it took years—or decades—before she could return? Erik would still be the virile male he was now and she would be old, frail, and decrepit. *One foot in the grave,* she thought as they drove past the cemetery. Too old to be attractive—

She blinked as her thoughts ground to a halt. Looking out the front window, she saw that sometime while she'd been lost in thought, the cabbie had turned off the main road and was now driving along the dirt road that led past the old cemetery.

Trying not to get too alarmed, in case it was an innocent mistake, she leaned forward in the seat. "Excuse me," she said, tapping the driver on the shoulder. "I think we might be going the wrong way."

"Are you sure?" the cabbie asked her politely.

"Yes," she said, looking around. "I'm positive. If you'll turn around, I think we can get back to the main road and I'll still make my train."

To her relief, the car slowed, but instead of turning around, it stopped. "Here now," she exclaimed, starting to get really worried. "What are you doing?"

"Small detour." When the driver turned around in his seat, he was holding a gun.

"Oh my God," she breathed, her gaze flashing to the door handle, wondering if she could possibly get away.

"Don't fash yerself, pet," he said, his proper accent gone. "This won't hurt ye none."

In a useless gesture, she raised her hands to shield herself. The noise of the gun going off was deafening. Almost immediately, she felt the biting pain in her side.

She looked down, expecting to see half her side blown away, but saw only a small feathered dart sticking out of her.

As her mind struggled to comprehend what was happening, an intense lassitude stole over her, sapping her energy and dulling her mind until she couldn't keep her eyes open.

Unable to even hold herself upright, she slumped sideways in the seat.

The next few hours passed in snippets of consciousness. Whenever Kacie woke up enough to begin to remember what was happening, an unseen hand shot her with another dart, knocking her out. By the time she was finally able to regain consciousness, she had no idea how long she'd been out or even where she was.

It took several minutes to clear the cobwebs from her mind and, without moving any other muscle, she opened her eyes to look around. She was lying in the back seat of the cab and it wasn't moving. Voices and music sounded all around her, and it took her a minute to realize the car radio was on. As the cogwheels of her mind started turning once more, she reasoned that whoever had gone to the trouble of kidnapping her wouldn't leave her alone, so there had to be at least one other person nearby.

Subtly testing her hands, arms, and legs to see if they were bound in any way, she decided they weren't. Every nerve in her body screamed at her to grab the door handle and make a run for it, but she knew she'd have only one opportunity to surprise her kidnapper and it would be nice to know first where he was. Shifting her gaze about, she tried to see as much as she could without moving, but it was no good. The grim truth was that she was either going to have to risk moving or wait to see what happened next. She knew she definitely didn't like the last option, so gingerly, she pushed herself up, freezing midway as the cab driver's back came into view.

He seemed unaware that she was awake, so she looked around for something she could use as a weapon. There was nothing. Surprise was the only weapon she had and she had to make it work for her.

Slowly, she finished pushing herself upright, taking care not to make any large movements that might be seen from the man's peripheral vision. As soon as she was sitting, the world started spinning and she had to close her eyes and take deep breaths before she opened them again.

When she did, she took a second to look around. The cab was parked inside some kind of old stable that clearly hadn't been used in a long time. Well-worn leather harnesses hung from nails in the wall and a thick layer of dust covered the tack lined up against one wall. She saw this all in a glance because that was all the time she allowed herself.

Summoning her courage, she leaned forward and slammed the unsuspecting cab driver's head against the side window just as hard as she could.

It made a sickening thud, but she knew it would only daze him, so she grabbed the door handle and threw her weight against the door. It didn't budge. She tried again, pushing harder, but with no luck. Fumbling with the lock, she tried again. Still, it wouldn't open. She tried the other side. Slowly she realized the childproof mechanism on the doors had been activated and they could only be opened from the outside. She was trapped.

By now, her heart was racing and she could no longer hear the radio for the sound of her own pulse pounding in her head. She glanced at the driver to see if he was coming after her yet and saw that he hadn't moved. Was it possible that she'd knocked him unconscious?

Daring to hope, she poked him in the back of the neck.

He didn't budge. Feeling more certain, she leaned forward and really shoved him. There was no reaction. Contorting her body so that she was standing bent over the front seat, she stretched to see his face. That's when she noticed the blood staining the left side of his shirt. With a growing sense of dread, she leaned over him a little farther—and saw the twin crimson holes in the side of his neck. Nothing could have motivated her to move faster.

Climbing over the front seat, she nearly fell out the passenger side when she pulled up on the handle and the door opened readily.

Her legs were unsteady when she tried to stand and she had to hold on to the door until the tremors in her muscles subsided. When she thought she could support her own weight, she let go and hurried for the stable door. Each step took effort and soon she was winded and gulping for breath.

It seemed to take forever, and when she finally reached it the door wouldn't open. She couldn't stop the small cry of despair that escaped.

Behind her, someone laughed.

Whirling around, she watched a form materialize from out of the dark corner of the stable. "Going somewhere?" a familiar voice asked. Squinting to bring his face into focus, she recognized him.

"Carrington."

He smiled, his fangs practically glowing in the dark. "I'm flattered that you remember me," he said, touching his heart in a mocking gesture.

"What do you want with me?" she asked, her mind quickly calculating the odds of beating him without a weapon. It didn't look promising.

"I believe we have some unfinished business," he said with an evil smile. "And I always finish what I start."

Erik woke after a troubled sleep and climbed out of bed. He tried not to think about Kacie, but as he walked into the living room, he couldn't help but notice the bathroom door with its large, gaping hole. It had been a childish thing to smash his fist through it and the pain in his hand had not eased the pain in his chest one bit.

He dragged a hand down his face, trying to wipe her from his thoughts, but everywhere he looked, he was reminded of her. There was the couch where they'd sat talking and watching the television together. There was the chess board with their last unfinished game still set up. The wall of paintings with the missing McLaughlin. The bathroom where he'd brushed up against her. The chair in the kitchen where she'd knelt between his legs. *Christ.* He had to get out of here or he'd go nuts.

Strapping on his sword, he left his apartment and started walking toward town. He knew Penny was still staying at Myrtle's, but he wasn't in the mood to see her. Instead, when he neared town, he veered off in the direction of the cemetery. He hadn't liked hearing that young boys were still foolish enough to spend the night there on The Dare. If any were there tonight, then he'd be sure to send them home with a message for others who might try.

When he got there, however, the cemetery was empty and Erik found himself walking up and down the rows of graves, silently greeting long-passed friends. When his cell phone rang, he was glad for the interruption.

"This is Erik," he said, answering it.

"They've got her," Ty said without preamble and Erik felt the cold hand of fear squeeze his chest even as he fought to stay calm. "Who has her? What happened? Is she all right?" *Please, God, let her be all right.*

"I don't know much. I just ran into one of Carrington's mates and he said Carrington had her. I think she's still alive, but I'm not sure what he has planned. Michael knows. He's on his way to meet them now."

"Carrington?" Erik asked.

"Yeah. I understand you had a run-in with him the other night."

"Right. I remember him," Erik said. "Where has he got her?"

"The stable at the old McPherson place."

"Okay. I'm on my way," Erik told him. "How long before Michael gets there?"

"He was in the lair when he found out, so maybe fifteen minutes. If you hurry, you might beat him there, but it'll be close."

Erik didn't bother to tell Ty that he wasn't at the castle. The old McPherson place was less than five minutes from the cemetery. With any luck, he'd be in and out before Michael arrived.

"Do you want help?" Ty asked.

Erik appreciated the offer but said, "No, it would be better if Michael didn't know I'd been talking to you."

"Okay, I understand. Be careful. Carrington can be dangerous."

"Save your warnings for them," Erik replied. "Because if they've harmed one hair on her head, they're going to wish they'd been more careful."

*   *   *

Kacie watched Carrington walk toward her with a confidence that had alarm bells pealing in her head. This was not a prime who would feed off her and leave her for dead. This was a sexual predator that preyed on women's fears. More than he frightened her, he disgusted her.

As he drew closer, Kacie's gaze darted around, evaluating every tool and piece of equipment as a potential weapon. She noticed then that Carrington wasn't alone. She counted three vampires lurking off to the side and reasoned that there might still be more.

Her odds of getting out alive were rapidly diminishing.

She started backing away, not moving fast because she didn't want to give Carrington any reason to lunge for her. She wanted him to think she was nearly crazed with fear, and it didn't take much acting.

"Don't worry, pet. I'm not going to kill you—yet. We're just going to have a little fun while we wait for Michael to arrive."

Michael. Now she *was* terrified. Remembering how he and Erik had fought for hours the other night, she didn't think she could beat him. Crazy though it seemed, she had better odds against Carrington.

"There's nowhere to hide, pet," Carrington continued to taunt her.

She cast a quick glance around and found what she was looking for—a potential weapon. "How did you do it?" she asked him, trying to keep him distracted. "How'd you arrange to have me kidnapped? You couldn't have known I was leaving."

"The fox always runs," he said. "Every hunter knows

that. So then it's just a matter of being prepared. Fortunately for me, there's really only one way off the bluff and it's a simple enough guess that you'll be calling a cab to get you during the day."

It was so obvious, she blamed herself for not thinking of it. The crunch of his shoe against the dirt brought her attention back to her immediate situation. The time to act had arrived.

Spinning, she raced the last couple of steps to the side where a pitchfork leaned against the wall. She grabbed it and turned just as Carrington closed the remaining distance between them. She raised the pitchfork and Carrington skidded to a halt, just short of impaling himself on the sharp tines.

"Stay back," she growled, "or I'll run you through."

For a second, his eyes grew round and then, just as she was starting to think she might have a chance, she heard a small cracking noise. Almost in slow motion, the aged wood splintered and the end of the pitchfork fell to the ground.

Carrington's laugh reverberated throughout the stable, but was cut short when Kacie stabbed him with the pitchfork handle. Her aim was dead on and if the wood hadn't been so rotted, Carrington would have been dead. Unfortunately, the wood splintered against his chest. He was as stunned as she was, swearing vehemently, his eyes blazing neon red. Kacie took advantage of the moment and ran.

In seconds, Carrington was after her. She raced around the cab, scanning the barn, looking for weapons or a place to hide. There was nothing.

Then she felt his cold grip on her arm and was spun

around so fast, she almost lost her balance. He hit her across the jaw and her head snapped to the side, exploding in pain. Her vision dimmed until it was little more than millions of sparkles of white light behind her eyelids.

It was the moment of truth. She was going to die and someone wiser or braver than she might accept it with quiet dignity. Kacie refused. Gritting her teeth, she brought her arms up, catching Carrington by surprise, breaking his hold. Taking a step back, she planted her feet and assumed a fighting stance.

She might not have a sword on her, but she was hardly defenseless. If Carrington wanted to kill her, she was going to make him work for it. Pulling on energy deep within her, she gave a battle cry and launched her attack.

In her various martial arts classes, she'd always been taught that the size and strength of one's opponent is irrelevant. She didn't think any of her instructors had had vampires in mind when they'd said it. Her first couple of punches and kicks did some damage, but Carrington was a quick study.

Finally, in desperation, she tried something she'd only done a couple of times—with success—when she'd been sparring with Erik as a teenager. Screaming at the top of her lungs, she waved her arms around in windmill fashion as fast as she could.

Erik heard Kacie's scream and his heart nearly stopped beating. Blind hot rage threatened to cloud his thinking and he had to exert iron control to keep from racing blindly into the barn. He couldn't help Kacie if he got himself killed.

The good thing about hearing her, he told himself, was that it meant she was still alive.

Going around to the back, Erik searched for the broken panel and open window. He, Michael, Sedrick, and Ty had used the barn many times in the past as a meeting place, so Erik knew it well. He used the panel to climb into the window and landed on the stall floor with a soft thud.

From the front, Kacie's scream still filled the night, but there was another sound accompanying them. Someone was swearing and someone else was—laughing? He made note that there were at least two others there besides Kacie and took advantage of their distraction to climb the side wall of the stall to the open loft above.

Once up there, he moved quietly across it until he reached the front of the barn and then looked down at the scene below.

When he saw what Kacie was doing, he wanted to laugh out loud. She'd pulled that crazy stunt of waving arms on him before and it had been so unexpected, he hadn't known how to react. Obviously, Carrington's reaction was the same because he was the one swearing as he stood by and waited for her to wear herself out.

Erik followed the sound of laughter and saw that there were three other vampires standing guard on the opposite side. Their placement was such that Erik wasn't sure he could eliminate any of them without alerting the others. He'd just have to do the best he could.

One of them was conveniently standing beneath the old pulley that had been used to lift the bales of hay to the loft. The last time Erik had been at the barn, the pulley had been loose. He didn't think it would take much effort now to bring it crashing down. It might not kill the vampire below it, but it would certainly slow him down.

Pulling his dagger from the sheath at his waist, he flipped it and caught hold of the blade. He tested the familiar weight and judged the distance to Carrington. One clean toss and Carrington would go down, but Erik hesitated. If Carrington moved, the dagger would miss and hit Kacie instead. Erik couldn't risk that.

He shifted his focus to the vampire across the way. It was a clean shot.

Below him, Kacie's screams were getting weaker. Any second, Carrington would get tired of her game and do something about it. Erik couldn't let that happen.

Finding inner calm, he sent the dagger flying across the barn, confident it would find its mark in the other vampire's chest. Launching himself through the air, he grabbed the pulley chain and rode it down, hearing a cracking sound as his weight proved too much for the ancient wood. As the pulley's mounting came loose, Erik landed, catching the vampire beside him off guard. Erik hit him and then leaped aside as the pulley and part of the roof crashed down on top of the vampire.

As the third guard rushed him, Erik swung the length of chain still in his hand and looped it around his attacker's neck. He pulled it tight and watched the vampire fall to the ground, his neck crushed.

Erik was already racing across the barn floor when Kacie ran out of steam. Fortunately, Carrington's attention was on her and Erik was able to land several good punches before Carrington started fighting back.

As he expended more energy, Erik's ability to keep the psychic shield in place weakened and he felt the hum of Michael's approach. He had to get Kacie out of there before the other vampires arrived because there was no way he could fight Michael and his army by himself.

"Erik, stop. He's not moving." Kacie's voice pierced his attention.

Erik stilled, his fist pulled back, ready to hit Carrington again if he moved. He didn't. His unconscious body slumped to the ground when Erik pulled away the hand propping him against the wall. "He's not dead."

Kacie came up behind him, her hands shaking as she rested them against his back. "I don't think there's time," she said, her voice sounding hoarse. "He said Michael was on his way."

The mention of others snapped Erik out of his temporary stupor and he turned, grabbing Kacie's arms. "Are you all right? He didn't hurt you, did he?"

"No permanent damage," she assured him.

"Good." He gave her a gentle squeeze and then looked about the barn. The humming along the link told him Michael was close and he slammed his shield back into place so Michael wouldn't know what he was up to. They had to escape and he needed every advantage. "Can you run?"

"Just point me in a direction," she said bravely, making him smile.

"That's my girl." He took her hand and led her to the back of the barn. "Behind here is an open field and beyond that is a ravine. It's dry right now, so we should be able to run along the bottom of it. No one looking for us will even know we're there because they won't be able to see us."

Erik, by himself, could outrun the vampires, but Kacie

couldn't. Getting to the ravine unseen was their only chance.

"Hold on to my hand," he told her. "And run like the devil himself is after you. It's going to be close, but we need to get to that ravine before the others arrive, all right?"

Kacie nodded, but looked worried as she stared out the barn's rear door at the open stretch of land. "Erik, it's dark out there. I can't see where I'm running."

"I know. You'll have to trust me. The ground is uneven, so expect that. Let's go."

He didn't give her any more time to doubt herself. They took off in a direct line away from the barn, straight back to the ravine. Behind him, Erik heard the sound of approaching footsteps along the driveway. With half an ear, he tracked them as they approached the barn.

Several times, Kacie stumbled and almost fell. Each time, he jerked her up and she kept running. With the ravine only a meter away, Erik started to think they might make it after all.

"Careful, here," he warned her when they reached the edge. "It's steep. Better take it sideways."

She nodded, turned, and froze as the beam of a flashlight hit her full on.

"There they are!"

Chapter
8

The alarm was followed by the sound of shouting and running feet. Erik jerked Kacie's hand and they practically slid down the side of the ravine to the bottom. The castle lay to the north and was probably only a fifteen- to twenty-minute jog. Logically, it made sense to go that way, but he knew they'd never make it. So he headed south, dragging Kacie behind him at a merciless pace, praying to God that Michael wouldn't put too much thought into following them and would lead his army north.

For ten minutes they ran until finally Kacie stumbled, fell, and didn't get up.

"I can't go on," she panted when he leaned over her.

"You have to," he demanded, keeping his voice hard. If he gave her the least bit of sympathy, she'd give up. "Damn it, Kacie. There was a time when you could run an hour and not complain. Maybe you shouldn't go into accounting if it's going to make you weak."

She glared up at him, her jaw set at a defiant angle. "I know what you're trying to do," she said.

"Yeah? Then get off your ass and do it."

She held up her hand and he hauled her to her feet. When she nodded, he took off running again, still holding her hand in case she fell again.

They were running past farmhouses, but Erik wasn't about to stop. He refused to endanger any more lives.

After another five minutes, he slowed them to a walk. Kacie hadn't complained but she was stubborn and would probably keel over dead before admitting to him that she couldn't go on.

There was a chill in the air that felt good after all their exertions. As they walked, Erik glanced up. The night was clear and the stars were out. Under other circumstances, he would have thought it a perfect evening for a stroll.

"Do you think they're following us?" she whispered.

"I don't know," he answered honestly.

"Too bad we don't have that horse."

Confused, he looked at her, eyebrows raised. "Horse?"

She smiled. "That white steed you ride."

He returned her smile and squeezed her hand.

"How did you know I was in trouble?" She asked.

"Ty called me as soon as he found out. I got there as fast as I could."

"I'm glad you did. I don't think I could have held them off much longer."

He hated how frightened she sounded. "I don't know. You looked like you had everything under control when I got there. Was that karate? Crouching tiger, whirling windmill—or something?"

Even under the moonlight, he saw her blush. "It used to work on you."

"Yes, it did, very effectively, I might add. I applaud you for thinking of it under the circumstances. It obviously threw Carrington as much as it used to throw me."

She gave a soft chuckle. "That was my plan. I—"

"Sshh." He cut her off as a new noise intruded on the night. He listened and the ease he'd started to feel vanished in an instant. "Damn." He should have known Michael wouldn't go north. He was too smart for that—and he knew Erik so well. "They're coming."

Kacie tensed beside him. "What'll we do?"

Erik raced to the top of the ravine and looked around. He recognized where they were. Town was another twenty minutes away. The cemetery wasn't far, but it offered no protection. They'd just passed the last farmhouse.

Kacie climbed the ravine and stood next to him. "We can't outrun them." It wasn't a question. She knew the situation as well as he did. "There's nothing out here except the funeral home."

"That's it." He started running and she fell into step beside him.

"The funeral home?"

"No, the chapel next door to it."

"I don't understand," she gasped, already winded.

"It's sacred ground," he explained.

"Oh. But what about you?"

It took him a second to understand what she was asking. "Sacred ground doesn't keep vampires away, Kacie. But Michael won't defile sacred ground with spilled blood. It's a personal code of his and as long as we stay in the chapel, we'll be safe."

The lure of reaching sanctuary seemed to give her a burst of energy because she sprinted forward. "Let's go," she challenged.

Kacie focused on putting one foot in front of the other, covering as much ground as she could before she passed out. She didn't know how much farther she could run but she knew what was coming and that helped.

Erik kept pace, running just behind her and even he was breathing hard. They had just reached the edge of the chapel's front lawn when a new sound caused her to turn around. When she did, she almost stumbled and fell. Michael was so close she could see the grim expression on his face as he raced forward. He was coming so fast, she hardly saw the point in trying to outrun him.

Then she was hit in the side with such force that it knocked the wind out of her. As she lost her balance, her world tilted. Shock kept her paralyzed and yet her body was bouncing. Then she realized that Erik had run into her and slung her over his shoulder as he made a last desperate race for the chapel.

The doors slammed open as Erik barreled inside. He charged straight up to the altar and only then did he stop. With a heaving chest, he set her down.

She stood a little unsteadily and turned to watch the chapel entrance. She wasn't sure what she expected to happen, but it wasn't to see Michael and his army of vampires charge in after them. As she stared, openmouthed, Erik stepped in front of her.

"Evening, Michael. Out for a stroll?"

Michael slowed his steps and casually walked forward. "Erik. How long has it been since you went to church?

Your sainted mother would die from the shock—if she were still alive."

"As would yours, I'm sure," Erik growled.

"Hello, Miss Winslow. How are you this evening?"

"Go to hell," she muttered.

Michael smiled and *tsk*'d at her. "Such language in the House of God—really, I'm quite shocked."

His superficially polite exchange baffled her. "I thought you said he couldn't come inside," she muttered to Erik.

"No. I never said he couldn't come inside. I said he wouldn't shed blood on sacred ground. Isn't that right, Michael?"

"True," Michael agreed as he continued to walk toward them. Behind him, his army of twenty or more vampires filled the pews of the church. She eyed them suspiciously, until Michael brought her attention back to him. "You see, Kacie—it is Kacie, isn't it? I didn't recognize you the other night. I apologize. As I was saying—you see, it's important to have a code by which one lives. Without honor and integrity, we are nothing. Live by honor; die by honor." He turned his gaze on Erik. "You used to live by the same code."

"I still do," Erik said grimly. "Only this time, my definition of honor differs from yours."

Michael's eyes grew brighter. "Turn her over to me, Erik," he said, sounding very grave. "I promise you that her death will be quick and painless."

Kacie's breath caught in her throat and she automatically stepped closer to Erik. He stood tall, with his feet apart, and reached behind with one arm to give her a reassuring hug. "Yours won't be if you harm her."

The two vampires studied each other for the longest

time and then Michael shrugged. "Okay. I guess we'll wait."

Kacie didn't understand. Judging from the expressions on the other vampires' faces, they didn't either, especially as Michael sat down in the pew closest to him.

"What's going on?" she asked Erik in a whisper.

"Michael is hoping to wait us out," he said simply. "You're wasting your time," Erik said in a louder voice to Michael. "Unlike you, I'm not afraid to die."

Kacie looked around and realized for the first time that the tops of the walls were lined with windows. When the sun came up, the chapel would be flooded with light—and she'd be alone with a room full of stone statues.

"Come on," one of the vampires cried from the back. "Let's kill them now. They can't go anywhere."

Michael held up his hand for silence. "Who said that?" he demanded, standing to look around.

"I did," one man in the back said. "Why are we waiting? This is stupid."

Michael stood, the expression on his face not one Kacie ever wanted to see directed at her. "Do you think so?" She watched him walk over to the other man while the others seemed to visibly shrink back. "When I say I don't want to shed blood in a church," he explained with exaggerated politeness, "I consider that a euphemism for death in general—whether or not actual blood is spilled. Do you think you understand?"

The other vampire looked confused. "Are we killing them or not?"

Michael shook his head. "You see, Erik?" he said over his shoulder. "So many of the old codes have been lost." Michael's fist shot out, catching the man across the jaw with a punch so hard, his neck snapped to the side. Even from where Kacie stood, she could see the man's eyes roll up into his head before he slumped to the floor. She didn't think he was dead, just unconscious. "Everyone outside," Michael ordered. "And take him." He pointed to the man lying on the ground. "I'm not finished with him."

Kacie watched as the group rose and filed outside. She couldn't believe they were actually leaving; was afraid to hope. When only Michael remained, he turned back to them. "Honor—it's a two-edged sword, isn't it? I'm afraid you've left me no choice." He walked to the double doors and then stopped. "In the end, all you've done is delay the inevitable. Good-bye, my friend."

After he left, Kacie felt the tension leave Erik's body. He turned around and placed his hands on her shoulders. "Are you okay?"

She looked from him to the door and then back again. "Is that it? He left? It's over?" She knew it couldn't be true, but hoped it was.

"No, he's outside—waiting."

She gripped the front of his shirt. "You're not going outside, are you?"

He shook his head. "No. I'm staying here."

"Then why is he waiting?"

He gave her a sad smile and suddenly, she understood. "He's there to make sure we don't leave, is that it? And when the sun comes up..." she looked around with growing despair. There seemed to be nowhere in the chapel to hide from the sunlight. "What are we going to do? We can't stay here—"

He placed a finger against her lips. "Hush, love. Everything will be fine."

She looked up into his dark brown eyes staring at her with such affection and knew that the talk about a code of honor and sacrificing his life to save hers wasn't just talk. The rest of Michael's words sank in. "He knew you'd stay here. He's going to wait until just before sunrise to leave and then it'll be too late. We'll never get home in time and you'll..." She couldn't bear the thought of it. "I'm so sorry, Erik. I'm so, so sorry. I never meant for any of this to happen. I know we've had our differences in the past, but I..." Tears gathered in her eyes. "I don't want you to die."

"Don't cry," he begged, cupping her face with both hands and using his thumbs to wipe away her tears. Then he lowered his head and kissed her.

It started out slow and gentle—unassuming—demanding nothing. Then, as if they both realized this might be their last kiss, the tone changed and it became more urgent. The world around her ceased to exist. There was only Erik, his body crushed against hers; his lips tasting hers, devouring hers...

"No," she rasped out, pulling away suddenly. "Not here. Not like this." She took an unsteady breath. "We have to think."

He stared at her with an awed expression on his face and brushed the back of his hand lightly down her cheek. "Aw, Kacie. Our timing has always been bad, hasn't it?"

Yes, it always has, she thought, blinking rapidly to clear the sudden moisture from her eyes. She knew crying wouldn't help—and would only make it harder for Erik— so she started walking around the chapel while she reined in her emotions. She didn't want him to die. She *wouldn't* let him die.

Harnessing her resolve, she studied every piece of furniture and item of décor in the chapel, looking for anything she could use to keep the sunlight from Erik when the sun rose.

"Can you sneak out?" she asked him after a while. "I could stay here and just walk home after dawn."

Erik walked over to the only door of the church and opened it. A second later he closed it. "No. Michael has his men encircling the place. This is the only exit and he's got it blocked. I'm afraid I'm here until dawn chases them away."

"Maybe you could race out as soon as they left. There's bound to be some cover close by."

"And if there's not, I'll be stuck outside. At least here, I die in a church."

"No. I'm not going to let that happen. Think harder. There has to be a way out of this."

For the next couple of hours, they discussed their options, but it always came back to the same thing. They had to stay at the chapel until dawn.

"Okay, if that's our only option, we'll make the best of it. How long do we have until dawn, can you tell?"

He looked grim. "Not long."

"A couple of hours?"

He shook his head. "I don't think so. More like thirty minutes."

"What?" Panic almost crippled her thinking. She wasn't ready. She glanced up at the windows and saw that the night sky had lightened considerably. She ran to the door of the chapel and looked outside, only to see that Michael and his army still stood sentry.

Closing the door, she studied the altar once more. The drape over the altar wasn't even as long as Erik was tall. It might provide some coverage, but not enough. She lifted it to see if there was any open space beneath the altar and saw that it was a solid block of wood. She looked across the room and studied the rows of pews. Slowly, an idea came to her.

"Kacie, before it's too late, I think we should talk," Erik started.

"No," she interrupted him. "I don't want to hear it. You're not going to die, so we can talk later. Right now, I need you to get on the other side of this pew."

He looked like he wanted to argue with her, but she gave him a stern look and watched as he slowly started walking.

"Today, Winslow. Get the lead out."

He gave her a look that said he was merely tolerating her tone, but he did as she asked. "What do you want me to do?"

"Lift up your end. These benches are heavy."

He used one hand to lift his end almost over his head, making it look easy.

"Show-off," she quipped. "We're carrying it up to the altar."

Erik put the pew back down. "I'm not defacing the church."

"You're not. Spraying paint on the walls would be defacing. We're not hurting anything." *Yet.* "Now help me, please."

They carried the pew up to the altar and set it on its side, so that the back of the pew formed a right angle to the altar.

"Let's get the next one," she said, glancing up at the

windows and seeing how much lighter it had grown outside. "We've got to hurry, Erik."

He shook his head. "When I envisioned my death, I saw it as doing something nobler than rearranging furniture."

"We're building a fort."

He glanced at her. "Excuse me?"

She gave an exasperated sigh as they carried the next pew to the front. "Didn't you ever play fort as a kid? Where you rearrange the furniture into a miniature fort?" They stacked the second pew on top of the first and she stepped back to examine it. The two backs were fairly flush and there was little light coming in.

Erik looked at the two pews, then gave her a speculative glance before looking over at the other pews. She could see him counting them as she had, judging that there were enough to build the sides up and still lay a couple across the top to form a box.

"And the drape?" he asked.

"To cover yourself, just in case we aren't able to block all the light." She looked at him expectantly, holding her breath to see what he thought of the plan.

She followed his gaze when he looked at the window. The sky was a light gray. "Stand back," he ordered her. Then he raced around the room faster than she could have moved, lifting the pews by himself and setting them down exactly as she'd imagined it in her head.

He finished just as the first ray of sun shot over the windowsill. "Erik!"

He dived for the center of the fort and crouched close to the altar. She rushed over there, grabbed the drape and snapped it out to cover him.

Then the sun was up and light was filling the chapel.

"Erik?" She couldn't stand the thought of him turning to stone.

"I'm okay." He sounded surprised and she wanted to laugh until she cried, though she did neither.

"All right. Don't move." She rolled her eyes at her own choice of words. "I'll be right back."

"Kacie! Where are you going?"

"I'm going to find a way to get us home—both of us—alive and well. We have to leave during the day or Michael and the others will be back and we'll be trapped here forever."

"Kacie." She heard the worry and fear in his tone and it sounded so foreign coming from the man she knew him to be that it tore at her heart.

"You once asked me if I trusted you. Now I'm asking you to trust me."

There was a long pause and then she heard him sigh. "Be careful."

"I will."

She rushed down the aisle and opened the door just enough to slip outside. As expected, Michael and the rest had disappeared. She was alone in the early morning sun and she raised her face to it, grateful for both the light and the heat. She wished she could stand there for hours and just let the sun warm her, but she thought of Erik, sitting inside, alone; vulnerable.

Looking around, she saw the funeral home next door and hurried over to it. The place appeared to be empty. She tried one of the doors and found it locked. Hurrying around the side, she tried each door until she finally found one that was open. Inside, the cool air hit her and, after the brightness of the sun, she was temporarily blinded.

She listened for sounds of anyone who might be around, but all seemed quiet. She looked around, not even sure what she was looking for. Maybe a phone, to call a cab. Then again, maybe not. The last experience was still too fresh in her mind. Besides, if Michael had known enough to send a fake cab to the castle when she called for one, he'd certainly find a way to arrange for a fake cab to come to the chapel. No, she needed some other mode of transportation.

She walked through the rooms, one at a time, starting with the front office. There was nothing there but a desk, computer, paperwork, shelves of books, a key rack, fabric samples... she stopped. She wasn't sure what all the keys went to, but plucked them off the rack to take with her, just in case, and then hurried to the next room.

This was the demo room, with four different caskets sitting open for inspection. She stepped up to one to take a closer look. Caskets were supposed to be airtight, weren't they? Airtight, in this case, would also mean sealed tight so as not to let in any light.

She raced to the next room, the seeds of an idea germinating in her mind. When she passed the window, she stopped, looked out, and smiled. Yes. She definitely had a solid plan.

She went outside and tried each key until she found the one that opened the hearse. She climbed inside and looked around. It was dark, but there was too much light coming in through the windows, so Erik couldn't just sit in the back as she'd hoped, but it didn't matter. She had that covered.

Going back inside, she went through the rest of the building until she found what she needed. Then she got to work. When she had everything loaded, she climbed into the hearse and drove it to the chapel, parking as close to the door as she could.

Going around to the back of the vehicle, she opened the doors wide, reached in and tugged on the casket she'd taken from the demo room. As it slid out, the wheeled legs of the gurney it was on automatically dropped and locked into place.

Once it was out, she pushed it up the handicap ramp and, after propping the door open, right into the chapel.

"Erik? Are you still here?"

"What the hell do you think?" His surly voice had never sounded so good to her.

"I think you'll be in a better mood once you're home, so I hope you're ready to go because have I got a ride for you."

Chapter
9

W e're almost there."
        Erik heard Kacie's voice call to him where he
lay in the back of the hearse. He was in the casket with
his face covered by the drape they'd "borrowed" from
the church. He gave her credit for creativity. Though he
wasn't crazy about riding in a casket—it was a little too
Lon Chaney for him—it *had* kept the light off him.

She'd rolled the casket right next to the fort and then
made a tunnel to it using a couple of additional pews that
she'd dragged over and the sheets she'd taken from the
funeral home. She'd called it a modification of the "fort"
game, which she called "tent."

He knew she'd never played either game growing up at
the castle and when he'd asked her about them, she mumbled something about watching Ben's nieces and neph-
ews play. The mention of the man's name had not helped
Erik's disposition any, but when he'd opened his mouth to

ask her about him, she'd closed the lid of the casket, effectively silencing him.

Now he felt the hearse slow down and come to a stop. Kacie's voice shouted to him from the front. "We're home. Can you lower the viewing lid yourself?"

"Yes." He steeled himself against the feeling of claustrophobia and told himself that he wasn't suffocating. Besides, it wouldn't be much longer.

A minute or two later, he felt the casket moving. They'd already discussed how to get it into his apartment and when he felt it stop, he knew she was running around to the stable for the planks of wood she'd use to make a ramp down the steps leading to the door of his apartment.

He still worried about how she was going to get him inside because the casket with him in it was much too heavy for her to control should it start to fall, but she'd told him not to worry about it, so, again, he'd decided to trust her.

It seemed to be taking her a very long time and with the sun being up the way it was, he was tired. He must have fallen asleep because suddenly, he was jolted awake by the sound of a loud motor. There was a grating sound at one end of his casket, followed by a muttered curse that could only be Kacie's. A moment later, he felt the casket tilt and slowly move downhill. He hit the bottom with a decided jolt and then he was moving again.

The next time he stopped, there was a knock on the outside of the casket. "You alive in there?"

He rolled his eyes at her choice of words and was about to answer when the lid was lifted and she plucked the sheet from his face. He blinked a couple of times to get used to the light and then opened his eyes to see Kacie's smiling face looking down at him. "Hey there."

"Hey, yourself," he said with a smile. "I take it we're inside?"

She stepped back and waved her hand around the room. "Safe and sound."

With her help, he lifted the lower lid of the casket and climbed out, grateful to move about again. "What was that loud noise I heard?" he asked her, noticing the fresh, deep scratches in the wood beneath the handle of the casket.

"I was afraid I wouldn't be able to control the gurney once it was on the ramp. Be too bad to get all the way back here only to have it take off and crash. Then I remembered your new winch and cable. I've never used something like that before and had a little trouble at first, but I figured it out."

"You drove my Hummer?"

"Out of everything I just told you, that's your big concern?" she teased. "Yes, I drove your Hummer. Had to. Nice ride, by the way. I like it."

He shook his head in awe. "Remind me to never underestimate you." He was still holding the altar drape in his hand and tossed it into the casket. "I guess I'll return all of this to the church tonight."

Kacie frowned. "I don't know, Erik. I kind of think you should keep it. Next time you invite a woman into your place and she asks if you have a coffin, you can say yes."

He rolled his eyes. "Yeah. I don't see that happening." He sobered. "Thank you for saving my life."

"It seemed the least I could do after you saved mine." She gave him a self-conscious smile. "Besides, I couldn't let anything bad happen to you."

Her words struck him as ironic and he laughed.

"Why are you laughing?"

"Because, there was a time, not too long ago, when I think you would have been happy to leave me in that chapel and watch me turn to stone."

To her credit, she didn't try to deny it. "Things are different now."

"Are they?" He searched her face, not sure if he was searching for answers to her emotions or his. He leaned close, his mouth centimeters from hers. "Kacie," he breathed, cupping her face, "I shouldn't want you, but God help me, I do." He kissed her, drinking deeply from her lips, knowing he'd never sate his thirst for her. When he finally came up for air, it was only to rain kisses down the column of her throat, hesitating when he reached the pulse throbbing in her neck. It had been almost twenty-four hours since he'd fed and the part of him that was vampire roared to life. He was consumed with the ravenous need to sink his teeth into her and savor the nectar of her blood. Fear that he might hurt her, or worse, kill her, rocketed through him and he abruptly broke the kiss, stumbling back. "No," he choked.

"Erik?" She reached out to him, but let her hand fall when he moved beyond her range.

"Get away from me. Now!" He shouted.

She looked momentarily surprised and then hurt. "Erik...?"

He couldn't take the time to explain. "Go to the guest bedroom and lock yourself in."

Something in his face must have registered with her, because she turned and ran to the guest bedroom. He saw her close the door and waited until he heard the lock slide into place. Only then, when he knew she was safe, did he go into the kitchen and sate his hunger. The animal blood he drank tasted sour after the temptation of her sweet blood.

When he was full, he headed for his bedroom, stopping outside the guest bedroom. He wanted to explain his behavior, but what was the point? He knocked on the door, but didn't wait for her to answer. "Kacie, I'm sorry I frightened you. I'm going to bed. I'd appreciate it if you stayed inside the castle." He didn't wait for her to answer, but continued on to his room. Once inside, he locked the door and, too tired to undress, lay on the bed and tried to sort through the mess he'd made of his life. It was bad enough that he was lusting after his friend's killer—a woman who hated vampires—but now it seemed that if he didn't keep that lust tightly reined in, he could end up killing her.

Kacie lay on the bed wondering what had happened with Erik. One minute, they'd been kissing—and the next he was shoving her away. Had he changed his mind? Lost interest? Or maybe he'd remembered that she was the one who'd killed his friend.

After thirty minutes of staring at the ceiling and finding no answers, she got up. She listened at the door for sounds of Erik but all was quiet. He'd said he was going to bed; since it was daylight outside, she assumed he was sound asleep.

She opened the door and saw that his bedroom door was closed. Relieved, she stepped out and headed into the kitchen. She was starving.

Searching the pantry, she found the bread to make toast. Not necessarily the breakfast of champions, but it would do.

When she'd taken the edge off her hunger, she went into the living room, feeling somewhat at a loss. She'd thought she would be tired, but her emotions were a mess, filling her with a restless energy. There was no way she would be able to relax enough to fall asleep.

Walking around Erik's living room, she stopped along the wall of paintings and felt a rush of despair. The McLaughlin sunrise that Erik had given to her had been in the back of the cab. Now, she'd probably never see it again. It was yet one more thing to be upset about.

Wondering if there might be something on the television to distract her, she was searching for the remote control when the phone rang. There was no reason to think he had a separate line, so it was probably the castle's phone ringing. Looking around, she couldn't see a phone lying about anywhere. She listened harder and thought the ringing might be coming from the direction of the hallway, so she headed that way. There were two closed doors beyond the guest bedroom and the sound seemed to be coming from the first. She hated to go into rooms that were clearly off limits, but it could be Gerard, or even Ben, calling.

Making her decision, she walked in, spotted the phone on the large antique desk, and hurried to answer it. "Hello?"

"Kacie? Is that you?"

She recognized her sister's voice. "Jess! Where are you?"

"I'm still in the States. I didn't know you were going home for a visit."

"It was a last-minute thing," Kacie explained.

"How are things going with you and Dad?" Jess asked sympathetically.

"Actually, he's not here," Kacie said. "He's at an armory convention."

"Oh, I'm sorry. Bad timing."

It was the story of her life, Kacie thought. She changed the subject. "So, how's everything in New Orleans?"

"Good, though busy. The baby chupa I helped deliver is a playful thing." Jess's voice rose with excitement.

"Jess, I hope you're being careful. Those creatures are dangerous."

"Oh, I never go to see them alone. John and Harris go with me."

"That's good," Kacie said. "Speaking of John—how's he doing?" Kacie couldn't begin to imagine what it must be like to be half-vampire.

Jess laughed. "You'd be amazed at the things he can do. He's stronger, faster—and he has great endurance, if you know what I mean."

Kacie smiled, hearing the laughter in Jess's voice. "Does it bother you that he's so much like a vampire? Or that his friend is a vampire?" Because of the attack, she and Jess had shared the same hatred for vampires.

Jess was quiet for a second. "At first it did, but John only looks like a vampire—he isn't one. I mean, he does drink blood, on occasion, but only during sex—and only from me."

"What?" Kacie found that disturbing.

Jess laughed. "It's not as bad as you might think. In fact, it's rather exciting. I don't know. I can't explain it."

"Never mind," Kacie muttered. "I'm not sure I want to hear the details. I'm just glad to know all three of you are still getting along."

"We are."

No one else might have picked up the hesitation in Jess's voice, but Kacie knew her sister better than most folks. "But ... ?"

"Sometimes I wonder if they resent having me around them. I insist on going on the patrols with them, but I'm not as fast or strong as they are. The only thing I have going for me is that I know how to use a sword."

"John loves you. He doesn't care that you aren't as strong as he is. I mean, you're only human."

"That's the problem," Jess said. "I'm *only* human."

"You can't blame yourself for that," Kacie told her. "There's nothing you can do about it."

"Maybe."

Kacie recognized that tone as well. "Jess," she warned. "What are you planning?"

"Nothing, yet," Jess assured her. "But I've been doing some thinking and I talked this over with Beth, who is Dirk's scientist wife. We think it might be possible to collect venom from the chupacabras and inject it into our bloodstreams. It might have to be done several times, but I think that with enough of it in our systems, we could turn ourselves into changelings."

Kacie thought about what she was suggesting. "Would you really want to turn yourself into a changeling?"

"Yes, I would."

Kacie was surprised that Jess didn't even hesitate. "Why?"

"Because then I'd be like John. I'd be as strong as him, as fast, and I could go on patrols with him and not have him worry about protecting me or get hurt because he was."

Injecting oneself with venom would certainly be a better

option than being attacked by a chupacabra, Kacie thought. "But how would you collect the venom?"

"I've learned that just after the sun comes up and the chupas turn to stone, they're not stone all the way through for about a minute. Once, when I was watching the transformation, I noticed that for several seconds after the colony had turned to stone, one of the creatures had its mouth open and a few drops of venom leaked out."

"But how are you going to get them to open their mouths for you at the exact right moment? I guess you could have John or Harris make the chupas do it," she surmised.

"Are you kidding?" Jess asked. "If either of them found out what I was thinking about doing, they'd throw a fit. No, I'm doing this on my own, but I've got that part figured out as well. You find an adolescent chupa whose adult fangs have just come in. They have a hard time adjusting to the new size and tend to leave their mouths open."

Kacie tried to find something wrong with her sister's plan, but couldn't. "Wow, it really sounds possible, but do me a favor and be careful, okay?"

"I will," she promised.

They talked for a few more minutes and finally hung up after promising to call each other next week.

Kacie looked around Erik's study, curious. She wasn't going to be so bold as to boot up his computer and nose through his files, but with time to kill, she searched through the papers on his desk. There was nothing much of interest, so she turned her attention to his massive floor-to-ceiling bookshelves.

She walked along the stacks, reading the titles until she came to several books without markings on them. Pulling one off the shelf, she opened it and flipped through the pages.

It appeared to be Erik's personal journal. She didn't know if he'd mind if she read it or not, but after reading the first couple of paragraphs, she was too caught up to care.

This particular book covered the time following his death, and she could tell from his writing that he had been filled with a lot of anger and resentment.

Fascinated, she skimmed the pages, reading sections at a time. He wrote about what it had been like to watch each of his brothers die. If it hadn't been for Michael, Sedrick, and Ty—and each successive generation of Winslows— he might have met the sun long ago. Her heart went out to him and she couldn't help but wonder if she'd been in his shoes, could she have been as strong?

Putting that book away, she selected another and leafed through its pages. She stopped when she saw the word *chupacabra* and took a closer look.

I found where the chupacabras are living. They are in a large chamber, deep underground, beneath the cliff. I followed one along the beach last night and saw it enter the cliff through an opening just past the fallen boulder. Low tide is the only time the entrance isn't underwater and that explains why no one has discovered them before now.

I must decide what to do with the discovery. It is dangerous for the residents of Hocksley to let the creatures remain, yet I sense they aren't inherently evil.

Kacie flipped through the pages, looking for other references to the creatures. She finally found another near the end of the journal.

Tonight, finally, I can rest. I believe the chupacabras

have left and in any event, I will spread the rumor of their demise.

That was all the entry said. Kacie put the book away and pulled the next off the shelf. When she opened it, she found that this covered the time of the attack on her parents and brother. She wanted to read it but not there in Erik's study. Taking it to the guest room, she sat on the bed and took a couple of breaths. She wasn't sure if she was ready to learn the details of her parents' and brother's deaths. As she mentally braced herself, her gaze fell on her sword resting in the corner where she'd left it. Erik had tried talking her into taking it with her earlier when she'd left, but she'd assured him that there would be no need for it in the States. She was glad, now, that she'd left it; otherwise it would probably be in the trunk of the cab with the rest of her things.

Her thoughts turned to the Death Rider swords both the Washington, D.C., Night Slayers carried. In her hands, those swords would be no different from hers. The magic of the Death Rider sword worked only for changelings.

Grabbing her sword by its handle, she lifted it into the air—and then almost dropped it as her muscles screamed in pain. She set it back against the wall in disgust. If she were a changeling, she could have lifted it easily, despite sore muscles. And her cuts and bruises would have already healed.

As soon as the thoughts entered her head, she couldn't let them go. What if Jess was right? What if a couple of injections of chupacabra venom were all it took to get the increased speed and strength of a changeling? She sighed. She needed that strength and speed now. There wasn't time to fly to the States and help Jess and Beth test their theory.

Putting aside the idea, she leaned back against her headboard, flipped open the book, and started to read. Erik wrote about the attack on the castle and she relived the horror of it through his eyes. He described her as a child and the guilt he felt for not protecting her. The passages became too personal and she had to flip past them. She would read them at a later date, when she wasn't feeling quite so raw and exposed.

Thinking of trying to get some sleep, curiosity made her turn to the book's last entry and the four words printed there made her breath catch.

The chupacabras are back.

Suddenly, she remembered some of the things Erik had said—about the growing number of vampires—not all of them progeny. The only way to create a prime was for a chupacabra to kill a human—so of course there had to be chupacabras around. He just hadn't wanted to tell anyone, maybe for fear they'd go looking for the colony. Obviously, it was a valid concern because that's exactly what she intended to do.

Just a little venom, she thought. That was all she needed. Not enough to become a changeling—just enough to enhance her strength and speed.

Immediately, she began working out the details. First she would need to find the colony, and she wondered if it was still in the same underground cave Erik had mentioned in his journal. It wouldn't be that hard to sneak into the colony during the day, grab a creature, and bring it back to the castle where she could collect the venom.

All she needed was a secure place to keep the creature

until she'd collected enough. She did a mental search of the castle, dismissing any place inside as impractical for keeping a wild creature. But the stables might work. Most of the outbuilding had been converted into a garage, but there was still one original section.

The stalls were constructed of solid wood and the sides were taller than she was. She didn't think a young chupacabra would be able to get out. As she thought about what she needed, she glanced at her watch. It was almost 1:00 p.m. At this time of year, low tide was usually in the early afternoon. Which meant she needed to hurry. She needed a flashlight and a harness to carry the chupacabra in case it was heavy. She wasn't worried about being attacked because she would be in and out before nightfall.

She hoped her dad still owned his four-wheeler; otherwise she'd never get down to the beach in time to catch low tide, nor would she be able to haul the creature back. She was not going to risk taking Erik's Hummer.

Disregarding Erik's orders to stay inside, she put on her shoes and left the apartment, hurrying through the castle and picking up the things she needed. When she was ready to go, she hesitated, debating whether or not she should leave a note telling Erik where she'd gone. In the end, she decided against it. If everything went according to plan, she'd be back before dark and he'd never know that she'd left.

As she'd hoped, the key to Gerard's four-wheeler was hanging on the key rack in the kitchen. She grabbed it and hurried outside to the barn where the vehicle was parked. After checking the gas in the tank and stowing the backpack containing her supplies on the back, she got on and started the engine. It purred to life and within minutes, she was racing down the road. She had to drive quite a distance before the sheer face of the cliff turned into a sloping hillside. At that point, she veered off the main road and took the more direct path down.

Once she was on the beach, she headed back in the direction of the castle. She stopped when she reached the end of the dry stretch, not wanting to take the four-wheeler where it would be underwater when the tide came in.

Getting off, she grabbed the backpack and headed for the base of the cliff. As she walked, she kept an eye open for the fallen boulder Erik had described in his journal. Many large boulders had fallen from the cliff since the time Erik had made the entry in his journal, and the entrance could have been behind any of them. As it was, Kacie almost missed the opening because it was so well hidden, appearing as nothing more than a dark crevice in the face of the cliff wall.

Excitement bubbled up inside her. This was it.

With the backpack slung over her shoulders, she inspected the crevice and saw that even though it appeared from a distance to be very narrow, it was actually wide enough for two people walking abreast to enter.

Before she went in, she listened for a second. Hearing nothing but the sound of the ocean, she dug her flashlight out of her backpack and flicked it on. It was a lithium flashlight, so while it was small, its beam was powerful.

Inside, she discovered a tunnel leading back into the cliff. The walls were damp, which was to be expected since the tunnel was submerged underwater so much of the time, and the air reeked with the odor of ocean and fish.

After walking several meters, she noticed that the tun-

nel started to narrow. It never got so small that she had to
crawl on her hands and knees, but there were a few places
where she definitely had to walk bent over. There were
also dips in the path containing standing water; places too
low to drain when the tide ran out.

After what seemed an eternity of walking, the tunnel
began to climb upward. Curious to know how long she'd
been walking, she shone her flashlight on her watch. She
couldn't believe what she saw. Allowing for the time spent
getting to the cave, she estimated that she'd been walking
nearly twenty minutes. She would have thought the chupacabras would prefer to be closer to the cave entrance,
but reasoned that their chamber might be more recessed
because that entire stretch of the tunnel leading in would
be underwater during high tide.

Another ten minutes passed and she started questioning whether she had the wrong cave. She'd give it another
five minutes—if she still hadn't found the colony, she was
turning back. She didn't want to be here when the tide
came in.

Directing the beam of the flashlight up ahead, she saw
that the tunnel made a turn. As soon as she reached the
bend, she saw that the tunnel ahead widened into a large
underground chamber. Shining the beam of her flashlight
over it, she was amazed at how open it was—almost like
a small underground amphitheater. And scattered around
like actors frozen in place were thirty or more granite-
like gargoyle-looking statues. Day-phase chupacabras.

Amazed, she could only stare. The chupacabras were in
all sizes and shapes. Some had wings while others didn't.
Some seemed light gray while others appeared almost
black. She would have loved to examine each and every

one of them at length, but there was no time. Already, she'd been in the cave longer than she'd intended.

Moving slowly, in case she was gravely mistaken about chupacabras being incapable of attacking during their day phase, she examined the smaller creatures, looking for one with its mouth open. She found a wingless chupacabra that looked more like a griffin than the feline shape she was familiar with, but its mouth was open and its front fangs looked too large for its head. This one would do. It was a small thing and she worried that it might not be old enough, but if it were any bigger she might not be able to carry it.

Shrugging out of her backpack, she took several deep breaths to steady her nerves. Even so, her hands shook when she pulled out the harness she'd brought along. Frozen like statues, the creatures were still intimidating. One good bite of those massive front fangs and she'd be dead.

No, worse, she reminded herself. She'd be a vampire.

She glanced around the chamber once more, making sure none of the creatures had moved and then set to work, moving quickly. It was awkward putting the harness around the creature. By the time she'd fitted it and strapped it on, she'd spent more time than she'd intended. When she tried to stand, she was relieved to discover that even though the creature appeared to be made of stone, it wasn't all that heavy.

With a final glance around, she started back down the tunnel, her thoughts already jumping ahead. She could keep the chupa in the stable through the night, then at sunrise tomorrow, she'd collect the venom she needed. It might not be enough to make her a changeling, but it might give her the added strength and speed she needed to help Erik against the vampires.

She'd been walking for some time when she noticed that the floor of the tunnel was more than damp. There was standing water. She couldn't remember any of the passage being this wet and hurried her pace, afraid that she'd misjudged the time of high tide. After another five minutes, the water was ankle-deep and rising fast.

She knew that up ahead, the tunnel sloped downward. The water would be even deeper—possibly to the point of sealing off the entrance.

She started rattling off the math in her head. *If the vampire hunter is a meter from the chamber after slogging through ankle-deep water for fifteen minutes, where will she be after ten more minutes if she's walking downhill?*

She didn't have to be a physics major to know the answer was *ass-deep in trouble.*

What did the chupacabras do at night when the tide was in? Surely, they didn't stay inside. The only possible answer was that there had to be another entrance to the cave that came out above ground.

She turned around, determined to find it. Even as she hurried, the water seemed to be coming in faster with every passing second. Briefly, she considered leaving the chupacabra behind in order to lighten her load and speed her progress, but she couldn't bring herself to condemn the creature to a certain drowning.

The going was slow. The only good news was that the closer she got to the cavern, the lower the level of the water became, until finally she was back on dry ground.

As she rounded the last turn to the cavern, she stopped to peek around the corner and was relieved to see that the chupacabras hadn't moved. Outside, it must still be daylight.

Looking around, she played the beam of her flashlight over the walls, hoping to find another entrance into the chamber. Everywhere she looked, though, the walls seemed solid.

The longer she searched, the more desperate she became. Finally, her beam hit a small fissure in the opposite wall. She took off running across the chamber and was about halfway across when a flicker of movement froze her in her tracks.

With a desperate, sinking feeling, she looked around and realized that she'd made a grave miscalculation on the time.

In the pit of her stomach, terror uncoiled until it had wrapped itself around her stomach and lungs. Her heart raced as adrenaline pumped through her system. Everywhere she looked, chupacabras were waking up. Despite what Jess had told her about the creatures' seemingly gentle nature, she wasn't seeing any evidence of it now as they growled at her.

When one of the chupacabras screeched, the hairs on the back of Kacie's neck stood up. She turned and saw the large gray, feline-looking creature stalking toward her on its disproportionately large hind legs. It opened its mouth to screech again and Kacie's gaze fixed on the two large fangs.

Afraid to break eye contact with it, she slowly backed away, but other chupacabras circled around, blocking her retreat. Deep down inside, she knew she wasn't going to come out of this unscathed. Probably she wouldn't even come out alive. Sheer, unadulterated terror caused her heart to race and her breath to come in short gasps.

When one particularly large chupacabra roared, the noise was ear-splitting, and it tore a scream from Kacie's very core. Then she felt her back being clawed and realized she'd forgotten about the baby.

After that, everything happened too fast for her to register anything more than feeling like a car had slammed into her. One minute, she was standing. The next, she was lying on the ground, her arms and back burning where sharp claws ripped open the flesh. By the time her mind registered the excruciating pain in her neck, she was already dying.

Chapter
10

Erik jerked awake, feeling panicked. He leaped out of bed, grabbed his sword, and prepared to face the danger—only there was none. Listening, he heard no screams or shouts. He could detect no sound or movement at all. Opening his door, he stepped into the hallway and, again, everything looked and sounded normal. Yet the urgency inside him continued to build, making him crazy.

He raced to the guest bedroom but found it empty. A quick search of his apartment told him Kacie wasn't there. Half hoping she'd gone to her own room, he raced out of his apartment, glad it was dark outside, and took the two flights of stairs to the second floor. Her door was standing open when he got there and it took only a quick glance inside to determine that she wasn't there either.

Trying to stay calm, he focused on the source of his feelings and noticed that it was coming to him over the psychic link. What really surprised him was that it wasn't coming from the vampires, but rather from the chupaca-bras—specifically, the alpha male who had created him.

Concentrating, an image began to emerge in his mind. It was distorted at first, but slowly began to grow sharper. The horror he felt then was all too real—through the chu-pacabra's eyes he saw Kacie's terrified face.

He didn't stop to question how she knew about the col-ony or how she'd found it. His priority was to get to her as quickly as he could. He didn't want to think about what would happen if he couldn't get there in time. Kacie being killed and then turning into a vampire was not something he was prepared to deal with.

He flew out of the house, sending thoughts to the alpha male, urging him not to attack. It had been so long since he had last communicated with a chupacabra he wasn't sure he re-membered how, but he sure as hell was going to try. With each pounding footstep, as he ran across the lawn to the stable, he bombarded the chupacabra with his mental pleas.

Jumping into his Hummer, he started the engine. Sec-onds later he was racing down the road toward town. The oceanside entrance to the chupacabra cave would be underwater by now, but that didn't matter. The entrance through the old cemetery was closer.

He raced through the night, fear clutching his soul. When he was almost to town, he turned onto the dirt road that led to the cemetery. He didn't even worry about whether or not Michael or the others were about. When he reached the cemetery, he drove through the entrance and took the main drive to the back. There he parked the Hummer and got out. Immediately, he jumped the fence and continued into the wooded area beyond until he found the outcropping of rock.

It took him precious seconds to find the opening because it had been so long since he'd last been there and the landmarks had changed with time.

Once inside, the passage was dark, but he hardly noticed. There was only one thing on his mind: Get to Kacie.

When he finally reached the main chamber, he stopped and stood still, giving the creatures time to register that he was there.

Looking around, he saw that there were easily twenty-five or thirty chupacabras moving about, and he felt weak. Fifty years ago, there had been half this many. Most of them seemed to be gathered at the far end of the chamber and Erik knew that Kacie was the object of their attention. Wondering how he was going to get past them, he drew his sword and started forward.

The closer he got, the more nervous the creatures seemed to become. They shifted about, keeping a wary eye on him. He slowed his steps even more.

Afraid to say anything out loud, he pushed feelings of peace and safety through the link. He spared a glance at Kacie and saw that her body was covered in blood. She moved and he breathed a sigh of relief that she was still alive. Then another creature moved out of his way and he was able to see more clearly.

What he'd mistaken for Kacie was, in fact, a small chupacabra tangled in some kind of netting. Erik moved forward. It seemed to take him forever to reach Kacie's body and even longer to bend over, because he didn't want to do anything to startle the creatures. Once he was there, he saw that the baby was caught in a harness strapped to Kacie's back. Before he could get Kacie out of there, he'd have to free the creature.

"Easy now," Erik soothed, reaching out slowly. He sent reassurance to the chupacabras through the psychic link, praying they understood he was trying to help.

As soon as he touched the baby, however, it panicked. Sharp fangs sank deep into his arm and it was everything Erik could do not to lash out at the tiny thing. Instead, he gritted his teeth against the pain and worked quickly to unsnap the fastening of the harness. It would have been easier to use his sword, but with the creature thrashing about like it was, he was afraid of accidentally cutting it.

By the time he finally worked the baby free, he'd been bitten numerous times and his arms and chest were streaming with blood—but he was hardly aware of it. His full attention was on Kacie.

Now that the baby was loose, all of the creatures moved off to the side, leaving Erik alone with Kacie. Sliding his hands under her body, he lifted her into his arms, remembering to retrieve his sword from where he'd laid it on the floor.

Getting out was a slow process, but as soon as they left the main chamber, Erik drew his first easy breath. Kacie's life was still in danger, but at least now he could move at full speed. Grateful for once that he was a vampire, he carried her through the tunnels faster than any rescue team could have.

He cleared the fence to the cemetery and hurried to the Hummer. There, he propped his sword against the side while he opened the back door and placed Kacie inside. Then sheathing his sword, he climbed into the front seat, shut his door, and with hands that shook, started the engine.

Erik was barely aware of driving back to the castle; all his thoughts were focused on saving Kacie's life. She had lost too much blood and there was no way to get her to the hospital in time. *He'd* have to save her.

Uttering a litany of prayers, he carried Kacie into his apartment and laid her on the bed. He wanted to clean the blood away, but the greater priority was replacing the blood she'd lost.

Going to his freezer, he took out all the frozen bags of Type O human blood that he'd kept for feeding emergencies.

Tossing them into the microwave, he set the dial to defrost, hoping that in doing so, he wasn't denaturing any important proteins or destroying elements her body might need.

While he waited for the blood, he searched for the rubber tubing and IV needles that were part of every Winslow's medical kit and carried them back to the bedroom. Next, he found a clean rag, towel, and antiseptic. Then he cut away Kacie's blood-soaked clothes, too concerned with her safety to notice her nudity with anything but a clinical eye.

Covering her with a blanket, he went back to the kitchen to check on the blood. It had thawed but was still chilled, so he put the bags back in, reset the timer for another minute, and hurried back into the bedroom to clean Kacie's face and body.

There were two large gaping holes in her neck where a chupacabra's fangs had sunk into her flesh. Even though he'd lived through a similar attack, the memory of it had long since faded with time. He hoped that when Kacie recovered, she'd have no memory of it either.

He finished treating the wounds and went back into the kitchen. The blood was completely thawed.

Carrying the first bag to her bed, he started the transfusion and waited as the bag slowly emptied. Every second that went by seemed to take an eternity. He sat beside her on the bed and combed the hair from her face, murmuring words of comfort.

When it seemed she was sleeping easier, he took the time to clean his own wounds. He'd lost a lot of blood and had no doubt been injected with a fair amount of venom, but he was already a vampire. There was nothing more the chupacabras could do to him—especially one as small as the one who'd bitten him.

The night passed slowly, but after the third bag of blood, Kacie's skin color was much improved. As her body began to heal, the nightmares started and her breathing grew rapid. She thrashed about on the bed as if she were fighting off an attacker—or a chupacabra. Erik watched, feeling helpless.

"It's all right, love. You're safe," he told her, stroking her head as he tried to ease her fears.

Her eyelids fluttered open and her gaze sought his face. "You're safe now, Kacie. I'm with you. It's going to be okay."

He repeated this several times until she quieted. At one point, she struggled to open her mouth, but couldn't get any words out. Then her eyes slowly closed and she slept.

Eventually her breathing evened out and he thought she might really be on the road to recovery. He knew enough about the chupacabra venom to know that it had amazing healing powers and already it was working in her system. She might not need another bag of blood, but he couldn't afford to take that chance, so he gave it to her anyway.

There was nothing more he could do for Kacie after that. Nature would have to take its course. As for himself, he was hungry. There were only two containers of pig's blood. It wasn't nearly enough to satisfy his hunger, but he was reluctant to finish off the last of his blood. There was no telling how soon he could get more.

He removed one of the containers and while he heated it, he placed a call to the butcher for more. The man had delivered containers of blood to the castle before; if he found it strange, he never said so. Of course, Erik paid him well not to be too curious.

After eating, he picked up the phone a second time. It was time to make the hardest call of his life.

"There's been an accident," he said when Gerard answered. "Kacie's going to be all right, but…" For the next few minutes, he explained what had happened. When he finished, the silence that met him was grim.

"Are you sure she's going to change?" Gerard asked finally.

"Yes. She'll need to make a few lifestyle adjustments, but she's going to be okay." Erik paused. "I'm sorry that I didn't do a better job of protecting her."

"What?" Gerard sounded genuinely surprised. "From what you've told me, you saved her life."

"She should never have gotten hurt."

"Don't beat yourself up. No one knows better than I do how headstrong Kacie can be."

Erik thought "headstrong" might be an understatement, but he let it pass. "Thank you," he said.

"For?"

"For not thinking I'd let something bad happen to her on purpose."

Gerard sighed. "It never occurred to me that you were responsible. I know that you'd do everything in your power to protect the members of my family—especially Kacie."

Erik wondered if Gerard suspected that his feelings for Kacie had changed. "What do you mean, especially Kacie?"

"I meant the promise you made to Vince. What did you think I meant?"

"Nothing." He sighed. "There is one more, rather significant, problem." He went on and told Gerard about the situation with Michael and the pact.

"Why didn't you ever tell us about the pact?" Gerard asked when he finished. He sounded angry.

"I was trying to protect all of you." Erik defended himself, though in light of what had happened, it sounded weak even to his ears. "I didn't think the family would understand why I'd made a deal with vampires."

Gerard sighed. "Perhaps not. On the other hand, if you had taken that chance, Kacie wouldn't have accidentally killed your friend."

Erik sighed. "Sometimes I think Kacie hates vampires so much, she'd kill them all if she had the chance."

"I noticed you're still alive."

Erik was silent as he thought about it. There had been several opportunities over the last couple of days when she could have killed him—or let him die—and she hadn't.

"I'm catching the next flight home," Gerard said into the silence. "I shouldn't be away at a time like this."

"Good. I think Kacie would like it if you were here. Call me when you get into Newcastle, we'll come pick you up. It'll be safer that way."

Eight hours after he'd brought her home, Erik dragged himself into the bedroom to find Kacie lying awake in bed.

"How are you feeling?" he asked.

"Like...run over...by train," she croaked in a voice still raw from the trauma.

"Do you remember what happened?"

He saw her start to shake her head and then wince from the pain. She closed her eyes and lay that way for so long that he thought she might have fallen asleep. Then her eyes snapped open and from the strange expression on her face, he knew some of the details were coming back.

As if to prove him right, she lifted a hand to the side of her neck. "How bad?"

"Bad enough."

"Vampire?"

"No, you're not a vampire. However, you've got a lot of venom in your system."

She listened to the pronouncement and then slowly exhaled. "Not exactly...how I...planned," she said in a hoarse whisper.

Planned? "Are you telling me that you purposely went to the chupacabra colony?" He was instantly livid. He wasn't sure what he'd thought—maybe that she'd been lured there—but to have gone there intentionally? "Are you fucking kidding me?" His yelling caused her to cringe, but he didn't care. "I've done everything I can to protect you and then you go and pull a stunt like this? If I hadn't been awakened by the chupacabras, you'd be dead, like me." He stopped talking long enough to take a deep breath. He had come so close to losing her. "Maybe you don't care what happens to you, but damn it, I do."

She had the decency to look contrite. "I thought I could...help you...if I was...stronger...faster."

"By becoming a prime?" He'd never heard of anything so crazy.

"No…changeling," she said, defending herself. She swallowed, winced, and then struggled to go on. "Wanted to… inject myself…with venom." She paused to catch her breath. "Still daytime…safe. Didn't expect the tunnel…so long. Tide came…before…finished. Trapped."

He stared at her in awe. She had gone into the chupacabra colony on purpose. He didn't care how rational it might have sounded to her at the time. "You're a damn fool," he chastised her, rubbing his head in frustration. "If you were going to do something that asinine, you should have told me."

"…talk me out of it."

"Damn right, I would have." He sighed. "I would have thought you'd at least be smart enough to use the other entrance."

She shot him a piercing look. "Didn't know…about other entrance…not in your journal."

He couldn't believe he'd heard her correctly. "You went through my private journals? In my office?"

She blushed. "Wanted to know…more about you. Curious."

He hadn't expected that answer and her interest in him helped mute his anger. "All you had to do was ask. I'll tell you anything you want to know."

"Promise?" She stared up at him with such intensity that he wasn't sure how to react.

"I promise. Now, you should try to get some rest," he told her, starting to feel sick. The blood he'd taken wasn't setting well and for the last several minutes, his vision had been tunneling. He didn't want Kacie to know, so he tried to keep his tone casual. "Next time you wake up, you'll feel better. At least that's one advantage to being a changeling—you heal quickly."

"Changeling?" Her eyes got wide as she squeaked out the word.

"Yes. Changeling. You were injected with enough venom that the change is inevitable. I've only witnessed one change and that was with Angus, my brother. Obviously, that was a long time ago. Charles kept Gerard and me apprised of the two American changelings, though, and from what I recall, your appetite will change over the next couple of days. You'll crave rare, bloodied meat, but don't worry, that will go away once your fangs come in."

"Fangs?" He could tell that the reality was finally hitting her.

Letting go of the last of his anger, Erik sat beside her on the bed and smoothed the hair from her face. It was a habit he couldn't seem to break because it gave him an excuse to touch her and right now, it soothed him too. "It won't be that bad," he assured her. "Just sleep for now."

As he continued to stroke her hair, her eyelids grew heavy. Several times they fluttered as she tried to keep them open.

"Michael?" she asked, barely above a whisper.

"Don't worry about him. He's not going to do anything to us here."

"Erik"—her eyes drifted closed—"don't leave me."

"I won't." He smoothed her hair and she fell back asleep. "Not as long as I still draw breath."

Kacie woke, feeling sore, tired, and weak. For several minutes she didn't move, taking inventory of the various aches and pains. She was lucky to be alive and knew it was thanks to Erik that she was.

Thinking of him, she turned and saw that he was lying beside her on the bed. He was unusually still and she hated to wake him, so she let her gaze linger on him, studying the contours of his face, the strong line of his jaw—the pallor of his skin.

She looked again, noticing the scratches on his neck that hadn't been there the night before. Had the chupacabras attacked him when he'd rescued her?

Feeling guilty that he'd suffered because of her, she laid her hand against his cheek in a gentle caress. He was burning up.

"Erik," she whispered, not wanting to startle him. When he didn't respond, she tried again. "Erik, it's Kacie."

"Kacie?" Her name came on a raspy whisper.

"Erik—you're running a fever. What's wrong?"

"Don't feel well," he managed to say. "Sick."

Kacie hadn't realized vampires could get sick. And if it was because the chupacabras were infected, why wasn't she ill? Questions tumbled around in her head, making her feel helpless, not knowing what to do for him. "Do you need blood? Medicine?"

He mumbled something incoherent, leaving her to draw her own conclusions. The first thing she needed to do was get his fever down.

Hurrying to the bathroom, she wet a cloth with cold water, wringing out the excess. She carried it back to Erik and laid the folded cloth across his forehead while she undid the buttons of his shirt. She laid her hands flat on his chest and pushed the shirt aside, noticing the male perfection of his chest. The dark hair covering it was soft and not so thick it obstructed her view of the muscled contours.

It was with an effort that she tore her attention away and rolled him to the side in order to pull the shirt completely off. As soon as his arms were bared, she caught her breath. Both arms bore puncture wounds and scratches. He'd obviously cleaned them sometime while she was unconscious, but they were hot to the touch and seemed to her to be the source of his illness.

For the next several minutes, she ran a cool cloth over his heated skin. Afterward, he seemed to rest more quietly, but she could tell he was still weak.

Covering him with a sheet, she went into his kitchen to look for blood. She saw the spent bags in the trash, along with bloodstained IV tubing. Glancing at the inside of her arm, she saw the faint mark where an IV needle had been inserted and realized he'd infused her with blood—and probably saved her life in doing so.

Her resolve to help him increased and she searched the refrigerator for other bags. All she found was a single pint of pig's blood. That would work to help restore his health but she knew it wasn't as good as human blood would have been.

She took it out and placed it in the microwave to heat. As soon as it was warm enough, she took it out. About to carry it in to him, a memory surfaced. The mythos around the energizing powers of blood freely given was well-known in the Winslow family. Typically, the story was told in reference to blood given to changelings, but hadn't Jess told her that she and John had given Harris blood once when he was ill? It had helped save his life.

It was worth trying.

She looked around the kitchen, wondering how much blood she would need—and how she was going to extract it. She grabbed the medical kit and searched the contents for a syringe. There wasn't one.

With the sense that time was running out, she looked around. Her eyes fell on the cutlery block. She looked from it to her open palm. The cut didn't have to be deep, just enough to bleed. And now that she was a changeling, it would heal quickly.

She pulled a knife from the block and tried to think of a better solution, but couldn't. Then, before she could change her mind, she dragged the knife across her palm.

The sting of the cut made her suck in her breath. Blood began pooling in her hand and she quickly grabbed a cup from the cupboard. Then she held her hand above it and let the blood flow into it.

"I give this blood freely," she said aloud. "I give this blood freely and pray it helps." *Because it hurts like a son of a bitch*.

A minute later, the pain started to fade and she noticed the bleeding had slowed considerably. Looking at her palm, she saw that the wound was already beginning to clot and close. She raised the cup and saw that there was enough blood for a swallow or two. It would have to do.

Running her hand under the water to clean away the last of the blood, she dried it and wrapped it with gauze from the medical kit. Then she carried both containers of blood in to Erik.

He was still lying with his eyes closed.

"Erik, I need you to wake up," she said, setting the containers on the bedside table. She needed to prop him up so he could drink.

With one hand beneath his head for support and the other on his shoulder, she pulled him into a sitting position. It was obvious he wasn't awake enough to hold himself like that, so she made a snap decision. Snaking a leg around him, she sat on the bed behind him. Then she let him fall back against her.

"Erik. You need to drink." With his head resting at the crook of her neck, she angled the cup with her blood to his lips. "I give you this blood freely. Drink." She tipped the cup until blood touched his lips. "Drink it, Erik, please," she said in his ear. His mouth opened and she tipped the cup a little more, pouring a small amount of blood past his lips. She wanted to shout with joy when she saw his throat work to swallow. "That's it, Erik. Drink. I give you my blood freely. Please let it help."

It took about fifteen minutes before he finished off the blood in both cups. After that, Kacie was exhausted. She decided she'd done too much too soon after her own injuries. She didn't even have the energy to try to get out from behind Erik, so she rested against the headboard and let him rest against her. That's how she fell asleep.

Chapter
11

Kacie woke when she felt Erik stirring. "Hey there," she said softly, not wanting to startle him. His head still rested in the crook of her neck and she laid a hand across his forehead. "I think your fever is gone. How are you feeling?"

"I should be asking you that," he said, sounding tired. "What happened?"

"I don't know. When I woke up, you were sick. I found some blood in your refrigerator and gave it to you. Then I sort of fell asleep."

"Have you been holding me like this all day?" His voice sounded husky, intoxicating.

"Yes," she said, unable to stop herself from running her hands across his chest, savoring the feel of him.

She felt his intake of breath right before he pushed himself up off the bed and headed for the door. "Where are you going?" she asked, feeling suddenly abandoned.

He wouldn't even look at her. "Back to my room."

"You don't have to go," she told him.

"Kacie, I...Christ. Yes, I do. You don't have any clothes on and right now, I'm feeling a little too alive." He disappeared out the door.

Pulling the sheet up to cover her, she felt her face heat. She'd been too worried about him earlier to notice her clothes, or the lack thereof. Now she wasn't sure if she was more embarrassed or disappointed that he'd run off.

Hoping a shower would wash away both emotions, she got out of bed. The clothes she'd worn into the chupacabra cave were missing. She imagined they had been covered with blood and Erik had probably thrown them away. That was fine, but it left her with nothing to wear. She'd deal with it after her shower. For now, she wrapped the sheet around her and headed for the bathroom.

Once there, she turned to close the door behind her and found herself staring through a hole. She remembered the crashing noise she'd heard—how long ago had that been? Now she knew what had caused it.

Hanging her sheet over the hole, she went to start the water. When it was hot enough, she stepped beneath the spray. As the water washed over her, it relaxed both her muscles and the mental restraint she'd kept around her thoughts. Her mind started replaying the entire attack sequence in slow motion—with all the horror and all the fear. She remembered the way the chupacabras had crowded her and felt the terror all over again.

She tried to force her thoughts to something more pleasant, but couldn't escape reliving that moment. Afraid the images wouldn't go away unless she got out, she picked up the soap and bathed so fast that she was done before the steam from the shower could build. Turning off the water, she pushed aside the shower curtain and reached for a towel. Her gaze fell on the mirror hanging across from her and she found herself looking straight into a vampire's red crimson eyes.

Adrenaline shot through her as she stumbled back, crying out in alarm. She lost her footing and fell, grabbing at the shower curtain for support. It came crashing down on top of her, making a huge noise—almost as loud as the sound of the bathroom door slamming open moments later.

Erik stood there, eyes blazing. Clutching a sword, he looked ready to do battle. He scanned the entire bathroom before letting his gaze settle on her. "Everything all right?" he asked cautiously. "Are you hurt?"

"Just my pride," she said, sitting sprawled in the tub with one leg hanging over the side. "I saw something in the mirror that startled me."

"What?"

"Me." She expected him to make fun of her, but he didn't. "I saw my eyes in the mirror," she explained. "They were glowing, like a—"

"Vampire's?"

She nodded.

"You'll get used to it," he told her.

"I don't want to get used to it," she told him, sharing some of her fears. "I look like they do."

"Oh, you mean, like me?" There was a bite to his tone.

"I don't mean you," she told him. "I know you'd never hurt anyone. No, I look like the ones who killed my family."

"No, you don't." He paused. "And you're wrong, you know. About me. Sometimes I hurt people without even meaning to." He lowered his sword and walked over to her.

"And sometimes I do it on purpose, in order to protect the ones I care about. I'm not evil incarnate, but I'm no saint either." He offered her a hand, which she pointedly ignored. "So you want up?"

"I'm...I'm not wearing anything."

"I hate to break it to you, but it's a little late for modesty."

He was right. Reluctantly, she clasped the shower curtain to her with one hand and placed her other in his so he could help her to stand. Then he grabbed a towel out of the cabinet and held it out to her.

She took it and waited until he'd turned his back to drop the shower curtain back into the tub. "How hard was it for you to adjust?" she asked, wrapping the towel around herself.

"It was hard, but there *are* advantages."

"Like...?"

"Well, for starters, those glowing red eyes you're so scared of? They'll let you see at night better than a cat."

She considered it and decided that could be a positive. "Go on."

"Then there's the speed and strength. Next time you pick up a sword to fight a vampire, I think you're going to be very happy with your reflexes and how well you fight."

Yes, she thought. Both of those were good.

"There are other things—better hearing and sense of smell."

"But on the downside, there's how tired I'll be during the day."

"Granted, but at least you won't turn to stone if the sunlight touches you, so count your blessings."

That was true, she thought.

"The bottom line here," he went on, "is that there's not a damn thing you can do about it, so you might as well make the best of it. Now, how about some clothes and then I'll fix you something to eat. Are you hungry?"

"A little," she admitted. "What about the shower? I think I might have broken the curtain rod." She stared at the damage, feeling bad about it.

He glanced at it, then at the door, which now hung at an angle from one hinge, and shrugged. "Forget it. I was thinking of remodeling anyway."

Smiling, he walked her back to her room, then left her while he continued on to his. He came back a few minutes later and handed her some clothes.

He glanced at his bare wrist like he was checking the time and then dropped it back to his side with a sigh. "I don't know what time it is, but it feels late. The butcher should have delivered the order I placed last night. I'll go get it and while you change, I'll start cooking you something to eat."

Leaving her in the bedroom, he headed for the door. So much had happened lately, he was having trouble absorbing it all. It didn't help that he wasn't quite feeling his old self yet. It wasn't that he was tired or sick, necessarily. He actually felt pretty good, but that probably had more to do with the time of night it was—and other things.

He undid the lock, his thoughts straying to that moment an hour ago when he woke up and realized he was resting against Kacie's nude body. She fit against him like they were made for each other. He imagined he could still feel her full breasts pressed against his back.

Pulling open the door, he wondered what might have happened if he hadn't left the room.

"Erik!"

Kacie's scream broke his reverie as daylight blinded him.

He slammed the door shut just as Kacie rushed up to him. Still unable to see, he felt her hands running over his face, his body.

"Oh my God, Erik. Are you hurt?" There was an urgent tone in her voice. "Did the sun touch you anywhere?"

He took a moment to brace himself. How could the sun not have touched him? There was a pain in his hand and he held it out to her. "My hand, I think," he rasped, blinking rapidly, willing his vision to adjust to the dark so he could see again.

He felt her cool clasp as she held first one hand and then the other, turning them over several times.

"Which one?"

The damage should have been obvious. "The right."

"No, no," she said, relief in her voice. "It's fine. They're both fine." Her hands returned to his cheeks and she stroked them. "I think you got out of the way in time."

Slowly, his vision returned and he studied his hands for himself. He did a quick inward check and decided she was right—he was untouched, but confused. In four hundred years, he'd never made a mistake like that.

"Erik?"

He saw the worry in her face and offered her a weak smile. "I'm fine."

"You're sure?"

"Yeah."

She hit him in the chest then, hard enough to knock him back a step. "What the hell were you thinking? You almost got yourself fried."

He stared at her in surprise and then smiled.

"Why are you smiling, you fang-toothed moron?"

He pulled her to him. "Why, Kacie. I believe you actually care."

"Of course I do," she said softly, a blush spreading across her cheeks.

He stared at her mouth, feeling its invitation. "Are you hungry?"

Her eyes widened and he heard her breath catch. "Yes," she breathed.

He smiled again and let her go, needing to put some distance between them before he did something she would regret. "Then if you'd go to the door and see if the butcher left my order by the door, I can make you something to eat. What do you feel like? Toast? Eggs and bacon? Steak tartare?"

Feeling a little off kilter at Erik's sudden change in mood—after nearly getting himself killed—it took her a second to process his words. When she did, she frowned, wondering if she'd heard him correctly.

"Raw steak?" The thought should have been disgusting, but wasn't, which bothered her.

"Not yet?" he said with a smile. "Oh well, it'll come." He looked at the face she made and smiled. "Don't worry, it won't last. Just a short spell where your diet changes and your fangs come in. After that, it's back to a relatively normal life—for a changeling."

"If you say so," she muttered.

"I do. Now get the food," he gestured to the door. "I've had about all the sunshine I care to have, thanks."

She made sure Erik had stepped well away from the door before she opened it. There, sitting just outside, was a Styrofoam cooler. She opened the lid and saw that it was filled with containers of blood, eggs, and bacon. She carried it inside to Erik and set it on the kitchen counter. He immediately set to work cooking her breakfast.

She stood and watched him, gradually becoming aware of a loud scratching noise. "What's that sound?"

"Mouse," he said without turning around.

"What? You have mice?" She looked around. "Where?"

"First, all old homes—especially castles—have mice, or rats. And second, nowhere close. They're in the walls probably up on the next floor."

"The next floor. No way, Erik. It's so loud. I think it must be coming from your cabinets." She cautiously opened the pantry door closest to her, expecting a rodent to jump out at her.

"You've got hypersensitive hearing now, Kacie. You're going to start hearing all sorts of noises."

She found the thought intriguing. "Really? Like what?"

He was at the stove and turned to glance at her over his shoulder. "I don't know. The smallest breeze. Hummingbird wings from across the yard. On a clear night, the dogs from town."

"No kidding. What else?"

"I don't know. All sorts of things."

She turned around and whispered, "What about you? Can you hear me?" She looked back and saw him giving her a tolerant look over his shoulder.

"Yes. I can hear you."

She smiled and walked into the living room, once again turning her back. "Can you hear me now?" She said in a softer whisper.

This time, he didn't turn around and she thought he

might not have heard her, then she heard a faint "yes," as if it floated to her on the wind.

"How about now?" she said even more softly.

"Yes." It was almost so soft she wasn't sure she'd heard it.

She moved to the farthest corner of the room. "How about—"

Before she could finish, the phone rang. She glanced around the room and saw the phone on the counter. She and Erik exchanged worried looks right before he answered it.

"Hello?"

"Erik?" Kacie heard Gerard's voice coming through. "I'm in Newcastle. How's Kacie?"

Erik looked at Kacie and then held out the phone. She went to it hesitantly. The last time she'd talked to Gerard, they'd exchanged hard words. Now, after everything that had happened, none of those things seemed to matter. "Hello?"

"Kacie." Gerard said her name like he was heaving a sigh of relief. "Are you all right?"

"I'm fine. Um... about last time—?"

"Plenty of time to talk when I get home," Gerard cut her off. "I'll get a car and be home in a couple of hours."

About to agree, Kacie saw Erik shaking his head. When he held out his hand, she gave him the phone.

"Don't drive out here. We'll come pick you up. There will be safety in numbers, I think. As soon as it's dark, we'll set out. Keep your cell phone on. We'll call you when we reach town."

They said good-bye and hung up.

An hour later, Kacie and Erik were in his BMW heading to Newcastle. They'd just left Hocksley and were driving along the short stretch of road south of town. The edge of the cliff was off to their left while the forest extended to their right. So far, there'd been no sign of Michael, Carrington, or any other vampire.

The atmosphere inside the car was tense. Kacie wished she could relax, but there were too many things weighing on her mind. Her body was changing—she was becoming half-vampire and half-human—and she wasn't sure how she felt about that. She'd wanted to inject herself with the venom to get some of the changeling abilities, but had never intended to turn herself into a half-vampire. Moot point now.

Suddenly the full magnitude of her actions hit her. Before she'd gone into the cave, she'd had a choice of whether she wanted to continue life as a vampire hunter or go to the States in pursuit of a normal life. There was no choice now.

She definitely couldn't go to the States with Ben. He would be disappointed because they'd already made so many plans. Worse still, she wondered if the two of them could even remain friends. *Hi, Ben. Don't freak out, but I'm half-vampire.* Yeah, that would go over well.

And then there was the small matter of finding employment. There weren't that many night-shift accounting positions to be found. If she couldn't find a job, she wouldn't be able to pay her bills. She could lose her apartment and worse, not have enough money for food.

She rubbed her temples as her head started to hurt and cast a furtive glance at Erik. His attention was focused on the road ahead of them, giving her a chance to study his profile. His face was so familiar to her and yet she never tired of looking at it. He was strength and nobility.

She had no trouble envisioning him as a knight in armor. Had she really once thought of him as being evil simply because he was a vampire? He was a good man who'd been in the wrong place at the wrong time, turned into a vampire against his will. And when that fate had befallen him, what had he done about it? Preyed on humans because it was the only way he knew to survive? No. He'd learned how to survive without feeding off humans, and in fact had spent his long, lonely nights protecting humans from those of his own kind.

She'd been so wrong about him. Gritting her teeth against her emotions, she noticed how her two upper canines were loose. It meant her fangs would be coming in soon. She was more like Erik now than ever before.

"You okay?" He asked, hearing her sigh.

"Yes."

"Worried about seeing Gerard again?"

"No. I was thinking about you."

That earned her a startled glance. "Anything you want to share?"

"I want to thank you."

"For what?"

"For everything you've done—for me, for my family." She gestured out the window. "The residents. I don't think any of us can ever repay you for all the ways you've protected us over the years."

"Here now, what's brought all this on?"

She smiled. "Guess more than just my body has changed as a result of everything that's happened."

He arched an eyebrow at her. "Really? Then maybe—"

A loud popping noise sounded and the car jerked to one side, throwing Kacie off balance. She threw her hands out to steady herself as Erik wrestled with the wheel to bring the car back on the road.

"Did we get a flat?" She asked.

There was another popping noise and a hole appeared in the front windshield.

"Erik, look out!" Kacie shouted and the car swerved dangerously close to the cliff side of the road.

"Get down," Erik ordered. "Someone's shooting at us."

"You're kidding!" Kacie ducked her head down below the dash. "Michael?"

"Or one of his vampires. There's no telling how long they've been waiting for us to leave town."

Kacie felt the car slowing down. "What are you doing? You're not stopping, are you?"

A small explosion sounded and the back end of the car fishtailed out of control. Kacie heard Erik's grunt and looked over. His face was locked in a mask of steely determination and his eyes glowed with the strength of his anger.

"Hang on," he bit out.

She had just enough time to brace herself when the car veered off the road and went into the ditch. It came to a sudden halt and the silence that fell was broken by their combined gasps.

"Get out," Erik ordered, already reaching for his door. "We can't stay here."

Kacie climbed out on unsteady feet. She looked around, but despite her improved night vision she couldn't see a thing.

Then Erik was there beside her, grabbing her hand and dragging her toward the woods. She'd only taken a couple of steps when the ground beside her suddenly kicked up some dirt. She was several steps past the spot when she realized how close she'd come to getting hit by a bullet. With new determination, she ran faster.

They entered the woods at breakneck speed. Kacie wanted to ask Erik if he had a plan or if they were running blindly, but she was afraid to hear the answer.

Despite the thick undergrowth, Kacie moved easily through the woods. They didn't take a straight path, but wove back and forth, hoping to lose whoever was pursuing them.

After a few minutes, Kacie noticed Erik was moving more slowly. She tried to urge him to move faster, but with each step he seemed to have a harder time keeping up with her.

Then he stumbled and fell, face down.

"Erik!" Kacie hurried to him. "What's the matter?" She turned him over and stared in horror. His entire left side was covered in blood. She pulled open his shirt and saw the bullet hole in his side. "Shit."

"Run, Kacie. Through here into town," he gasped. "If you hurry, you'll get there before they do. Take the wooded path to the castle."

"Save your breath," she told him, pulling him to a sitting position. "Can you stand?"

She thought he'd weigh a ton, but found she was stronger than she'd expected to be. Her muscles ached with the change but she found it easy enough to pull him to his feet. Once he was up, she draped his left arm around her shoulder and then more or less carried him as she started into the woods.

Behind them, she heard the faint rustle of their pursuer

and knew there was no way they were going to make it back to the castle in time.

"Leave me," Erik gasped.

"Shut up and run," she countered. It was taking all her energy to carry him but she wasn't leaving him behind.

She scanned the woods around them as she ran and saw a dip ahead of them. She raced for it, thinking it might offer a place to hide.

To the left, a fallen tree lay on its side. Kacie hurried them to it. The tree didn't lie flat on the ground, leaving a small space beneath it. She helped Erik over to it and eased him to the ground behind it. Then she went back to the other side and looked around.

To a careful observer, their trail could be seen. She needed to cover it. Grabbing a nearby branch, she went back to the point where she and Erik had hit the dip in the ground. Then, dragging the branch behind her, she raced off in the opposite direction. She didn't want to go too far—just far enough to throw whoever was shooting at them off the trail.

As soon as she thought she'd gone far enough, she circled back around to where Erik lay. He was deathly still. She was afraid he'd bleed to death, though she wasn't sure if that was possible. After all, technically, he was already dead.

Taking the branch she'd been using to help make a new trail, she propped it on the ground in front of them, hoping to provide more coverage. She swept some leaves up in front of it and then went behind the fallen limb to sit by Erik.

"I don't know if you can hear me," she whispered in his ear. "But we need to be quiet."

She stroked the hair from his face and leaned over him, wanting to protect him as best she could. When she heard the sound of running footsteps, her entire body grew still in anticipation.

She watched as three vampires came into view—Carrington and two others. In his hand, Carrington carried a rifle. The gun ban in England had obviously not affected the vampire population. The weapon looked old—not that Kacie knew that much about guns—but it made her wonder when Carrington had been turned. Had it been around the time of World War II?

The three men stopped when they reached the dip and looked around. For a brief, horrifying second, Kacie thought Carrington looked directly at her. She tensed for his attack—then one of the other men found the fake trail she'd made and the three were off and running.

Kacie let out a sigh and turned her attention back to Erik. He was lying so still and quiet, already so weak from his recent illness that she worried he might not even survive long enough for her to get him back to the castle. She'd given him her blood before and it had helped. Would it do the same now?

"Erik, wake up." She stroked his cheek and received a faint moan. "Come on, baby. I need you to drink."

She lifted him into a sitting position and propped him against her. She had no way of cutting her palm now to get him to drink, so instead, she took his head in her hands and positioned it over her neck at just the right angle. "Drink, Erik."

She waited, braced for the pain of his fangs breaking her skin, but it never came. "Damn it. Drink. I'm giving you my blood to heal you, but you have to help."

When he still didn't respond, she gritted her teeth and pressed his head down, forcing his fangs to pierce her skin.

Thinking the blood would drip down his throat and slowly revive him, she was totally unprepared when he grabbed her to him, sank his fangs deeper into her throat, and started sucking her blood with a fervor that was too reminiscent of Carrington's attack.

This was Erik, she told herself over and over. He would never hurt her. As she fought to stay calm, she noticed that the pain of the bite was already fading. Instead, she was conscious of the warmth of his lips pressed against the side of her neck, sending little tendrils of awareness skittering through her.

Erik's hands came up to hold her tenderly, one at her shoulder and the other at the back of her head where his fingers were buried in her hair. Her breasts grew heavy and she arched into him, her breathing ragged. She'd expected this experience to be disgusting or terrifying. Certainly, she hadn't counted on it being so arousing.

"Erik," she whispered. It came out sounding like a plea, but for what, she was afraid to say.

Almost as abruptly as he'd started, Erik withdrew his teeth, but he continued to hold her in that intimate way. He was breathing hard; she knew he was working hard to control himself. "Kacie...," he began and then stopped. He rubbed her shoulder and tried again. "Kacie, I...thank you."

"You had me worried there for a minute," she told him, trying to make her tone light to cover her worry.

He stiffened beside her. "Did you think I wouldn't stop?"

"No," she told him softly. "I was afraid you wouldn't start."

She felt his intake of breath. Since they were still sitting so closely together, she couldn't stop herself from leaning forward to press a kiss against his lips. "You scared me. I thought they had killed you." The hunger in his eyes had her pulse racing. "Do you think you can stand?"

He let her help him to his feet and they stood, listening.

"They went by a little while ago. I don't know if they still think they're following us or not."

"Then we'll have to be smarter than they are."

They set off through the woods, taking the most direct route back to the castle. They were almost there when they heard Carrington and the other two vampires talking nearby.

"You let them get away," Carrington was barking at the others.

"No more so than you did," one grumbled back.

"I've had enough of this," the third said. "I don't remember Michael saying anything about shooting them. I thought he wanted them alive."

"They were alive," Carrington said. "How else do you think they were able to run into the woods and get away from us?"

Erik put his hand on Kacie's arm, making her hold still until it was clear the group was walking away from them. As soon as their voices faded, Erik and Kacie hurried on to the castle.

"That was close," Kacie said once they were safely inside. "Maybe my leaving isn't such a bad idea—I don't think they're ever going to stop."

Erik shook his head. "It doesn't matter anymore. Whether you leave or not, they're after me now as well."

Guilt rode her and she felt herself bending under the weight of it.

Erik, obviously sensing how she felt, came up and gave her a reassuring squeeze. He was looking at her so tenderly she didn't know why she'd ever thought he was hard and uncaring. He plucked a small twig from her hair. "Why don't you go bathe? I'll call Gerard and tell him we're not coming."

It didn't take her long to shower. When she got out, she found another one of Erik's shirts laid out for her.

Erik was standing in the living room staring at the pictures on his wall when she joined him. "Thank you," she said, gesturing to the shirt. "At this rate, you won't have anything left to wear."

"I'm not worried about it."

"How did Dad take the news?"

"Like he usually does—calmly. We decided it might be better, after all, for him to hire a cab on his end and drive up tomorrow."

"Good. Now what?"

He smiled. "Now, I'm going to take a shower and try to wash off some of this blood and dirt."

He disappeared into the bathroom and Kacie had barely enough time to go into the kitchen to retrieve the first aid kit when she heard the sound of the shower turning off.

She went to the bathroom door, careful not to look through the hole. "How bad is your wound? Do you need me to dig out a bullet?"

"I'll live, thanks to you. Looks like the bullet went all

the way through. The bleeding stopped before we headed back and I can tell it's already starting to heal." She heard the smile in his voice. "There are some advantages to being a vampire."

At that moment the phone rang.

"Can you get that?" Erik asked through the door. "It's probably Gerard calling to let us know what time to expect him."

Kacie looked around the living room and found the phone. "It's dead," she shouted a moment later. "Do you have an extension?"

"Studio," he answered absently.

That had to be the room beyond the study, she thought, heading for it.

She was almost to the door when she heard Erik's quick intake of breath.

"Kacie—wait."

Too late. She'd opened the door and discovered his big secret.

Chapter
12

W hat's this?" she hollered, walking into the room. "You paint?"

"I, uh, dabble a little bit." Erik had come down the hallway and stopped in the doorway, a towel hurriedly tucked around his waist. She felt his gaze following her around the room as she looked around, the phone now silent and completely forgotten.

In the center of the room stood a large cloth-covered easel. Beside it was a table, on top of which sat an array of oil paints and brushes.

"Looks like you do more than dabble," she said, noticing the stacks of finished canvases leaning against the walls. They were facing away so she couldn't see the subjects. She moved closer, hoping he wouldn't stop her. She was in his private domain, but now that she had breached its secret, she was fascinated. This explained why he was so proud of his collection of works by famous artists like Rembrandt, McLaughlin, and Monet.

Imagining Erik garbed in a painter's smock and beret, standing at the easel, leaning back with his arm out in front of him, one eye closed and his thumb stuck up in the air as he studied the subject of his painting, she tried to meld the image with the blazing red eyes and fangs—and couldn't.

"May I look at what you're working on?" she asked, walking over to the big easel.

He shifted nervously. "I'd really rather you didn't."

She noticed that he hadn't moved from the doorway so she pressed her luck. "Please," she scoffed, "how bad can it be?" She grabbed the cloth before he could stop her and pulled it off. "Oh, Erik," she breathed in admiration, studying the finished landscape. "It's wonderful." She glanced at him and smiled. "I had no idea you were so talented."

She'd thought he'd be pleased with her praise, but it seemed to make him even more uncomfortable, so she tried again. "I really like the way you combined the colors. And the angle—it's terrific—it's—oh my God." She stepped closer to look at the all too familiar signature at the bottom. "Erik, this is a McLaughlin."

She heard him sigh behind her and turned to face him, feeling confused. "I don't understand." Then she realized her mistake and, embarrassed, smiled. "I'm sorry. I assumed this was your work," she said, adding lamely, "because of the cloth and the easel. When did you buy this?"

"I didn't buy it."

"Someone gave it to you?" She gaped at him. "Oh, wow. It wasn't McLaughlin, was it?" Now she was really impressed. "Do you know him personally?"

He came to stand beside her as she continued to study the picture. "Yes, I know McLaughlin."

"What's he like? I've been to his Web site, but it doesn't show a picture of him."

"He's a vampire."

"What?!" She turned to see if he was kidding and saw that he wasn't. Then she realized exactly what he was saying. "*You're* McLaughlin?"

She could hardly believe it. She went over to a stack of framed canvases leaning against the wall and began flipping through them. They were all McLaughlins.

She looked at him pointedly, aware that he hadn't answered her.

"McLaughlin was my mother's maiden name," he said finally.

"I never would have imagined," she mused, feeling overwhelmed. "How long?"

He shrugged. "I've been painting for centuries, but I've only been McLaughlin for about thirty years."

"What made you start painting?"

"You try living four hundred years and see if you don't get bored. The first thing I tried was music and I enjoyed it, but there was always something missing." He smiled. "I tried other things, but nothing held my interest for long. Then, one day, I was missing the sight of a sunrise so badly that I decided to sketch a picture to remind me what it looked like. I showed it to Gerard, who asked if he could have it. Since I could paint another, I gave it to him. He added the McLaughlin signature to the bottom and took it to an art agent. The rest, as they say, is history. Even now, I'm surprised that anyone buys them."

"I'm not," she said with conviction. "They're wonderful paintings."

"Thank you." He sounded so sincere that she wondered if he knew just how great an artist he was. "The money from the sales helps pay the bills on this old castle," he went on to explain. "What's left over, I put into the Winslow Trust for the extended family to live on."

"You fund that trust?" She'd never seen the financial books on the family trust, but knew it had to contain several million dollars.

He nodded. "From the sale of the paintings, as well as the returns from several investments I've made over the years."

She nodded. "I'd always wondered. I mean, I know the Night Slayers don't hold regular jobs, so they had to get money from some—"

The phone rang again. This time, Kacie let Erik answer it. As she watched, a hard, unreadable expression crossed his face. "Just a moment, please." He held the phone out to her. "It's for you."

She took the phone from him, wondering who would be calling her. "Hello?"

"Hi, Kacie. How's your visit home going?" The familiar voice was from another life and so unexpected that she almost didn't recognize it.

"Ben?"

He laughed. "Yeah. Who did you think it was?"

Being in the room with Erik standing so close, wearing nothing more than a towel and looking sinfully sexy, Kacie felt her face heat up. "No—I knew it was you. Don't be ridiculous." She tried to cover her discomfort with a laugh, but it came out sounding forced.

"Kacie—is something wrong?" Ben's voice was laced with concern.

Kacie looked up and found Erik watching her closely. The intensity of his gaze made her pulse race. Ben's gaze never did that to her. "No, everything's fine."

She felt Erik's disapproval slam into her right before he walked out, closing the door behind him. Kacie sighed. She didn't want to have this conversation over the phone, but she didn't see that she had any choice. Ben deserved the truth. And more than Ben, Erik deserved it.

"Actually, Ben. Everything's not all right."

Erik went into his room and closed the door. The wound in his side didn't hurt nearly as much as his chest did at that moment. The phone call from Kacie's fiancé was probably for the best. It helped remind him that she was off limits and would soon be leaving. He wondered if Ben would understand when she told him about the chupacabra incident.

He pulled off the towel and put on a pair of jeans, his mood dark. When he left his room, he paused outside the studio door. When he heard the soft click of the phone being turned off, he hurried into the living room, not wanting her to come out and think he had been eavesdropping.

He waited a full minute for her to come out, and when she didn't, he became concerned. Going back to the studio, he knocked softly on the door. "Kacie?"

"Come in," she called.

He walked in and found her staring at one of his paintings, holding it in front of her. "Everything all right?"

She glanced over at him and smiled. The effect of her

expression rocked through him. "These really are beautiful. I can't believe you're McLaughlin."

He went over to stand beside her, unwilling to be sidetracked by compliments. "How'd he take the news?"

She leaned the painting against the wall with the others and looked around. "Pretty well, actually."

"Really?" Erik frowned. The guy must be a saint. Erik really hated him.

"Yeah. He was disappointed, of course, that I wasn't moving to the States with him, but promised to e-mail me once he got there." She turned and gave him an embarrassed smile. "I lied earlier about being engaged. We never were. I just wanted you to think I was."

Erik couldn't stop his smile. "Is that right? What about the job you were going to take over in the States?"

She shrugged. "I couldn't take it anyway—not now." She sighed.

"You could always become a Night Slayer and live off the family trust," Erik suggested. He hoped his voice didn't sound too eager.

"I'll probably have to," she agreed. "The thing is—I kind of liked doing the accounting work. It made for a nice change from all the slaying."

"Well, I don't know if you're interested, but as it happens, I'm having a hard time juggling the accounting for the Winslow Trust as well as my painting. Would you consider working for the family? Our hours are flexible and you could work at night."

"Really?" Her eyes lit up. "You're offering me a job?"

"Sure, but only if you want it."

"I think I'd like that."

"Good. Great." He heaved a sigh, not even realizing

how afraid he'd been that she would leave and he'd never see her again. That wouldn't happen if she worked for him. Of course, he'd have to find another job for his current accountant because he didn't want to leave the kindly old man unemployed.

Kacie continued to walk around the room. When she stopped before another stack of canvases, he was too preoccupied with watching her to pay much attention to what *she* was looking at. When he finally did, his heart skipped a beat.

"Kacie—wait!" A part of him wanted to turn and run but he knew it was time to face the consequences. She was reaching for the one picture he didn't want her to see. He'd started working on it the day she'd been kidnapped—if anything was an invasion of her privacy, this one was. It had never been meant for public viewing. It was for him to have after she left. "I'd rather you didn't."

She looked at him, her hand ready to pluck off the drape. "Why? What's under here? Something I won't like?"

"Something you won't understand."

She arched her eyebrow and before he could stop her, she pulled the drape off the canvas. "Oh my God."

"I can explain." Erik stared at the portrait of a nude Kacie. "Or maybe I can't."

She blushed, but her expression wasn't one of outrage or horror as he'd expected. "Do I really look like that? It's beautiful," she breathed. "I mean, the way you painted me, I'm beautiful."

He looked at the picture again. "It's the way I see you."

She turned to him with eyes opened wide in surprise. "You do? I thought you hated me."

He looked deep into her eyes, willing her to understand

him. "Hate you?" He wanted to laugh. "Kacie, a man doesn't paint pictures of a woman he hates. He doesn't feel a need to be with her every second he can and he doesn't fight with her simply because that's the only way he can get her attention. When I'm with you, my palms are sweaty, my heart races, and all I can think about is how much I don't want you to leave."

She gasped. "You don't?"

"No. I want you to stay here, with me." *Forever*. He was already feeling too vulnerable to say that last bit out loud.

"But what about your girlfriend?" she asked, taking him by complete surprise.

"What girlfriend?"

"I saw you with her at Myrtle's the night Carrington attacked me."

It took Erik a minute to think of who she meant. "You must have seen me with Penny. Penny Lockwood. She's not my girlfriend. She's my business manager and art agent."

"You kissed her." Her words sounded like a jealous accusation and he couldn't help but be amused.

"Yes, I did. It was a kiss between friends, not lovers, but if it bothers you, I'll never do it again."

She took a step closer and laid her hand against his chest. "The only person I want you kissing is me." She rose up on her toes and placed a small kiss on his lips that shot straight through him.

He nearly groaned aloud. "Careful. Another kiss like that and I'm liable to lose control."

"Is that right?" She feathered a kiss on the side of his neck, sucking at the skin until he shuddered.

He gripped her tightly on the arms, holding her still. "I mean it, Kacie. I'm not doing a repeat of the other night. This time, we finish what we start."

"About damn time," she whispered.

He couldn't keep his eyes from glowing and the desire to taste her blood was almost as strong as the need to bury his swollen flesh deep inside her. He pulled her against him, kissing her with unrestrained need. She responded without hesitation and when she opened her mouth for him, his tongue swept in to taste her sweetness.

Picking her up, he carried her to his room and laid her on the bed. Pulling off his jeans, he tossed them to the side. He saw her eyes widen when her gaze fell on his engorged member, standing at eager attention. He hesitated, worried about frightening her with the intensity of his need, but then she looked up at him and he saw the passion and anticipation in her eyes.

He needed no further encouragement. Joining her on the bed, he held her in his arms, showering her with kisses as he slid his hand up her side. When he reached her breasts, he worshipped each one, savoring their fullness.

She arched into him. Unable to resist, he lowered his head and pulled one of the dusky rose tips into his mouth. He drew on skills honed over centuries, wanting this experience to be as special for her as it was for him.

He was as hard as he could ever remember being and he rubbed against her, hoping to find some small measure of relief in the action. Her delicate gasp pulled an echoing moan from deep inside him and when he felt the tentative touch of her hand on his shaft, he nearly exploded.

Running his hand along her waist, across the gentle swell of her stomach and down along the curve of her hip, he couldn't get over the way she felt. "Perfection," he whispered in awe.

He used his knee to open her legs and settled his weight between them, his shaft probing her swollen flesh, finding her moist and ready.

Every nerve in his body hummed. He could hardly believe he was with her like this. "Kacie, are you sure?"

"Yes." Her voice sounded seductively husky and breathless. "Now, Erik." She pulled at him with her hands and yet he resisted. He had no expectation that she was a virgin, but it was her first time with him and he wasn't about to rush things if he could help it.

Kissing her deeply, enjoying the sensation of her breasts pressed against his chest, he took her hands and raised her arms above her head. Then he fit himself at her entrance and, moving with deliberate slowness, pushed himself into her.

Kacie was already wound so tight with wanting him that when he finally entered her, she nearly came. She didn't think the nerves in her body could be wound any tighter and yet, as he filled her a little at a time, the tension inside built until she was nearly shaking with need.

When he pulled out, she felt the entire length of him sliding inside her. He pushed into her again and with each successive stroke, went deeper than before.

When he released her hands, she clutched at him. "More." She could hardly form the word and yet he seemed to understand her need.

His tempo increased as he repeatedly drove himself into her, but she had the sense that he was restraining himself. "Give me all of it, Erik. No holding back."

"Kacie," he gritted out her name, breathless from

exertion. "It's everything I can do now not to bite you. Christ, I want to taste you so bad." He drove into her again and she nearly came off the bed.

"Do it," she begged, feeling like a spring that had been wound too tight. "It's all right. You know it is." She grabbed his head and brought his mouth to her neck. She was skirting the edge of something wonderful and there was only one way she could enjoy it. "I give you my blood freely." She felt her orgasm coming and didn't want to go there alone. Driven by a need greater than any she'd known, she tightened her inner muscles around his shaft. "Now, Erik," she cried.

When his teeth sank into her flesh the sharp pain triggered her orgasm, and it hit her like a supernova. Her vision turned blood red and the spaces where her two upper canines had fallen out during the walk home were suddenly filled with fangs. She barely noticed them over the sudden craving she had for blood. Acting on an instinct that was foreign to her, she angled her head and sank her fangs into Erik's neck.

As the blood flowed into her mouth, he surged into her one final time. Raising his head, he gave a primal roar as his body tensed and he found his own release.

Chapter
13

How long they stayed frozen in that position, letting their orgasms carry them, Kacie had no idea. Slowly, as she became aware of her surroundings once more, she noticed the coppery taste of blood in her mouth. She looked up and saw that Erik was staring down at her, looking completely stunned. His mouth was also covered with blood.

He bent to kiss her, licking the blood from both their lips in the process.

"A week ago, that would have totally grossed me out," she said with a shaky laugh. "Now I find it erotic."

He smiled down at her tenderly. "Are you all right? I didn't hurt you, did I?"

"The man gives me the best sex I've had in my life and asks if I'm all right. No, I'm not all right. You've ruined me. No human male could possibly satisfy me now."

His expression grew ferocious. "Good, because I'll kill any man who tries." The possessiveness of that statement sent chills along her spine. There was no teasing, no humor in that statement. He was dead serious.

Though her tone had been light and joking, the truth was that their lovemaking had left her shaken. She'd never experienced anything like it before and she didn't like the thought of any other women getting the opportunity—at least not from Erik. "I hope you enjoyed it, too, because I feel the same way."

As her words registered, a smile spread across his face. "Enjoy is not a word I would have used to describe a life-changing experience such as that. I think I just found a whole new religion." He lowered his head and dropped a kiss on her lips.

She wrapped her arms around him and kissed him back as thoroughly as she knew how, until they were both breathless. It amazed her that just kissing someone like this could be so arousing and yet, with him, it was. Her entire body tingled all over and she wondered how long they'd have to wait for a repeat performance.

She got her answer almost immediately when Erik, already hard, teased the opening between her legs. She raised her eyebrows at the obvious invitation in his expression. "Really? So soon? I didn't think you could—I mean, I didn't think men could . . ." She stopped at his smile, his fangs showing. She had her answer before he said it out loud.

"There are a few advantages to being a vampire," he informed her with a promise in his eyes as he slowly entered her.

It didn't take Kacie long to become addicted to sex with Erik, but it wasn't just because he was an excellent lover with tireless stamina—though that certainly didn't hurt. She suspected that her emotions might run deeper than her current infatuation with him, but she'd had enough earth-shattering revelations for a while and didn't try to analyze the way she felt.

For the rest of the night and well into the morning, they made love. Each time, they exchanged blood because that seemed to make the experience that much more powerful for both of them. Kacie was amazed that their necks didn't hurt from the biting, but then reflected with a mixture of amusement and embarrassment that neither of them had restricted their bites to the neck area. Despite that, there seemed to be something in the commingling of the changeling and vampire blood that caused the cuts, bruises—and bites—on both of them to heal at a much faster rate.

By the time they fell asleep in each other's arms, both were exhausted, well sated, and, for the first time in a long time, blissfully happy.

"What do you want?" Michael asked when Erik called him on his cell phone the next evening.

"I want to talk to you, in private." He'd convinced Michael and the others to get cell phones several years back, securing postal boxes, with Gerard's help, where the bills could be sent. Now he was grateful for a way to communicate with his former friend besides the psychic link, which was shared with too many others.

"So talk."

"Not like this," Erik went on, glancing at the bathroom door. He could still hear the sound of Kacie's shower water running. "In person. At the Point," he added, referring to the highest spot on the cliff, about halfway between the castle and the lair.

"If you think you're going to change my mind about Sedrick's killer—"

"Just hear me out."

There was a long pause before Michael spoke again. "How do I know this isn't a trap?"

Erik sighed. "I give you my word that I'm coming alone—that is, if my word is still worth something to you."

Again there was a prolonged silence. "What time?"

"In an hour."

"Fine."

"Good."

He was about to disconnect when Michael stopped him. "Don't you want my word that I won't trick you?"

"No."

"Why not?" Michael sounded like he was looking for an excuse to be offended, but Erik wasn't going to give him one.

"Because I know you live by that code of honor we talked about in the church." Erik disconnected the call, not waiting to hear Michael's response. Honor and integrity—that was the code—now he was going to break it by lying to Kacie.

The sound of the shower stopped, so he went into the bathroom and caught Kacie stepping out, her skin glowing from the heat of the water and, he hoped, from the three orgasms she'd had before getting out of bed. "Now that you know I paint," he said, taking the towel from her so he could dry her off. "How about posing for me instead of making me paint you from memory?"

She glanced at him in surprise. "After seeing the real thing, you still want to paint me?"

"Are you kidding? Now more than ever."

She blushed but there was a gleam in her eye. "It might be fun."

He kissed her, surprised at how easily she came into his arms. Only in his wildest dreams had he thought this possible. "I would love to stay here all night, making love to you, but I can't."

She leaned back and he prayed they weren't about to get into their first fight. Well, not their first fight, he amended, but their first one since the start of this new relationship.

"Where are you going?"

Once again, he considered telling her the truth, but knew there was no way she'd let him go if he did. "I have to run into town to meet Penny. Wait; before you get upset, we're discussing business, nothing else. And while I'm there, I'm going to tell her all about the new woman in my life and how much I love her."

He watched her eyes grow wide at the announcement. "You do?" Her voice was filled with wonder and doubt.

"Yes, I do—more than life itself," he assured her, kissing the tip of her nose. "Which is why I want you to stay here and be safe. I don't think I could stand it if anything happened to you."

She kissed him then and he savored the sweet taste of her lips until he knew if he stayed even a moment longer, he wouldn't be able to leave.

"I have to go, love. I'll be back as soon as I can." He walked out, hoping his parting words wouldn't be the last he spoke to her.

* * *

Kacie watched him leave and turned back to the mirror. She was fascinated by her new fangs and leaned closer to get a better look.

Compared to her other teeth, the fangs were twice as long. Like the canines they replaced, they narrowed to a point at the tip. They appeared solid, even sounded that way when she tapped on them with her fingernail, but she knew they were hollow because when she'd tasted Erik's blood, not only had she tasted it on her tongue, but she'd tasted it through the fangs, though she had no idea how that was possible.

She turned again in the mirror, getting a different angle on her new appearance. She concentrated on her eyes and when they started to glow, she smiled so her fangs showed. "I vant . . . to drink . . . your blood," she intoned, then quickly looked around to make sure Erik hadn't sneaked back in behind her.

Thinking about him reminded her that he was with that woman and she couldn't help feeling a definite spark of jealousy. She had a good mind to go down to Myrtle's to make sure that Miss Penny Lockwood understood that Erik was off limits. But she'd promised him she wouldn't go out and as much trouble as she'd caused him these last couple of days, she owed him that much at least.

Still, how much trouble would she get into if she ran upstairs to her room? Now that she was a changeling, she had the strength and speed to fight off a vampire. What she didn't have was something decent to wear. She couldn't keep wearing Erik's oversized sweats. For one thing, they were too big; for another, they didn't exactly show off her figure. It was hard to feel attractive when you looked like a sack of potatoes.

Not seeing how she could come to any harm if she hurried, Kacie left the apartment and went up to her room. After doing a quick search, she realized that her figure had changed over the last three years. None of her old clothes fit.

Before she gave up, however, she decided to check out Jess's room. They were close enough in size that her clothes might fit. It was worth searching her sister's closet to see what Jess had left behind before traveling to America.

She was thrilled to discover that not only were there clothes, but they fit. As a bonus, Kacie even found some clean undergarments and shoes. Stepping into the attached bathroom, Kacie discovered perfume and makeup. Gathering up all of it, she carried it down to Erik's apartment and sealed herself back in. Then she set about making herself look nice for when Erik returned.

Unfortunately, the entire primping process didn't take long, especially at changeling speed. All too soon, she was standing in the living room, bored out of her mind. She was too restless to sit and watch the television, so she wandered around his apartment, ending up in his bedroom. They'd made love in his bed at least a dozen times, enough so that she'd thought she'd be sore for a week, only to discover that each exchange of their blood left her so energized that she could have made love a dozen times more. A familiar warmth stole over her at the recollection.

Ignoring the bed, she looked around his room, trying to get a feel for the man himself. His room was nicer than she would have expected, but that was mainly because the furniture was antique. He'd probably purchased it new—a couple hundred years ago.

She also noticed that he didn't have a lot of clutter about, except for the corner bookcase, which seemed to be filled to overflowing with journals and scrapbooks. Those piqued her curiosity, so she pulled one out and sat down on the floor to look through it.

The first book was filled with sketches of people and places, which she assumed Erik had drawn. There were no photographs in these books, but that made sense given the dates scratched at the bottoms of the pages. These drawings were done in the years prior to the development of photography.

Quickly flipping through to the end, she closed one book and put it back on the shelf so she could take out another. This one was more modern, filled with sepia-toned pictures from the late 1800s to the early 1900s. Below each of the prints, someone—presumably Erik—had written in names and dates.

She was most intrigued by the photographs of Erik. He appeared just as he did now, not a day older and not a day younger.

There were also pictures of Michael and Ty. She studied their pictures, trying to mesh the happy, smiling faces with the same men who'd tried to kill her.

Giving up, she turned the page and glanced at the next set of pictures. One in particular caught her eye. She thought she was seeing an example of early trick photography until she read the caption. She took a closer look, studying the picture to make sure there was no error.

A low-grade humming started in the back of her head

as she realized the significance of her find. She needed to tell Erik right away.

Rooted precariously near the edge of the cliff at its highest peak was the old tree that marked the Point. As Erik approached it, he extended his senses, trying to pick up the essence of other vampires. He'd meant what he said about Michael being an honorable man and trusting him to show up alone. In fact, Erik was so sure of Michael's integrity that he was literally betting his life on it. However, that didn't mean he should throw caution to the wind and not be careful.

To his relief, Michael's essence was the only one he detected. As he neared the top, he saw Michael approaching from the other direction.

They stopped a short distance from each other and Erik saw that, like himself, Michael had a sword strapped to his back. This was a habit left over from the first two centuries of their lives, when a man lived and died by the sword.

"Why did you want to talk to me?" Michael asked.

"I want to put an end to this," Erik said.

Michael glowered at him. "Fine, bring me the woman and it'll be over."

Erik shook his head. "She didn't know about the pact when she killed Sedrick."

"Do you think it would have made a difference?"

"Maybe not," Erik admitted. "At least, not at first, but things are different now. She's not the same person she was."

Michael studied his face and his expression changed to

one of understanding. "I gather the situation between the two of you has changed. She no longer hates your guts?"

Erik actually felt embarrassed. "No, she doesn't."

"Congratulations. I'm happy for you," he said, though he didn't sound it. "Is she good in bed?"

Erik bristled at the question. "Careful. You're talking about the woman I love."

"Come on, Erik," Michael chastised him. "How gullible are you? Of course she's going to be suddenly agreeable. You're the only thing keeping her alive. What's sex with a vampire compared to losing your life?"

"That's enough, Michael," Erik warned him.

"No, Erik. I don't think it is. Damn it. She killed Sedrick."

"Don't you think I know that?" Both of their voices were getting loud.

"Well, you sure as hell don't act like it bothers you. My God, you're sleeping with my brother's killer."

Erik shook his head, disgusted with himself, not trying to deny it. "I know. But I never told them about the pact. Sedrick's death is as much my fault as it is hers." He took a deep breath. "So, if we can't reconcile, then let's finish this, here and now."

"I don't want to kill you, Erik," Michael said. "*She's* the one I want."

Erik shook his head. "As long as I live, I won't let you have her." He stepped back and pulled his sword from the scabbard on his back.

"You'd better hope you kill me," Michael told him, pulling his own sword. "Because when this is over, I'm going after her. Not only did she kill my brother, but she took away my best friend."

"I understand," he said with the same lack of enthusi-asm he heard in Michael's voice. Then he slashed the air with his sword in a practice stroke. "Let's do this."

They came together, and the clashing of their swords rang out loudly in the night. It hadn't been that long ago that they'd stood on this same stretch of ground, similarly engaged. Only then they'd been practicing, not fighting to the death. Unfortunately, being equally matched, there would be no quick victory for either of them.

"Let me know when you want to stop playing around," Michael goaded him after an hour. Erik clenched his teeth a little tighter and thought that he'd never felt this depressed before in his life. Even if he beat Michael, he'd lose.

"When I finish with you," Michael continued, "and go after Kacie, maybe I won't kill her. Maybe she'd like to sleep with a man who knows how to pleasure a woman. What do you think? Should I fuck her?"

Erik felt rage color his vision and lunged at Michael, who easily blocked him and then countered by trying to slice open Erik's midsection. Erik jumped back, but not far enough. Michael's blade sliced open his shirt and grazed his skin, leaving a nasty cut behind. As blood oozed through and soaked Erik's shirt, Michael laughed. Erik knew then that Michael was only baiting him in order to break his concentration. It was a trick they'd used on each other many times in the past and Erik would have anticipated it if he'd been thinking clearly.

With renewed vigor, he pressed forward, forcing Michael precariously close to the edge of the cliff.

On the next blow, Erik surged forward, bringing his

sword down in a mighty strike. Michael blocked it, but the effort sent him stumbling back.

Erik stared in horror as Michael's foot caught on a root and he teetered on the edge of the cliff, his arms beating the air as he tried to regain his balance. Then, as if in slow motion, Michael disappeared over the edge.

Without thinking, Erik flung his sword aside and dived after his friend.

Chapter
14

The save was more luck than anything he'd consciously done, but Erik wasn't about to question it. He dangled off the side of the cliff, holding on to Michael's wrist with one hand and a tree root with the other, praying the root—and his strength—held out long enough for him to figure out how to get them both safely to the top.

"You're a damn fool," Michael hollered up at him. "You should have let me fall."

"No," Erik bit out, barely able to spare the energy to talk.

"I'm too heavy," Michael continued. "I'm just going to pull you down with me. Let me go. I won't have your death on my conscience."

"Shut up, Michael. You're not helping." He groaned under the strain and then felt the root move. With their imminent deaths came a moment of clarity he hoped he would live to reflect on later. For the moment, he wanted only to get them both to the top. "Brace your foot against the cliff and scale it. Do it now."

"You're crazy. The extra drag will pull you down for sure. Let go, Erik. It's okay. Hell, I might even survive the fall."

"Scale...the damn...cliff."

Michael stared up at him for a second longer and then, thankfully, did as he was asked. There were several false starts as Michael's foot repeatedly slipped against the smooth surface of the rock. Finally, though, he was able to get enough purchase to start climbing.

The going was slow and Erik thought the strain would rip his chest apart, but he knew the pain would be far worse for him if he let go and Michael died.

When Michael had climbed high enough, he used his free hand to grab hold of the tree root. At that point, Erik was able to let go of Michael's wrist and use both hands to keep himself from falling.

Soon, Michael was able to use the other tree roots as a ladder and climb to the top. Once there, he lay on his stomach and extended a hand down to Erik.

It was Erik's turn to trust Michael with his life, and he did so without hesitation, letting go of the tree root with one hand so he could use it to grab Michael's.

Minutes later, back on top, they collapsed on the ground side by side.

"That was too damn close," Erik said, trying to catch his breath.

"Why didn't you let me fall?" Michael asked. "That could have been the end of your problems."

"You think I have so many friends that I can afford to lose another? No. Anyway, as I watched both of our lives pass before my eyes, I had an epiphany. I don't want to kill you. If you still hate me and want my life, then grab your sword and take it now while I'm too tired to move. I only ask that you give me your word that my life will be price enough and you'll leave Kacie alone."

Silence weighed heavily between them, then Michael got to his feet and picked up Erik's sword from the ground. Erik's muscles tensed, but he could do nothing except lie there and wait for the killing blow.

"You had your chance," Michael told him. "You should have let me fall."

"Stop gloating and just do it if you're going to," Erik told him calmly. "The sooner you do, the sooner I'll be out of pain. My arm hurts like hell. I think I dislocated my shoulder when I caught you."

Michael stood glaring down at him, the point of his sword scratching the skin of Erik's throat. The men's gazes locked and held.

"Bloody hell," Michael swore, dropping the sword as he once more lowered himself to a sitting position beside Erik. "I don't have that many friends either."

"So now what?" Erik asked.

"I don't know. I guess we take it one day at a time."

"And Kacie?"

Michael sighed. "That's going to be a little harder for me. I understand how you feel about her and I'm happy for you, really—especially if she's returning your affection, but she killed Sedrick. That's always going to be there between us."

Erik knew this was true and he hated it. "Okay," he agreed. "One day at a time."

They sat in silence a few minutes more before Michael asked, "How's your shoulder?"

Erik struggled to sit up, wincing. "It hurts."

"Sorry about that. I didn't remember the edge of the cliff being quite that close." He smiled. "That was a good move, by the way."

Erik smiled. "'Let me go, Erik,'" he mocked Michael. "Bloody hell. You didn't really expect me to let go, did you?"

Michael's face sobered. "No. I knew you wouldn't but I meant what I said about not wanting to be the cause of your death."

Erik turned to face Michael and the two men clasped hands and leaned forward, giving each other an affectionate slap on the back.

"So, tell me about you and Kacie," Michael said. "What brought about this sudden change in her feelings for you?"

"She found a painting I did of her."

Michael furrowed his eyes. "So?"

Erik gave him a pointed look. "It was a nude."

Michael gave a hearty laugh. "I would have liked to have seen that."

"Forget it."

They spent the next hour talking. When they parted, they were on better terms and promised to talk again soon.

Erik left his friend and returned to the castle, where he hoped to find Kacie still waiting for him. With luck, she wouldn't be too angry when he told her the truth about what he'd been doing.

"Where have you been?" Kacie was beside herself with worry and had been pacing the living room floor for a good hour. "Don't even try to tell me your business with that woman took this long because I called Myrtle's and talked to her. She said she hadn't seen you all night."

Erik didn't know whether to be pleased that she was so worried or mad that she was checking up on him. "No, you're right. I didn't go see Penny."

"Where did you go? And what is that all over your shirt? Is that...?" She stepped up to him and took a closer look. "My God, is that blood?" She took his hand and pulled him into the living room. He winced as pain shot along his sore muscles. "Erik, what happened? Here, sit down."

She helped him to sit on the couch and then hurried to the bathroom to get a wet cloth to wipe away the dirt and blood covering his face and arms. "You're a mess. Did you get into a fight?"

"Yes, with Michael."

She heaved a sigh. "I knew it. Did he trap you? How'd you get away?"

Erik tried to brace for her reaction. "I asked him to meet me."

She stared at him like he had just grown a second head. "Excuse me?"

"I asked Michael to meet me at the Point, so we could talk."

"About?"

He sighed. "About you. I wanted him to agree to a truce. If that didn't work, then I was going to fight him."

"Judging from the cuts and bruises all over you, I'm guessing he didn't go for the truce idea."

"No, he didn't. At least not at first."

"What happened?"

For the next several minutes, she cleaned his wound and listened quietly while he told her about fighting with Michael. When he got to the part about both of them going over the side of the cliff, she almost lost it. Tears welled in her eyes hearing how close she'd come to losing him.

"Don't be upset, Kacie, love. I'm fine. In fact, I'm better than fine because after Michael and I got back to the top of the cliff, we no longer felt like killing each other. We talked and everything's fine."

"No, it's not, Erik," she said, remembering the reason she'd been so desperate to find him.

"Yes, it is. Michael's going to reinstate the pact and we're not going to have to worry about him trying to kill you anymore."

She reached over to the end table and picked up the photo album she'd been looking through earlier. She opened the book to the page she'd marked.

"Who is this?" she asked, pointing to one of the pictures.

"That's me and Michael, standing in front of the Eiffel Tower." He smiled. "It had just been built. He pointed to the printed caption below it. "See? It says so here."

"I know, but I wanted to make sure. So that means this"—she'd turned the page and pointed to another photo—"is a photo of Michael and his brother Sedrick?"

Erik looked like he was trying to be patient. "Yes. It says so right there on the page."

"Michael and Sedrick were twins?"

"Yes." He furrowed his brow. "I'm sure I mentioned it before. Michael and Sedrick were twins and Ty is their half-brother."

Kacie smiled, barely able to contain her excitement. "Erik, this man in the photo is not the vampire I killed."

"What?"

She nodded. "No. The vampire I killed was shorter, leaner, and had dark hair."

"You're positive? After all, it was dark and you were probably more focused on severing his head from his body than the color of his hair."

Kacie felt her jaw drop open and had to consciously close it. "He was decapitated?"

Erik's brow furrowed. "Yes."

"Erik, I've never cut off anyone's head. I don't have the upper arm strength—or at least I didn't while I was human—to be able to cut through the spinal cord. You know that—it's why you had always insisted I use a shorter sword for fighting—it wasn't as heavy."

Erik pushed himself off the couch and started pacing, trying to process this latest revelation. "This is incredible," he muttered, kicking himself for not asking for more details earlier. He'd assumed when she took credit for the killing that they were talking about the same vampire. He wondered what happened to the body of the vampire she'd killed and then remembered finding her knife beside Sedrick's body where someone had placed it.

Pulling his cell phone from his pocket, he keyed in Michael's number. Michael picked up after the fourth ring.

"Michael—are you alone?"

There was a pause before Michael answered cautiously, "I am right now, but I'm expecting Ty to show up. Why? Is something wrong?"

"Yes and no. Kacie was going through an old photo album and came across a couple of pictures of you, me, Sedrick, and Ty at the Eiffel Tower."

"How sweet," Michael said with a slight edge to his voice. "No offense, but I'm not quite ready to hear all the details of your new domestic lifestyle."

Erik ignored him and went on. "Kacie didn't know that you and Sedrick were twins or this would have come out sooner. The vampire she killed was short, thin, and had dark hair."

"What?"

Erik knew he had Michael's full attention now. "Yes, and there's something else. She impaled the vampire she fought; she didn't decapitate him."

"You believe her?"

"Yes."

There was a long pause. "I'm glad it wasn't her," Michael finally said, sounding relieved.

Erik wanted to reach through the phone and throttle Michael. "Don't you see? Someone else killed Sedrick and then went to a lot of trouble to make it look like Kacie did it."

"But why?" Michael asked. "It doesn't make sense."

"It does if someone was trying to start a fight between us."

"But who would do that?"

"I don't know," Erik said. "Someone who knew that Kacie was family and I'd protect her, even if she was responsible for breaking the pact."

"Then that means it had to be someone familiar with the pact—which means it's someone from my lair."

Erik had come to the same conclusion moments earlier. "I think it's best if we let whoever it is think their plan is still working. Don't tell anyone that we've reconciled or that we know the truth about Kacie. There's no telling what the killer might do next—or who they'll go after."

"Okay," Michael agreed. "Not a word to anyone."

"And make sure you block your thoughts," Erik cautioned, thinking of the psychic link. "We can't take any chances. Use your cell phone to get in touch with me."

After Erik disconnected the call, he turned to Kacie. "You heard all that, right? So I don't need to repeat it."

"I heard." Rising from the couch, she came over to him, a frown creasing her forehead. "Why would anyone set me up? I've been out of town for three years. Who hates me that much?"

"Oh, no, love," he said, gathering her into his arms, though his shoulder screamed in protest. "I don't think it has anything to do with you." He placed a kiss on her forehead. "It has to be someone who hates me, Michael, and Sedrick."

"But who would that be?"

"Where the hell is he now?" Carrington demanded, pausing long enough in his pacing to glare at Ty, who was draped over the arm of a chair. They were the only two in the main living room of the lair. The others were out trying to find a decent meal, and that was now the problem. As Carrington saw it, there was no such thing as a decent meal when humans weren't on the menu.

Despite the fact that the pact had been broken, Michael had refused to lift the restriction on hunting humans, and most of the others in the lair had abided by his rule. Carrington hadn't. After getting his first taste of human blood, he'd sworn never to go back to "sucking on steak," as he called the practice of feeding off cow's blood.

The difference between human blood and animal blood was like night and day. After drinking human blood, he felt stronger and more energetic. He'd be crazy to ever go back.

"Someone needs to do something," Carrington muttered, more to himself than Ty, but Ty responded.

"About...?"

"About Michael, of course. None of us asked for this life, but here we are. Might as well make the best of it."

"How?" Ty raised his eyebrow, which always made Carrington think that Ty considered himself to be better than him, somehow. He wasn't. He'd been born out of wedlock just as Carrington had. Neither one of them, from what Carrington had learned over the years, had exactly had an easy life. What was more, to him Ty was just a kid.

"By letting us be what we are," Carrington replied. "Vampires. Michael is so busy trying to be human that he's not taking advantage of the situation."

"Maybe he doesn't want to exploit it," Ty offered.

"If you ask me, it's more like he's afraid—and well he should be."

"Why's that?"

"Because his brother's not here to protect him anymore. When Sedrick was alive, anyone who went against one brother went against both. Together, it was impossible to fight them." He cast Ty a speculative glance. "If you ask me, Sedrick was the tougher of the two. With him out of the way..."

"What are you saying, exactly?" Ty asked, swinging his legs off the chair and finally giving Carrington his full attention.

"I'm saying that it might be time for new leadership."

"And who do you think is going to be man enough to go up against Michael?"

Carrington pulled himself up taller. "I think you're looking at him."

"Why are you telling me? You've got to know I'll go to Michael with this."

"Of course, that's to be expected. Tell him the time is coming—it's closer than he thinks. As for you, Ty, my young friend, you might want to start thinking about whose side you're going to be on."

The next evening Kacie sat on the couch, leafing through the pages of a magazine without even reading them. Her father had called hours earlier to tell them he had gotten a much later start than expected, but was finally on his way. Now, with each passing minute she waited, her nerves frayed a little more.

Part of her was trying to figure out exactly what she wanted to say while another part of her was worried about Erik, who'd gone into town.

She didn't like the idea of him being out alone while the killer was out there. It wasn't that he couldn't take care of himself—he'd proven time and again that he could—but this killer was smart. Worse yet, they had no idea who it was, although if she had to cast her vote, it would be for Carrington. Hadn't Ty warned Erik earlier about him?

A part of her wanted to strap on her sword and go after Erik. She felt fully recovered from the chupacabra attack and now that the sun had set, her body fairly hummed with energy, which made it nearly impossible for her to sit still.

She stood up and tossed the magazine aside. She had to do something, and she began pacing about the room. She tried to calm herself with thoughts of Erik; that worked for a while.

It amazed her to think how much their relationship had changed over the last week. If anyone had asked her before, she wouldn't have thought it was possible. If ever there was a doubt in her mind, she had only to look at how happy she was now with him. Even her nightmares had stopped—of course, that could be because they tended to stay awake until long after sunrise, making love.

She wondered what her father would say about that and felt herself get nervous all over again. Glancing at her watch, she saw that her father should arrive any minute.

Heading back to the couch, she picked up the magazine and started flipping through the pages again. After the fifth or sixth page, she sighed and turned it right side up. After another page, she closed it completely and thought about what she wanted to say to her father.

Erik settled Penny into a cab and said good-bye after promising to call her about when he would send her his next piece of artwork.

"Are you sure you won't reconsider?" she asked him, referring to her invitation to give up this new girl—whoever she was—and spend the evening with her.

"Thank you for the offer, but I think we need to keep our relationship strictly business. Besides, I'm in love; what can I say?"

Penny smiled. "Well, all right. You look happy and I'm thrilled for you. I suppose it would never have worked out anyway. You keep odd hours and it's really your art I'm in love with, so I guess it's good that I'm just your agent."

He smiled, knowing that everything would work out. "I'll call you."

A second later, he watched the cab drive off. That was

one less person he had to worry about. Pulling out his cell phone, he called Michael.

"Where are you?" he asked when Michael answered.

"I'm at the lair. Why?"

"I left you a message to meet me in town. Didn't you get it?"

He heard a pause and imagined Michael looking at the screen of his phone. "No, there's nothing showing up. Must have got lost."

Erik sighed. Using the cell phones might be safer, but they certainly weren't as fast as the link. "Can you meet me? I'd like to see if we can flush out our killer. I'm outside of Myrtle's."

"Sure. I'm on my way."

Sitting in the back seat of the cab as it pulled down the driveway of his ancestral home, Gerard Winslow, Earl of Hocksley and veteran vampire hunter, was a nervous wreck at the prospect of seeing his daughter again. He'd already loved her as a niece when Vince died, but he'd quickly grown to love her as his own child after he adopted her. To have been estranged from her these past three years had been horrible. Now he had a chance to patch things up—if only he knew what to say.

Still lost in thought, he paid the cabbie and climbed out. He only had the single piece of luggage with him because his collection of hand-forged and crafted swords would be delivered sometime later in the week.

Standing in the drive, he waited for the cab to drive off and then took a deep breath. There was no point in putting it off any longer, he supposed.

The crunch of gravel caught his attention. He turned,

expecting to see Kacie, and barely had time to register the red glowing eyes of the vampire before he was hit over the head with something hard and blackness engulfed him.

Kacie glanced at her watch again. Her father was late—at least an hour—maybe more.

Picking up the phone, she tried calling him, but he didn't answer. More than a little concerned, she keyed in Erik's cell phone number and waited for him to answer.

"Hello, love," his velvety voice answered, instantly soothing her.

Momentarily distracted, she couldn't hide the smile in her voice. "How do you do that?"

"What?"

"You know perfectly well what. That thing you do with your voice that makes me feel like you're caressing me."

He groaned. "I wish that's what I was doing right now."

She sobered. "Are you all right?"

"Yes—in fact, it's downright boring in town tonight in terms of vampire nightlife. I'm waiting for Michael. He was supposed to meet me, but I guess he's running late."

"He's not the only one."

"Gerard's not there yet?" His tone told Kacie she was right to be concerned.

"No. And there was no answer on his cell phone."

"Okay. Try not to worry. I'm on my way."

"Thank you," she said, feeling better already. She was still worried, but felt that with Erik by her side, she could handle anything. "Be careful." She disconnected the call and mentally added, *I love you.*

Maybe one day, she'd have the nerve to say it out loud, but not yet.

The phone rang again and she hurried to answer it. "Hello?"

"I have something of yours," a stranger's voice said.

"Excuse me? Who is this?"

The voice on the other end of the line sounded vaguely familiar and she tried to remember where she'd heard it before.

"Kacie?" A new voice came on the line. This one was very familiar.

"Dad?" Alarm shot through her. "Are you all right? Where are you?"

"Not so fast." The first voice came back on. "If you want to see your father again—alive—you'll meet me at the old cemetery, near the Winslow mausoleum. Come unarmed and alone. If I see you with a sword—or if I see anyone else at that cemetery—I'll kill the old man."

"How do I know that if I do as you ask, you won't hurt him anyway?"

"Oh, I assure you that I have every intention of hurting him and I will continue to hurt him until you arrive, so I suggest you hurry. The longer you delay, the more likely it is that in a couple of nights, when you go vampire hunting again, it'll be your father you have to kill. So Kacie? Don't take too long."

The line went dead but not before she heard her father's strangled cry of pain.

Chapter
15

S tress and worry caused her head to ring. She gripped the back of the nearest chair to make sure she didn't fall.

Could her father's kidnapper also be Sedrick's killer? With her father's cry still echoing in her head, she knew there wasn't much time. Picking up the phone, she punched in Erik's number and then hung up. Maybe she shouldn't call him. If Erik got to the cemetery before she did, her father could die.

On the other hand, it was foolish to try to rescue her father by herself. She picked up the phone again and dialed Erik's number. It rang several times before clicking over to voice mail. She tried once more, but when she still couldn't reach him, she had no choice but to leave a message.

"Erik. Dad's been kidnapped. I got a call to go to the old cemetery—to the Winslow family mausoleum—alone. If I don't, he'll hurt Dad. Please hurry."

She prayed he would check his messages soon and raced out of the castle. She longed to take her sword, but even without it, she had one ace up her sleeve—she was a changeling. She hoped she would have an opportunity to try out her new skills.

"I don't know what's going on," Erik said to Michael over the phone. "There's no activity in town at all."

"Where are you now?" Michael asked.

"I'm headed back to the castle. That's why I'm calling. There's been a change of plans. I talked to Kacie a little while ago and she's worried because Gerard hasn't shown up yet. Frankly, I'm a little worried myself. It could just be a coincidence that he's late tonight, but—"

"Tonight's not a night to believe in coincidence."

"My feelings exactly, so I'm headed home to check it out. Can you meet me there instead?"

"I've got to take care of something first, but then I'm on my way."

"Thanks."

Erik disconnected the call and then dialed the number to the castle. He knew Kacie was upset and he didn't like the idea of her sitting there alone. He waited for her to answer. With each unanswered ring, his anxiety grew. He quickened his pace until finally he was racing along the backwoods path to the castle.

Kacie approached the cemetery slowly, alert for signs of trouble. The last thing she needed was to have a random vampire appear out of nowhere and attack her. Worse yet would be the ones who weren't random; the ones who'd been sent specifically to kill her.

She headed toward the Winslow mausoleum and had almost reached it when a movement in the shadows caused her to pull up short.

"You," she spit out the word as Carrington appeared, holding her father.

"You don't seem surprised," he said, smiling to show off his pearly fangs. With her new night vision, Kacie saw that her father's neck bore twin puncture marks, indicating that he'd been bitten.

"Let him go," she ordered. "You don't need him anymore. You have me."

"I don't think so," Carrington said.

"Why are you doing this? What do you want?"

He laughed. "You, of course." He gestured with a tilt of his head and two vampires appeared from out of the shadows. One was carrying a set of handcuffs. "Now, be a good girl and put these on."

When the first of the two vampires reached for her, she kicked out and caught him in the stomach. He doubled over and collapsed to the ground. Kacie didn't wait to see if he stayed down, but turned to face the other as he rushed her.

He was too close to kick, so with fingers folded, she flattened her hand and jabbed him as hard as she could. He stopped in his tracks, clutching his throat and gasping for air. Kacie was about to hit him again when her father's pained cry caused her to look around.

Carrington's mouth was pressed against the side of her father's throat. A small amount of blood oozed out from beneath the vampire's lips and ran down her father's neck. White-hot rage filled her and she charged, shouting.

She'd only taken a step or two when she was hit with

what felt like a battering ram. She landed on the ground, the air knocked out of her.

For a second, she was too stunned to do anything more than lie there gasping. When she was able to catch her breath, she rolled onto her hands and knees. Her stomach and lungs burned and she felt sick.

"You all are pathetic," she heard the voice from the telephone snarl. "Do I have to do everything myself?"

She looked up and saw the familiar face. The nausea in her stomach grew worse at the depth of betrayal she now witnessed. "How could you do this to him? He's your friend."

His eyes grew ice cold. "I have no friends."

With a gesture of his hand, he summoned the two vampires she'd attacked earlier. They came forward eagerly and before she could gather her thoughts for a plan of attack, they grabbed her. She fought them, thrashing out with hands and feet—anything to get free.

Her efforts against three vampires, however, proved futile. Before long, she'd been cuffed and forced to her knees.

She looked up into the smiling face of her captor. "You don't need my father anymore," she pleaded. "You have me. Please let him go."

He laughed. "How naive do you think I am? If I let the old man go, he'll go tell Erik. No, you'll both be my guests."

"Just tell me why," she asked. "Why are you doing this?"

"Why, revenge, of course."

Erik stood in his apartment, feeling lost. He'd searched the entire castle for Kacie and came up empty. He had no idea where she was and it was killing him. When his cell phone rang, he practically pounced on it.

"Hello?"

"Erik." Ty sounded panicked. "You have to stop him. Michael's kidnapped both Gerard and Kacie. I think he might be planning to kill them."

Erik couldn't believe what he was hearing. For a second, shock caused his mind to lock up. "What? Where are Kacie and Gerard?"

"They're here," Ty told him. "Chained up in the old dungeon in the back of the lair."

Erik felt his gut clench. "Are they still alive?"

"They were when I saw them, although I think they've both been knocked around a bit."

The thought of anyone hurting either Kacie or Gerard made Erik crazy.

"I'm sorry, Erik," Ty continued. "I tried to talk him out of it. I . . ." His voice broke with emotion. "I'm sorry. I don't know what to do."

"Don't do anything." There was just one more critical piece of information that he needed to know. "Where's Michael now?"

"He's here, at the lair."

"You're sure?"

"Positive," Ty said.

"All right. I'm on my way."

"Be careful."

There was a resounding click as Erik disconnected the call. For a few seconds, all he could do was stare off into space and absorb the pain and shock of this latest betrayal. Then he turned to Michael, standing beside him. "I know who's behind all this."

* * *

The dungeon they were in was dark and smelly. Kacie and her father had been locked in two of the five sets of manacles bolted to the dungeon walls and she didn't want to think about what the vampires used this room for.

There was a small amount of light coming in through the hallway, where someone had mounted lanterns. She could have seen without them, but knew her father wouldn't have been able to. Listening for the sound of approaching footsteps, she heard only her father's rattled breathing.

"I'm sorry I got you into this," she said. "How are you feeling?"

"Tired—and a little sore."

"This isn't exactly how I envisioned our reunion."

"Me either." He sighed. "I missed you."

"I missed you, too."

"I should have insisted you come home." He took a breath and winced, making Kacie wonder how badly he was hurt. "At the very least, I should have put more effort into convincing you to visit," he continued. "I thought, at the time, that I was respecting your decision—and your privacy. That I was giving you a chance to forget the past."

She rattled her chains against the wall, wishing they were having this discussion anywhere else but here. "When I met Ben, I thought I'd finally found what I was looking for—a large family to be a part of. I thought if I stayed with him, his family would fill the hole I felt in my life. But the truth is, that hole only existed in my mind. I created it when I alienated myself from you." She took a breath. "I don't need a big family to feel at home. I need my family—you and Jess. I love you, Dad."

"I love you, too, Kacie. I never stopped hoping that one day you'd be back. I'm glad you decided to come home."

She yanked on the chains again, as if by doing so, she could loosen them. "There's something I should tell you, just in case...you know...we don't get out of here." She paused to take a breath and gather a small measure of courage. "Erik told me the truth about my parents—about how they knew about vampires. I wish that they had given it up while they raised their children, but I can also understand why they didn't. And I know that the reason you lied to me was so I wouldn't hate them."

"Erik shouldn't have told you."

That made her mad. "No, he shouldn't have. *You* should have. It would have saved years of hurt feelings on both sides. Maybe then I wouldn't have thought the only reason you adopted me was out of guilt."

"What? Kacie, that's crazy." He took a step toward her only to stop short when he reached the end of his chain. "I adopted you because I wanted you for my daughter," he said. "I could have found a good family to adopt you and you would have been well taken care of, between the trust your father had set aside for you and the portion of the Winslow Trust that Erik and I would have given you. But Vince was more than my best friend. He was like a brother to me and I loved you and Robbie as if you were my niece and nephew. You *were* my family. When your parents died, there was no doubt that you would stay with me. Out of respect for your parents, I tried to keep my affections in line with those of a favorite uncle.

Only I failed, miserably, because I came to love you as a daughter."

He stopped talking, winded from his long speech. Kacie searched for the right thing to say, her feelings in turmoil. "I'm glad you became my father." The confession hung in the air, leaving emotions on both sides raw and exposed.

Then her father sighed. "I haven't done such a great job of taking care of you lately, have I? How are you feeling?"

"You mean aside from being beaten and chained in this place by a psychotic vampire who will probably kill us?" He smiled at her attempt at humor and she went on. "Oh, you mean the chupacabra attack?"

"Yes. It must have been horrible."

"'Terrifying' is maybe a better word, but now I guess it's not so bad. I have these cool new teeth"—she smiled to show him—"and I can see and hear things I never thought possible."

"Still, I should have been there," he said.

"It's okay. Erik took good care of me."

At that pronouncement, her father arched an eyebrow. "Speaking of Erik—how are the two of you getting along? You didn't stake him, did you?"

Thinking of Erik, she prayed he knew where they were and had a plan to save them. "No, Dad. I didn't stake him."

"That's good to hear."

"Someone's coming," Kacie whispered, hearing approaching footsteps.

"What have we here? A surprise for me?" Michael strolled into the dungeon, and Kacie had never been so glad to see anyone before, until he stopped in front of her and backhanded her across the cheek.

"That," he sneered, "is for killing my brother."

The blow looked worse than it felt, but it still hurt. Even more, it confused her. She'd thought Michael and Erik had reconciled. Apparently not. She wondered if Erik knew that both of the vampires he'd considered to be his friends had betrayed him.

"How could you?" she asked, eying him suspiciously. "If you do anything to hurt Erik, I'll—"

"What?" he asked. "Chained to the wall, what *exactly* do you think you'll be able to do?" He leaned close to her. "Not a damn thing." He shook his head and then looked around. "Ty! Where the hell are you?"

"I'm right here," Ty said matter-of-factly, appearing at the entranceway. "Do you like my little surprise?" He sauntered forward, gesturing to Kacie and her father.

"I do. How did you manage it?" Michael sounded impressed.

"It was really more of Carrington's doing, if you must know."

"Wonderful. And where is he?" Michael asked. "I must be sure to thank him."

Ty shrugged. "I don't really know. Around, I'm sure."

Michael walked over to Kacie and she braced for another blow. Instead he grabbed her hand and held it up, studying the manacle about her wrist. "Where's the key?" he asked, glancing around.

"I have it; why? You're not thinking of taking them somewhere, are you?"

Michael smiled. It wasn't a very nice smile. "Oh, I'm

definitely taking this one someplace where we can...talk... in private."

"You leave my daughter alone, you bastard!" her father shouted, struggling to grab Michael, who stood just beyond his reach. Her father was not easily deterred, though, and fought against his bonds until Ty stepped forward and cuffed him hard enough that he dropped instantly to the ground, unconscious. In that second, Kacie saw anger spark in Michael's eyes as he turned on Ty.

"What the hell are you doing?"

Ty's eyebrow shot up, but he only shrugged. "You're going to kill them anyway, so what do you care if they get a little beat up first?"

Kacie watched the byplay between the two carefully. It was to her advantage if the two of them fought.

Michael's gaze turned cold and empty. "If you keep hitting them like that, then there won't be anything left for me to kill." He turned his attention back to Kacie's manacles. "Now, can you get me the key?"

"Of course, but I really think you should leave her chained."

Michael held out his hand and glared at Ty. "The key. Now."

Kacie kept an eye on both of them, wondering if she'd have a chance to attack once she was free. The problem was that there were two of them and her father was unconscious. She couldn't leave him behind.

Ty handed the key to Michael, who used it to unlock one of the manacles around her wrist. As it came off, he handed her the key and stepped beyond her reach. "Slowly, unlock the other one."

She didn't have a choice. There was no way to fight them if she was still chained to the wall.

As soon as she was free, she faced Michael again, her expression openly defying him, but he only smiled.

Then she heard the sound of running footsteps and she turned, along with the two vampires, to see Erik appear in the entryway.

"Michael!" Erik shouted, running forward and then coming to a stop just inside the dungeon. "Don't do this."

In a burst of speed too fast to follow, Michael was behind her, holding her captive much the same way Carrington had held her father earlier.

"It's a trap," she shouted before Michael jerked her to silence.

"Have you come to say good-bye?" Michael sneered.

"Let her go, Michael," Erik said, his voice carefully controlled. "Let them both go and I'll stay in their place."

"Why would I do that?" Michael asked. "She's the one who killed Sedrick."

"I'm offering myself in trade," Erik said. "I'm the one who failed. I'm the one who didn't keep an eye on the family and allowed Sedrick to be killed."

"True," Michael agreed. "Ty, undo the old man's chains."

Kacie couldn't see the other vampire's face, but she heard the shock in his voice. "Michael, you can't be serious. You're not actually thinking of trading them for him, are you?"

"Just do as I say, Ty," Michael ordered, snatching the key from Kacie's hand and tossing it to his brother.

Kacie tried to catch Erik's eye, needing to know that he had a better plan than trading his life for theirs. Try as she might, though, he wouldn't look at her. His attention was focused on making sure Ty actually unlocked the manacles on her father's wrists.

She heard the clank of metal against the rock floor as first one and then the other manacle came off.

Erik walked slowly forward.

"Ty, help Gerard to his feet," Michael ordered.

Reluctantly it seemed, Ty complied. A second later, he appeared in her line of vision, supporting her father.

"Take him," Michael told her.

Michael was still holding her, so she accepted her father's weight as best she could, grateful she was a changeling. As soon as she did, she was surprised to feel Michael loosen his grip. Was he really going to let her go?

She searched Erik's face, wondering what he expected her to do. There was no way she was leaving him behind and yet, she had to save her father.

The wheels of her mind started turning as she tried to think of a plan.

"Okay," Michael said, still not releasing her entirely. "They're both free. It's time for you to keep your end of it."

Erik nodded and walked forward. When he reached her, he cupped her face between his hands and peered deep into her eyes. "I want you to leave and don't stop until you get to the castle. Lock the doors and wait for morning."

"Not without you," she whispered, unable to keep the catch from her voice. She didn't want this to be the last time she saw him.

"I have to know that you're safe," he responded.

"Enough," Michael said, cutting off the rest of what they might have said. "Put on the manacle, Erik. I can't have you changing your mind as soon as she walks out of here."

Kacie watched as Erik obediently went to the wall, picked up a manacle, and snapped it around his wrist. Then Michael took the key from Ty and locked the manacle in place. Then, to her utter amazement, he gave her a small shove toward the archway. "Go, before I change my mind."

Kacie didn't know what else to do. She knew she had to get her father out of there, but she vowed to come back.

Starting for the entrance, she had only taken a couple of steps when the sound of slow applause caused her to stop and look back.

"Bravo! Bravo!" Ty shouted, looking at all of them, but Michael in particular. "I haven't seen a performance like that in years." His tone was heavily laden with sarcasm. "But please. How gullible do you think I am?"

Confused by what was happening, Kacie looked first at Ty, then at Michael and finally at Erik. When she saw the look on his face, she finally understood. He and Michael were still reconciled. This had been their rescue attempt. And it had failed.

"What gave me away?" Michael asked, sounding grim.

Kacie watched Ty pretend to give the question some thought.

"I'd have to say it was when you set your brother's supposed murderer free and agreed to kill your best friend in her place."

Chapter
16

T y shook his head as he stared at them. "It was that last phone call, wasn't it? That's what gave me away."

"Your plan might have worked," Michael agreed, "if Erik and I hadn't already reconciled."

Ty laughed. "My plan *might* have worked? Dear brother, maybe you should take a look around. Do you really think you stand a chance against us?"

"I think we stand a better chance than you think," Erik said, pulling his hand free of the manacle that had been around his wrist. The look of surprise on Ty's face would have been more satisfying if he hadn't then laughed.

"Very nice sleight of hand, Michael. Pretending to lock Erik in chains. Are you ready for *my* next trick? Carrington," he said loudly. "Won't you join us? And bring our friends."

Carrington came into the room, a smug expression on his face. He was followed by thirty vampires, ten of whom were wearing collars and leashes, like dogs, and were restrained only by the combined efforts of the two vampires holding them. Their eyes shone with a wild red light and their faces were twisted as they snarled and pulled against their handlers.

"These poor creatures are progeny that we converted months ago." He gestured to the leashed primes. "They've completely lost their capacity for rational thought. Now, all they're interested in is feeding. Of course, we don't let them feed often, so they're ravenous."

There was a sudden blur of movement as the handlers released the progeny, who rushed forward. One creature fixated on Kacie. Still holding her father, she couldn't move out of the way fast enough. She waited to feel the creature's talons ripping her flesh and his teeth sinking into her neck, then Erik was there, swinging his fist. The creature's head snapped to the side, but even as it went down another attacked.

"Stay behind me," Erik told her, his attention on the progeny. Not far off, Michael was fighting a losing battle.

Kacie wanted so badly to lay her father down and help, but knew the moment she did, he'd be vulnerable to attack while her back was turned. She couldn't risk that.

A guttural cry drew her attention and she watched as Michael disappeared beneath a pile of the creatures. Erik dived into the melee to help.

Kacie gave a small cry when he was also dragged under as she stood by watching helplessly.

"Call them off," Ty ordered. Carrington issued commands in a language she didn't understand and the handlers surged forward, deftly catching hold of the collars and bringing the progeny to heel.

Michael and Erik lay on the floor, bloody scratches

covering their bodies. They weren't moving and Kacie feared the worst.

Keeping an eye on the handlers to make sure they didn't release their charges, she eased her father to the floor and hurried to Erik's side.

"Erik?" She smoothed the hair from his face and gingerly laid her hand on his chest, waiting to feel the slow rise and fall that would tell her he was still alive. When it came, she felt like she could breathe again herself.

"Get them up," Ty ordered, coming over to her. Carrington clapped his hands and several more vampires walked into the room. Kacie didn't know what Ty had planned, but she knew she couldn't let him hurt Erik any more. She prepared to defend his life with hers and turned to keep the approaching vampires in sight.

"Get away from him!" Ty shouted, catching her by surprise. He grabbed her hair and jerked her up. She stumbled to her feet, but didn't have time to collect herself before he shoved her against the wall so hard she saw stars.

Her field of vision narrowed and a ringing started in her ears. She felt as if she were on the verge of passing out. When a pair of hands hauled her up, she tried to hit her captor, but failed. Within minutes, she'd been manacled to the wall again.

By the time her head cleared, she had company. Erik had been manacled to her left and Michael and her father had been manacled to her right. All three had regained consciousness and were straining against their bonds.

"I'm sorry it has to end this way," Ty said, not sounding the least bit sorry.

"At least tell us why," Michael bit out. Then he gasped. "You killed Sedrick, didn't you?"

"I hadn't planned to," Ty admitted. "I'm afraid he was in the right place at the wrong time. He ran into me in town while I was enjoying a particularly tasty little dish. I'm afraid he wasn't happy with me for breaking the pact and insisted I come back to the lair for my punishment." He raised his hands to make quotation marks in the air as he said that last phrase. "That's when we saw that Kacie was back in town. Since Erik usually tells us when she's coming back—so we can avoid her—we figured he didn't know."

Kacie glanced at Erik and Michael to see how they were taking Ty's revelation. Both of their faces were blank masks, revealing no emotion.

"When we spotted Kacie, she was fighting a progeny," Ty continued. "Sedrick reminded me of the vow Erik had made to protect Kacie and said in his absence, we should help. We pulled our swords and started to cross the street. That's when inspiration struck me." He chuckled. "Or rather, it struck Sedrick." He looked at Michael. "If it's any consolation, *brother,* Sedrick never even knew what happened. When the deed was done, I looked up to see if Kacie had seen or heard anything, but she had disappeared and the progeny she'd been fighting lay dead. The little silver knife was lying nearby; I don't think she knew she'd lost it. I saw an opportunity to turn you against one another and took it. The rest you can probably guess. I arranged for it to look like Kacie had killed Sedrick and then I disposed of the other body."

"But why?" Erik asked.

"Because when you and Sedrick went on your big hunt to find the creature that would make you immortal, you invited *me* to go along without bothering to tell me why.

I was so excited just to be included, I didn't stop to question you." He paused to catch his breath. "I was seventeen! Too old to be a child and too young to be a man. Did you really think I'd want to be *trapped* in this body for all eternity? Talk about torture. Give that a try." His laugh sounded crazed. "Four hundred years later, I'm still being treated like a kid. Really, when we're all over four hundred years old, does the eight years between us really make that much of a difference?" He paused and looked around the room like he was trying to steady his emotions. "You stole my chance to be a man—an equal. Hell, I didn't even get an ossuary in the family mausoleum. *That's* why."

"But you liked Sedrick," Michael pointed out, sounding both exasperated and deflated.

"I did," Ty agreed. "But when he started scolding me like I was still a kid—I'm afraid I just snapped."

"The minute you killed him, you had to know that Erik and I would eventually learn the truth and come after you," Michael told him quietly.

"Yes, I did," Ty agreed. "But really"—he gestured to the chains imprisoning them—"you'll forgive me if I don't consider you much of a threat."

"Nice room you have here," Erik commented as if they were sitting around taking tea instead of standing in an underground chamber chained to the wall. Ty had walked out of the room an hour ago and there'd been no sight or sound of him since. Though many of Erik's wounds still oozed blood, that wasn't his primary concern. He rattled the chains and pulled, testing their strength. "Is this early Spanish Inquisition? Or maybe it's French Revolution.

I'm a little fuzzy on my history of manacles and chains in home décor."

"Damn it," Michael swore. "I knew I should have gotten rid of this shit."

"Why didn't you?" Erik asked.

"Because Ty thought they were an important part of our history—at least, that's the argument he used at the time."

"So, how old are they?" Erik asked, focusing on that critical bit of information.

"A couple hundred years, at least," Michael said. "Sedrick and I brought them over before the old estate was sold back in the 1720s. Why?"

"Because I'm hoping we can pull them out of the wall." He clenched his hands into fists and extended his arms as far in front of him as the chains would permit, straining against them. After several minutes, he stopped to catch his breath. The bolts hadn't even budged.

"Dad?" Kacie called out, catching Erik's attention. He leaned forward to see Gerard, who looked decidedly worse for wear. He wasn't a young man anymore, and he was human, which made him the most vulnerable of the four.

Erik saw the older man blink as he looked around and managed to catch his eye. "How are you doing?"

"Is Kacie...?" Gerard tried to ask.

"I'm fine, Dad," she hurried to assure him. "I'm worried about you."

"My fault," he mumbled.

"What is?" Erik asked.

"This. If I'd been more careful coming home, they might not have caught me by surprise—"

"It's not your fault," Michael told him. "Ty would have found another way to lure us here. Isn't that right, Ty?"

"Indeed," Ty said, coming through the archway and into the room. "Sooner or later, an opportunity would have presented itself and, as I've told you, I've learned to be very patient."

"Let's go, Ty," Carrington shouted, walking into the room carrying a small device in his hands. He was followed by several other vampires walking in pairs, each couple carrying an unconscious body between them. "Put them there," he ordered, gesturing to the far wall.

"What's this?" Michael asked.

Ty turned to him and smiled. "This is good-bye, brother. Carrington and I have decided to move the lair and I really can't afford to leave you and Erik alive to try and stop us, so we've arranged a proper send-off for you." He pointed to the ten male bodies on the floor. "These unfortunates were killed the other night. That means, of course, that they'll be rising sometime tonight. When they do, your blood will be the first thing they sense. The four of you should provide a tasty meal for them. You and Erik will naturally take a little longer to die, simply because"— he smiled—"you're already dead. The process, according to our earlier experiments, should take several days."

Erik listened to the plan with a new appreciation for how much Ty really hated them.

"And just to make sure you don't escape," Carrington added, holding up the small device, "we're going to seal the entrance to the lair." He set the device down and Erik could see red numbers, frozen at 15:00, on its face.

"You planted a bomb?"

"Don't worry," Ty assured him. "The explosion is small

enough that you won't be touched here in this room. Just the main entrance will be affected. I want these crazed creatures to be able to feed off you for a long, long time."

"You bastard," Michael swore.

Ty shot him an irritated look. "Yes, I think we've already established that." He turned to Carrington. "Is it set?"

"I still say we should put the bomb in here," Carrington grumbled.

"No," Ty said quickly. When he looked at Michael, Erik thought he caught a flicker of regret in his expression, but it was quickly masked. "The entrance to the lair will be good enough."

"It's set then," Carrington assured him.

"Then we should be off," Ty said.

"Ty, it's not too late to change your mind," Erik told him. "You can still put an end to this."

"That's exactly what I'm doing, Erik." He looked at Kacie. "It was nothing personal. You just happened to be in the wrong place at the wrong time." He turned and headed for the arch, but stopped when Carrington walked over to Kacie. "What are you doing?"

"I'm not leaving without her," Carrington said, pulling a key from his pocket. "She and I have unfinished business."

"Leave her here," Ty argued. "She'll just slow us down."

"She's not going to be a problem," Carrington growled. When he turned, he backhanded Kacie so hard that her head snapped around and slammed against the wall of the cave.

Impotent rage coursed through Erik as he watched Kacie collapse. Only the chains holding her kept her from hitting the ground. "I'm going to kill you, Carrington," he shouted.

Carrington shot him a sideways glance and smiled. "Is that right?"

"Don't touch her."

He started unlocking the cuffs around her wrists, laughing. "Oh, I'm going to do a lot more than touch her."

"Leave her here," Ty commanded, striding forward. "Leave her here or you can stay with them."

Carrington turned and Erik saw a look of irritation cross his face. "Careful, Ty. I put up with your orders because they served my purpose. Don't push me."

"Step away from her. Now."

Carrington had succeeded in getting both of Kacie's cuffs off and as her unconscious body started to slide to the floor, he lifted her to his shoulders. Then he turned to face Ty.

"I mean it," Ty said. "Put her down, or else."

"Or else, what?" he drawled. He made a show of shifting Kacie's weight across his shoulder and then suddenly he was pointing a gun at Ty. "You have to be willing to back up your threats."

"You can't kill me with that," Ty pointed out.

"Yeah? What kind of quality of life do you think you'll enjoy with your brains splattered across that wall there? Think about it—while you still can."

Erik watched Ty struggle with his decision. There was more at stake than Ty's life. If he backed down, he was, in effect, conceding his authority to Carrington. If he didn't—

The gun went off and Ty clapped his hand against the side of his head, his eyes growing wide. Then Erik smelled the sweet scent of copper and saw blood oozing between Ty's fingers.

"That was my ear, you stupid git!" he shouted.

"I could just as easily have put that bullet between your eyes," Carrington told him. "You see, I wasn't just a soldier in the war before a chupacabra got me. I was a sniper. Now—you've wasted five of our minutes and the clock is ticking. I don't really want to be in this cave when the bomb goes off. After you." Ty gave Erik and Michael a final look and then, with a grim expression on his face, walked out of the room with Carrington following him.

Erik immediately began pulling on his chains, desperation driving him. "If I can just get these loose..." He pulled as hard as he could. Across the way, the digital numbers of the bomb's timing mechanism mocked his efforts.

Erik's shoulder muscles still ached from saving Michael the night before and they screamed in agony as he strained against the chains. Tearing the bolts out of the wall seemed impossible.

Beside him, Michael and Gerard were trying to work their bolts free as well. Erik renewed his efforts and felt one of his chains shift. Encouraged, he grabbed the chain closer to the wall, used his feet as leverage, and pulled, first one way and then another.

Slowly, the bolt slipped out partway, giving him the encouragement to keep trying. Finally, with a loud grating sound, it came out of the wall.

"You did it," Gerard breathed. "Hurry, Erik. Only three more minutes."

There was no time to enjoy his victory. If he couldn't find the strength to pull the next one out, he wouldn't be able to stop Carrington from performing atrocities on Kacie that were too horrible for Erik to imagine. He wasn't sure that her being a changeling would be enough to keep her safe.

Putting everything he had into his next effort, he pulled on the remaining bolt. Slowly, it also started to loosen. Erik let go of the chain and, stepping closer to the wall, wrapped the slack around his arm, giving him a better grip. Then, using both hands, he pulled. With the added strength of both hands, the bolt screeched in protest but slowly it slid out.

Erik let his arms fall to his sides. His muscles would barely move, but he still rushed to Michael's side to add his strength to Michael's. "There's no time," Michael said, pushing him away. "You have to go after them."

"But—"

"No," Michael interrupted. "We'll be fine. You can come back for us."

"But..." He didn't want to point out that Gerard would not survive the progenies' attacks, but Gerard obviously understood the situation. "Go after my daughter, Erik. Save her if you can."

Glancing at the clock, Erik saw that the time for making decisions was up. As the last five seconds ticked down, he raced for the entrance to the lair and leaped through just as the bomb went off.

The impact of the explosion propelled him through the air and he hit the ground hard enough to be stunned. Small bits of rock and stone pelted him and he rolled onto his stomach, covering his head with his arms until it seemed safe to look up. By then, the ringing in his ears had faded and he was able to look around.

The entrance to the cave was almost completely sealed. There were gaps near the ceiling, large enough to let in air, but not large enough to see through.

Michael! He called through the psychic link.

We're fine, Michael thought back.

Then Erik felt Michael shut down the link and knew he had to do the same, before Ty picked up their thoughts.

He hated to leave them behind, but with every passing second, Carrington and Ty were getting farther away.

Michael felt a deep, dark despair. His twin was dead and his only other living relative had killed him. No matter how things turned out, Michael was now completely alone.

"Are you all right, son?" Gerard asked with such sympathy Michael was caught by surprise.

"Son?" Michael asked.

Gerard smiled. "You looked lost."

"I'm fine. How are you?" He did a visual check of the man beside him and saw that he was covered in dust and had a few cuts. Physically, he would live, but Michael could tell from Gerard's face that he was worried about Kacie. "She'll be all right," he tried to reassure the older man. "Erik will save her and everything will be all right."

"I know," Gerard told him. "They have to be. I've just patched things up with her. And I think Erik and Kacie might be on the verge of mending their differences, too. It wouldn't be fair if something bad happened to her now."

"I hate to break it to you, but I think Erik and your daughter might be well beyond *mending* their differences."

Gerard's eyebrows shot up. "You don't say. All the more reason for us to get out of here, because if that bloodsucker thinks he's living with my daughter without marrying her, he's got another think coming."

Michael found the man's reaction slightly amusing under the circumstances.

"What are you laughing at? It's not like you get off scot-free. He'll want you to be his best man, and then there's the night patrol. You don't think I'm doing that alone, do you?" He paused to catch his breath. "First thing I'm doing when we get out is remodel the west wing so it's protected from the sun."

Michael could hardly keep up with the man's ramblings. Maybe he'd been hit on the head by a falling stone after all. "What are you talking about?"

"Your rooms at the castle. Erik's already taken over the basement, but there's plenty of room on the upper levels once we get them sun-proofed."

"You want *me* to come live with you?" He could hardly believe it. It was his dream. To belong.

"Well, you can't live here anymore," Gerard pointed out.

"But you don't even know me."

"Of course I do. We might not have formally met before, but Erik's talked about you and your brothers so much, I feel like I've known you for years. Hell, son, in my mind, you're practically family."

Michael smiled. "There's that word again. *Son.* You do know that I'm practically eight times your age."

"You don't say? Then, if you wouldn't mind, you old fart, can you help a young man out? I have plans for both of us and none of them are going to be possible if we can't"—he tugged on his chains and groaned—"get out of here."

The future Gerard painted for him was far better than

the one he'd pictured for himself, and Michael grabbed his chains with renewed vigor. "I think the bolts are finally starting to loosen," he said after a minute. He heard Gerard's quick intake of breath and looked over. "What's the matter?"

"We might be out of time."

Michael followed the direction of Gerard's gaze to the pile of bodies on the floor and watched first one and then another progeny stir to life. As the growling, mewling noise of hungry vampires filled the air, he couldn't help but think how close he'd actually been to having his dream.

With an energy born of desperation, he gripped the chains and pulled. A pulse beat along his temple, faster and harder as he labored. Sweat broke out along his brow and pain lanced through his palms where the metal dug into his skin.

The sounds of the creatures grew louder. It was impossible for Michael to double his efforts, and yet he tried.

With agonizing slowness, the bolts eased from the wall. Then pain burst along his neck when one of the creatures rose and attacked.

Michael jerked his body to the side, trying to throw off his attacker. Beside him, Gerard cried out. Three of the creatures had smashed the older man against the wall with such force, he sagged against his chains. Now he was defenseless against the creatures and if Michael didn't get to him soon, Gerard would be killed.

With a final tug, the bolts holding Michael burst from the wall, sending the chains flying.

Michael grabbed the creature that was almost on top of him and threw it against the wall. Then he grabbed one of the creatures attacking Gerard and twisted its neck. He did the same thing with the other two, letting their bodies drop to the floor with a heavy thud. They weren't dead, but they wouldn't be moving any time soon.

He turned to free Gerard, but at that moment, the rest of the creatures rose and attacked him.

Gerard watched the battle before him with a sense of helpless dread as the six progeny bore Michael to the floor. Gerard said a quiet prayer that both his daughters would have long and happy lives, and prepared to meet his maker. When he heard a low droning noise, he wasn't sure at first where it was coming from. Then suddenly, like a crazed animal fighting for his life, Michael threw off his attackers. Gerard saw a blur of movement accompanied by howls of anger and blood-chilling cries. With a feral growl, Michael went from being the hunted to the hunter.

When the proverbial dust had settled, the progeny lay dead all around them. Michael turned to Gerard. His eyes still shone with their wild crimson light and his arms, neck, and body were covered in blood.

Gerard wasn't even sure Michael recognized him, and when Michael rushed forward, he braced himself. To his surprise, however, Michael grabbed the chains securing him and pulled them from the wall.

Both men collapsed then, too tired and beat up to move.

"Are you all right?" Michael asked, his voice barely above a hoarse whisper.

"I'm still alive, so I'm good." He studied Michael, noticing the pallor of the vampire's face. "What about you?"

"I'm . . . fine."

Gerard could tell he was anything but fine. "You've lost too much blood. You need to feed."

"Later." Michael took a breath. "First, I need to get you to the castle. Then . . . help Erik."

"Sounds good, but what about the entrance? I don't know about you, but I don't think I have the strength right now to dig my way out of this cave."

Michael sat with his eyes closed and his head bowed. He was silent for so long, Gerard thought he might have passed out—or worse. "There's another way out," he finally said in a raspy voice. "Behind the tapestry in the outer chamber. A secret passage . . ."

"A secret passage? Where does it come out?"

"Trap door in the Ellington family mausoleum. Right behind the altar."

Gerard was stunned. "Did Ty know about this?

Again, Michael was still for so long, Gerard wasn't sure he'd heard the question. "Guess he forgot about it."

"I don't think so," Gerard said. "I think that maybe he didn't want to be responsible for killing another brother. He wanted to leave you an escape route."

"Maybe. Doesn't make things better." Michael weaved a bit where he was sitting and Gerard had to put out a hand to steady him. "Dizzy."

"You need to feed." Gerard wasn't in great shape himself, but he rolled up his sleeve and held his arm out in front of Michael. "Here."

Michael stared at the arm and then looked at him in horror.

"Don't look at me like that. I'm not offering you all of my blood," Gerard clarified. "Just enough of it to sustain you until we can get you more."

"What if I can't stop?"

Gerard smiled then. "You will."

Michael hesitated only a minute and then bit Gerard's arm. The pain was intense, but was over in a matter of seconds. As Gerard knew he would, Michael pulled away after only a few swallows and wiped his mouth.

"Thank you," he said, clearly humbled.

"It's the least I could do. Now, why don't we both rest here for a bit and then we can go find that secret passage you told me about."

"What about Erik?"

"I don't think either of us is in any shape to help him. If anything, we might prove a liability and he's already got his hands full. No. The best thing we can do for him is stay out of his way."

Gerard also knew that the last thing Michael needed was to go after Ty. No man should have to kill his own brother—even if he deserved it.

Chapter
17

She was dying. It was the only possible explanation for the way she felt, Kacie thought. Every time she caught a breath, someone knocked it out of her. Her head felt near to exploding. When she tried to move her hands, she found that she couldn't. Her weary mind tried to figure out why; with the realization that her wrists were bound tightly together came the rush of memories.

She was Carrington's prisoner and Erik and her father could already be dead.

Draped over Carrington's shoulder like a bag of potatoes, she tried to raise her head enough to look around. Making out the underbrush of prickly vines and tree limbs, she knew they were at the edge of the woods, not far from the castle.

Closing her eyes, she prayed for the ability to endure more of this jostling because she wasn't sure how much more of it she could take without groaning aloud.

Then suddenly she caught the faint sound of a twig snapping.

When she opened her eyes, she saw that they were just leaving the woods. Erik was racing toward them, chains still dangling from his wrists. Hope flared inside her, then Carrington whirled around and she lost sight of Erik altogether.

She tried to twist in Carrington's grip and as she did, she spied the gun in his hand. He was aiming it at Erik— any second he would pull the trigger. There was no way she could reach it and knock it from his hand, so she did the only thing she could. She bit Carrington on his side, sinking her fangs deep into his skin.

He screamed and twisted, trying to get away from the pain. Then she was flying through the air as Erik knocked Carrington to the ground. She couldn't get her bound hands out in front of her in time to break her fall, though, and she landed on her side with such force, the air was knocked from her lungs.

She heard fighting nearby. Looking over, she saw Erik hit Carrington in the jaw and send him stumbling back, but Carrington wouldn't stay down.

While they used their fists to beat each other senseless, Kacie looked around for the gun Carrington had dropped. There wasn't much time. She systematically ran her gaze over the ground around her until she spied a glint of metal reflecting the moonlight. At the sound of pounding foot-steps, she looked up and saw Ty racing toward her. She put on a burst of speed and dived for the gun.

Her fingertips brushed against the metal just as Ty snatched it up. Crushed, she looked up at him. His cold, hard eyes stared at her with a smugness she wanted to wipe from his adolescent face.

"Get up," he ordered, pointing the gun at her. Off to the side, Erik was still fighting Carrington and she knew she was on her own.

She nodded her head and slowly pushed to her feet, but when she went to stand, she pretended to stumble, falling forward into Ty. As she did, she rammed him with her shoulder just as hard as she could. When she heard his breath whoosh out, she spun around and ran.

With every step, she imagined Ty pulling the trigger. She expected to feel the bullet ripping into her flesh, spilling her blood, ending her life.

Her foot hit a dip in the ground and her ankle twisted. She couldn't stop her cry of pain as she fell. With Ty practically breathing down her neck, she pushed herself up and felt her heart lurch. There, in front of her, was the edge of the cliff. Instead of running toward the castle, she'd gotten confused and run the wrong way. If she hadn't tripped, she might have run off the edge. She turned around and froze as Ty raised his gun, blocking her escape.

Frozen in fear, she watched him move toward her. When he was close enough to grab her, he pulled her to the very edge of the cliff.

She thought he was going to push her off, but then he spun her around and held the gun to her temple—and waited.

From where she stood, Kacie could see Erik holding Carrington off the ground by the scruff of his shirt. He hit him in the face and Carrington fell back. He stayed down; unmoving.

Kacie waited for Erik to look for her and when he did, she knew the exact moment he realized the grave danger she was in because his expression reflected his horror and desolation. She wanted to cry. If only she'd run the other way.

"How many times do I have to kill you, Erik?" Ty shouted.

"At least once more," Erik called back, climbing to his feet and walking slowly toward them.

"I think this time your luck has run out. You know as well as I do that only one of us is going to make it off this bluff and, well, I think it should be me."

"Okay," Erik agreed. "You win. Let her go and you can shoot me. Then you walk out of here."

Ty laughed. "I have a better idea. Go to the castle, get your car, and bring it over here. *Then* I'll shoot you and drive away."

"What about Kacie?"

"I'll drop her off down the road, safe and sound. You have my word on that."

"The word of a murderer doesn't hold much weight with me."

Ty gave a dismissive shrug. "I don't really see that you have a choice, do you?"

Kacie felt the pressure of Ty's grip tighten on her arm and she turned to see his face. He seemed more nervous than he let on and she wondered why. When she turned her attention back toward Erik, she saw that he was still moving slowly forward.

"You know that if anything happens to her, I'll come after you," Erik said.

"Not if you're dead. But maybe you don't care if she dies first, because if you take one more step, she's going to suffer a fatal accident."

Erik and Ty locked gazes and waged a silent battle of wills. The tension between them was almost palpable. "You had your chance," Ty said, cocking the gun as Erik took another step forward.

"Duck!" Erik's shout filled the night and Kacie dropped to her knees. Beside her, Ty shouted and pulled the trigger just before Erik plowed into him, driving both men back— and over the side of the cliff.

The horror of seeing Erik go over was so unreal that for a moment Kacie couldn't believe it had really happened.

"Oh, God. Erik!" she screamed, scrambling to the edge on hands and knees, taking care not to slip and fall after them.

She looked over the edge. At first, all she could see were shadows. "Erik," she moaned.

"Kacie." His voice was faint, as if coming from a far distance down.

"Erik? Where are you?"

"I'm down here. I don't know how far."

"I'm coming down," she said, searching for a way.

"No! Kacie, it's too steep. It's a sheer drop all the way down."

That didn't make sense. "Then where are you? Is there a ledge?"

She heard his groan of pain. "The chain around my wrist caught on something on the way down. I'm more or less hanging in midair."

"And Ty?"

She heard a strangled sound. "I've got him," Erik said.

Kacie leaned a little farther out, trying to distinguish what was the side of the cliff and what wasn't. "Oh, I see you," she called. The ring and bolt that had secured his chains to the wall in the chamber were wedged between two boulders on the side of the cliff. If he hadn't still had the other end manacled to his wrist, he would have fallen all the way down.

"Is there any way you can pull yourself up? Maybe climb the chain?"

"No. I think this time my shoulder really is dislocated. It hurts like hell."

She leaned to one side and noticed that the ring was standing straight out. If she could hook something into that end, maybe she could pull him up.

She sat up and looked around. The castle wasn't that far if she ran. "I'm going to get the Hummer. I can use the winch to pull you up."

Silence met her suggestion. "Erik?" She leaned out again, afraid that the chain might have broken loose, but he was still there, dangling, and using his free arm to hold Ty around the throat.

"It's too late, Kacie."

At first she didn't know what he meant, then she glanced out over the horizon and knew. What she had taken for new and improved night vision hadn't been that at all. The sky had been growing lighter with the approach of dawn. Even now, there was a decided glow on the edge of the horizon. If the sun came up before she could save Erik—

It was too horrible for her to contemplate. "You hold on, Erik Winslow. Do you hear me? I am *not* going to let it end this way."

Then she turned and raced for the castle, running as fast as she could, ignoring the drain of energy brought on by the coming daylight. She was a changeling, by God. She could do this.

Hands still bound together, she ran faster than she'd ever run in her life. Under other circumstances, she might have enjoyed the accomplishment, but now, all she could think about was saving Erik.

The stables loomed ahead of her—she didn't even slow down as she raced inside. As expected, the Hummer was where she'd left it. She started to climb in and stopped when she had to reach for the door handle with both hands. She wasn't going to be able to work the winch with her hands tied together.

She looked around and spotted several old gardening tools. Hurrying over to them, she picked up the hoe, as it seemed to have the sharpest blade.

It was awkward, but she managed to brace the tool against the wall with her feet, blade facing out, so she could rub the ropes tied around her wrists over the hoe in a sawing fashion.

It seemed to take forever; the entire time she worked, she had the sense of time passing too quickly.

Finally, the rope frayed. Exerting pressure by pulling her wrists apart, she managed to free herself. She let the hoe fall back against the wall of the stable and rubbed her wrists, trying to restore circulation. Then she turned around and nearly jumped out of her skin.

"Miss me?" Carrington snarled.

Erik dangled helplessly, Ty's weight dragging him down. The pain radiating throughout his body was almost as strong as his sense of helplessness. Even if he let go of Ty and managed to pull himself up the chain, he was too far down the face of the cliff to be able to scale it the rest of the way. And reaching the top was a secondary concern as the dawn's arrival drew imminently closer.

This was the end for him. He'd contemplated his demise so many times and in so many different ways, but now that it was here he found the prospect a little anticlimactic.

Ty jerked and Erik tightened his grip around the man's throat, knowing he couldn't choke him to death. "Hold still," he grumbled and then loosened his hold enough for Ty to catch his breath.

"I can't...believe it," Ty gasped past the restriction on his throat. "After everything...you would still...save my life?"

"You give me too much credit," Erik grunted, trying to ignore the pain in his arm. "I'm not trying to save your life. I'm afraid that if I let you go"—he tightened his hold around Ty's throat—"you might survive the fall."

There was a moment of silence. Then, when Erik's words registered, Ty kicked his feet, trying to break Erik's grip on him. Erik gritted his teeth and focused on hanging on.

"You can't...hold on...forever," Ty choked.

I don't have to, Erik said through the psychic link because he no longer had the strength to talk. *I just need to hold you for another ten minutes. Now shut up and enjoy the sunrise with me.*

When he heard Ty's horrified gasp, he knew the other man had finally realized the time. He had to give Ty credit for the effort he put into his struggles, but it did no good. Erik had lost all feeling in his muscles and the arm around Ty's throat was locked in place.

Erik kept his gaze on the horizon. He'd longed to see the sunrise again and now he was finally going to. It was the perfect way to die, if he'd still wanted to. Now, however, he'd give up a thousand more sunrises just to have one more night with Kacie.

Closing his eyes, he pictured her face in his mind. The line from a Tennyson poem ran through his mind—'Tis *better to have loved and lost, than never to have loved at all*. Well, he had loved—and loved deeply—even if the time had been too short.

When he felt the lethargy of the coming dawn fill him, he knew it was time. It was harder to face than he'd ever thought it could be. He didn't want to die.

He opened his eyes and saw that the sky had lightened and there was a bright orange line along the horizon. Despite his dire circumstances, he couldn't suppress the thrill that raced through him. He'd missed seeing the sunrise.

A single, brilliant spot of light emerged, blinding him. The sun. His breath caught in his throat. It was as lovely as he remembered it; lovelier than his finest painting. After hundreds of years, he finally felt the sun's heat on his face.

Even if he could have spoken aloud, there were no words to describe it. Ty's gasp told him that he, too, had found the sight captivating. Then Erik felt the hardening of Ty's skin beneath his arm and knew that his end had finally come.

Chapter
18

Still bleeding from the pounding Erik had given him, eyes blazing and fangs showing, Carrington looked like something straight out of a horror film. Desperate to get away from him, Kacie stumbled back, straight into the workbench. Keeping her eyes on Carrington, she reached behind her and blindly felt along the top for anything she could use as a weapon. There was nothing within reach but dust.

She grabbed a handful of it and flung it in his face. As he tried to blink it away, she ducked out of his way and raced across the stable.

"You can't run from me," he taunted her, rubbing his eyes. "Sooner or later, you'll get tired."

She could have run out of the stable, to the castle. There, she would be able to lock herself safely inside where Carrington couldn't reach her. But that plan had one insurmountable flaw—it left Erik on the cliff to die. That was unacceptable.

So instead of racing to safety, she hurried around to the far side of the Hummer, trying to keep the vehicle between them while she figured out what to do. The clock was ticking.

After considering and rejecting several plans, she finally realized that she'd have to deal with Carrington head on. A full-out attack. But she needed a weapon.

Giving herself a nanosecond to mentally prepare herself, she raced to where she'd left the hoe propped against the wall.

She reached it with Carrington a hairbreadth behind her. Grabbing it, she spun around.

"Get away from me," she demanded, feinting with the hoe and forcing Carrington back several steps.

He only laughed at her efforts. "That's it, baby. Fight me all you want," he taunted her. "I like it rough."

She held the hoe at an angle and tried to stab him with the corner of the blade, but he blocked her effort. The impact of the long wooden handle hitting his arm broke off the end of the hoe and it clattered to the ground in a horrible replay of their earlier confrontation.

As she contemplated her next move, Carrington reached out and grabbed the wooden handle, yanking it from her hands. Horrified, she tried to run, but he caught her and threw her up against the side of the Hummer.

"The time for games is over," he told her, leaning into her, his rank breath hitting her in the face so that she felt like she was suffocating. "It's time to finish this." His mouth came down on hers in a brutal kiss. When she tried to twist her head away, he grabbed it and held her still. She bit down, her fang piercing his lip. As he pulled back in surprise, she shoved him as hard as she could and escaped, running once more to the side of the stable that held the tools.

He stumbled after her, but she kept running, grabbing an old shovel as she hurried around to the front of the Hummer. There, she stopped and waited. Carrington came crashing around the corner and seeing her standing there holding the shovel, he pulled up short, his eyes glowing and his lips curling back in a snarl.

Kacie waited, holding the shovel up in the air with both hands wrapped around the base of the handle.

"You like to play games?" she sneered. "I've got a game you'll like."

"Is that right?"

"Yeah. It's called baseball." She glanced up at the old pulley hanging above Carrington's head and then smiled, praying her bluff worked. His eyes widened momentarily and then he, too, glanced up. In that moment she swung the shovel as hard as she could against the side of Carrington's head. Now that she had changeling strength, the blow was considerable.

She watched as he stood frozen, his expression going blank and his eyes rolling back. Then, he dropped like a stone.

She tossed the shovel to one side and jumped into the Hummer. The key was still in the console, so she dug it out and started the engine. She had to look down to make sure she'd put it in the right gear, and when she looked up Carrington was standing in front of her, blood dripping down the side of his head.

He gave a furious roar as she slammed her foot on the accelerator. The Hummer jumped to life, hitting him square on.

Instead of falling under the Hummer's wheels as she'd hoped, he jumped up and landed on top of the hood. His snarling face and bloodthirsty glare filled her vision as she drove out of the stables.

It was much lighter outside and Kacie's fear that she would be too late to save Erik spurred her to drive faster than she ever had before. She hit ruts in the ground so hard she literally came out of her seat. And still Carrington held on. Each rut she hit bounced him a little farther down the hood but he kept climbing up, relentless in his attempt to get to her.

Trying to ignore him, she turned the steering wheel, angling the vehicle so it was headed toward the spot where Erik waited for her. As soon as she made the slight turn, the sun hit her eyes. As the significance of the light set in, the expression on Carrington's face turned to one of horror.

As she watched, a rough, light gray substance spread over his form, turning him to stone. Stunned, Kacie let her grip on the steering wheel slip and the Hummer hit another rut. At the moment of impact, Carrington's body slammed against the windshield and exploded into dust.

Kacie stood on the brakes and the Hummer slid to a stop. Her heart was pounding so fast she thought it might burst from her chest. She looked at the dust covering the hood of the Hummer and then looked behind her. Nothing. Carrington was gone. Turned to dust by the sun.

By the sun.

A fresh horror hit. She was too late.

If the sun was up high enough to turn Carrington to stone, then . . . Erik was dead.

She stepped on the gas and drove to the place where he and Ty had gone over the edge. She moved about as if in a dream state, her body doing what needed to be done while her mind sat in a private corner, screaming endlessly over the pain of losing Erik.

Though it was too late, she refused to leave his body hanging from the cliff. She fed the winch cable down the side and then tried several times before she finally succeeded in hooking the ring wedged between the two boulders. Then, returning to the winch, she flipped the switch that would retract the cable.

It didn't take as long as she thought. When Erik's lifeless body reached the top, she shut off the winch and pulled him up the rest of the way on her own.

His skin had turned the same grayish color Carrington's had. Unhooking the winch, she knelt beside him, afraid to touch him the way she wanted to for fear that despite surviving the trip up the rocky cliff face, even the smallest gesture would turn him to dust and she'd lose him forever.

Now that she knew he was dead, the numbness that had carried her this far began to recede. She tried to call it back, not wanting to feel the hurt and pain. The last time she'd felt such a magnitude of sorrow and despair had been on the night her parents and brother had been killed. And even then, she'd had Erik to comfort her.

"Go to sleep, little one. I'll protect you," she whispered, her voice catching. She hadn't protected him at all. He'd protected her, just as he always had. And now he was gone. It wasn't fair. As a changeling, she had the potential to live as long as a vampire. They could have had a long, happy life together and now she was facing an eternity alone. She didn't think she could bear it. She missed him so badly.

Once the tears started, they wouldn't stop. She cupped

her face with her hands and great, gulping sobs racked her body until she thought the pain would kill her, and still she cried.

She didn't notice the gentle brush against her hand at first, until it came a second time. Then she stopped crying as quickly as if someone had turned off a water spout, every part of her alert.

The third time she felt the caress, she knew that she hadn't imagined it. Opening her eyes, she stared down into Erik's face. It wasn't possible for him to be alive, was it?

There were splotches on his body where her tears had fallen and pale skin showed through. She stuck out her hand to touch him and then hesitated. What if she was wrong? What if touching him destroyed what little of him she had left?

She had to know. Touching the spot where one of the tears had landed, she softly rubbed it. To her utter amazement, the powdery gray substance came off on her finger.

Hardly daring to hope, she ripped open his shirt and saw that his skin—was skin. Lowering her head, she pressed her head to his chest and cried out. His heart was beating.

"Kacie." The word was barely above a whisper but she heard it.

"Erik," she cried. "You're alive. How is this possible?" She bent to kiss his lips, his face, whatever she could reach.

"I want to hold you, Kacie, but I can't move my arms."

"No, no. You can't turn to stone. Not now."

She heard the rumble of his chest. "No, I don't think that's it. Muscles ache, that's all. Help me sit up, will you?"

She started to reach for him and noticed that there was a dusty red stain on his shirt. "You're hurt."

"Yes, I know."

"No, I mean, you've been shot," she said, getting even more worried.

"When Ty fired the gun, he hit me."

"We have to get you to a doctor." She helped him to sit up, but when she tried to help him stand, he resisted. "I'll be fine. We both know that one little bullet isn't going to kill me."

She reached her arms around him and hugged him as if she might never get the chance to again. "I thought I'd lost you."

"To be honest, I thought you had, too."

She sniffled, still not over her scare; afraid that this might be the dream, that harsh reality awaited her.

"Don't cry, love. Everything's all right," he told her, turning his head so he could press a kiss to her temple.

"Maybe we'd better get you inside," she suggested. "Just in case."

"Actually, I'd like to sit here for a while. I'm not sure how it's possible for me to be out here while the sun is shining, but I haven't seen a sunrise in four hundred years. To be able to sit here and share this one with the woman I love—well, it doesn't get any better than this."

"What about my dad and Michael?"

Erik shook his head. "No, I prefer having only you by my side."

"That's not what I meant," she said, then saw his smile. "I take it they're all right?"

"Yes, they're fine. Michael contacted me on the link and

sends his regards. He's at the lair with Gerard. We'll see them tonight."

She settled in beside him. "Would it be terribly painful for me to hold your hand?"

"Let's see."

He winced when she started to slip her fingers through his, but when she tried to pull back, he stopped her. "No, hold my hand."

She did, pulling it into her lap because that seemed to be a more comfortable position for him. "Where did all this powder come from?" she finally asked. "When I saw it I thought you had turned to stone." She rubbed her finger across the top of his hand, wiping away the top layer. "You're covered in it," she said, reaching over with her free hand to ruffle his hair, creating a soft gray cloud of dust.

"Ty wasn't as fortunate as I was," he said quietly.

"Oh, Erik. I'm so sorry."

He squeezed her hand. "There's no need to be. He found the justice he deserved."

She shook her head. "I'm not sorry for Ty. I'm sorry for you. I know you cared about him, despite the horrible things he did."

"Thank you." He groaned and pulled his arm away from her lap. Before she could protest, he slipped it around her shoulders and pulled her closer to his side.

"I have to tell you something," she said, getting his attention.

He looked at her with a quizzical expression on his face. "What's that?"

"I love you."

He looked at her in surprise and then smiled. "I know you do, love."

She smiled back. "I wanted to say it to your face, so you'd never doubt it. And I'm going to keep saying it to your face until you're tired of hearing it."

"That could take a long time," he warned her.

"I'm prepared to say it for as long as it takes."

His expression grew serious. "We could be talking hundreds of years."

Her tone had been light before, but not anymore. She wanted him to know that she was as serious about this as he was. "I think we're talking a lot longer than that."

He kissed her then, taking his time, so that when he finally pulled away, she felt like she'd been kissed very thoroughly.

"Maybe we should go back to the castle?" she suggested, hoping he'd take the hint.

The look he gave her was troubled. "Would you be horribly insulted if I asked you to sit here with me a while longer?"

She smiled up at him as understanding dawned. "Not in the least."

"Thank you." He turned to stare at the horizon while she continued to watch him. "I've never seen anything as miraculous as a sunrise," he said almost reverently.

"I have," she said, her gaze fixed on him.

Epilogue

Y ou're what?" Jess screeched over the phone when Kacie
   called her several days later. "I can't believe it."

Kacie furrowed her brow. "Somehow, I thought you'd
be more surprised to find out that I'm a changeling, not
that Erik and I are getting married."

"Well, I admit that all of it's a shock," Jess said, "but
Dad called me the other day to tell me about the chupacabra attack and what happened with Erik. You should have
heard my scream then. I've never seen John and Harris
move quite that fast to see what was wrong."

Kacie smiled, imagining how strange a life her sister must lead, living with a changeling and a vampire.
It couldn't be any more bizarre than hers now, *being* a
changeling and living with *two* vampires—or maybe they
were two *changelings* and a vampire. After all, whether
it was the infusion of baby chupacabra venom—the same
stuff that had restored Lanie Weber to life and had made
Erik so sick—or the vast quantities of blood that she—a

changeling—and Erik had been sharing, Erik had definitely changed. There was no other explanation for why he had survived the sun. Whatever the reason, life would definitely be different.

From upstairs, she heard the sounds of her father and Michael working on Michael's apartment upstairs. She was amazed at how quickly the two had become friends. Neither had shared the exact details of how they'd escaped, but judging from the scratches and bite marks, it hadn't been easy.

"Dad failed to mention anything to me about you and Erik," Jess said, interrupting her thoughts. "So...?" she asked. "How is it?"

Kacie had a feeling she knew what her sister was asking and felt herself blush. "I'm not the kiss and tell type," she said with a laugh.

"Oh, please," Jess scoffed. "The man is four hundred years old. He's got to have developed some great technique by now."

"Well, that goes without saying," Kacie said, smiling as Erik, standing at his easel close by, heard everything and rolled his eyes.

She and Jess talked a few minutes longer and then hung up after promising to call one another soon.

"Everything all right?" Erik asked, coming up behind her. His hands stole around her bare waist and she leaned back against him.

"Everything's great," she sighed, feeling the familiar stirrings that came every time he touched her.

"Good." He kissed her. "Now, please go back to the couch where you were posing so nicely for me. I'd like to finish this picture before the sun comes up."

She rolled her eyes but went and sat down, arranging herself as closely as she could to the way she'd been sitting before the phone rang. "How's this?"

"Perfect," he said, picking up his brush and getting back to work. After sitting quietly for several minutes, she had to ask him the question that had been bothering her for a while.

"Erik?"

"Yes, love," he answered absently, his attention still focused on his work.

"I'm almost afraid to ask, but what exactly have you been doing with all these nudes you've been painting of me? I really don't want to walk into a gallery one day and see my naked body all over the place."

"You don't? I can't think of anything I'd like more."

She smiled, remembering how self-conscious she'd been the first time she'd posed for him. Now, it seemed that she spent more time naked in front of him than wearing clothes. "Seriously. What are you doing with them? And when do I get to see one?"

"Love, you can see what I'm painting any time you desire."

"I can?"

"Of course. I never said you couldn't."

"But when I asked before, you said it wasn't finished yet."

"It wasn't, but that didn't mean you couldn't see it."

Feeling slightly miffed, she got up from the couch and walked across the room until she was standing beside him. She studied the picture, feeling her cheeks heat up. "This is a beautiful picture, Erik."

"Thank you, my love. I'm glad you like it."

"It's not really a nude, though," she observed.

"No, it's a landscape."

"I see." She turned to him, hands on her hips. "Would you mind telling me, then, why it is I've been sitting nude on that couch for the last couple of days?"

He gave her a sheepish grin and shrugged. "I love being with you and I love looking at you. And as long as you were willing, I saw no reason not to have both while I painted. It's as simple as that." He gave her an endearing look. "Are you angry with me?"

She laughed. "How could I be? Although to be fair, I think that if I'm going to sit nude for you, you should start painting in the nude for me."

The light in his eyes grew brighter and her own vision took on a reddish haze. "If I did that, I'd never finish a painting." He gathered her to him and kissed her thoroughly.

After a while, she felt a familiar drain on her system. "It's almost time," she said, pulling back. "Shall we?"

"Only if you're sure you don't mind."

She left him long enough to put on clothes. When she came back, he was waiting for her by the door. "We'll need to hurry," she said.

"Not a problem."

He opened the door and like kids after the ice cream truck, they ran hand in hand into the night. Once they reached the bluff, Erik pulled out a large wool blanket and spread it over the ground.

"Hurry," Kacie said, sitting down and patting the spot next to her.

Erik joined her and together they stared out over the

cliff. Kacie thought she would never tire of seeing the look of love in his eyes when he looked at her or the wonder on his face when he faced each new day.

It was the reason she came out every single morning with him to sit on this blanket and watch the sun rise.

About the Author

Bestselling author **Robin T. Popp** has built a reputation of delivering highly sensual, action-packed reads. Three-time *Romantic Times* Reviewers' Choice finalist, she is best known for her Night Slayer series, which combines mythology with vampire lore. The first two books of the series, *Out of the Night* and *Seduced by the Night,* were both *Romantic Times* Top Picks.

Robin grew up watching *Star Trek* and reading science fiction. She was amazed that anyone could dream up stories so enthralling and aspired to do the same. Though forced to take a thirty-year detour through the real world where she earned two master's degrees, took on a full-time job, married, and started a family—all of which brought a fair amount of adventure—she's now also pursuing her dream of being an author.

Robin lives southwest of Houston with her husband, three kids, two dogs, two frogs, a rabbit, and a mortgage. She is living the American dream.

To learn more about Robin, go to www.robintpopp.com.

THE DISH

Where authors give you the inside scoop!

♥ ♥ ♥ ♥ ♥ ♥ ♥ ♥ ♥ ♥ ♥ ♥ ♥ ♥ ♥

Dear Reader,

While rummaging together through an antique store full of furniture and clothing, we came across two curious books. The first, bound by leather so soft and worn it almost fell apart in my hands, was the journal of Highland laird. The second book was more modern with sketches in the margins written by an ancient vampire bent on revenge.

Paula Quinn

Laird of the Mist

Robin Hogg

Lord of the Night

Dear Reader,

When yer called the Devil, there isna much to prove to the world anymore save that the title is a deservin' one. I am an outlaw, a murderer, and a legend to be feared. I dinna seek fergiveness fer my many sins. My road to perdition has been long and my iniquities too numerous and too savage fer redemption. There is naught in my soul but darkness, and I am driven by one purpose: to kill those who have created this beast no one dares call a man.

I wasna born from my mother's womb as such a detestable creature. I was formed in the dank dungeons of Kildun castle, home of my kin's lifelong enemies the Campbells. Taken as a young lad by the Earl of Argyll, after his men slaughtered everyone in my village, I was shackled to a wall and tortured fer my faither's crimes against the realm. My faither was an outlaw as I am. His crime was refusing to surrender his name during the MacGregor proscription. Mayhap, some would find my faither guilty. But I was sinless as was my sister, who bore his punishment with me and grew to adulthood in the caverns of hell. It took many years, but we did escape. When all that made me human was finally stripped bare, I massacred Kildun's mighty garrison and fled north with my sister to the misty Isle of Skye. But I canna escape what I have become, and my hunger fer revenge against the Campbells is all I have left.

Fer six years now I have ridden forth from the obscure mists to exact payment fer that which was robbed from me and from my clan. I have killed withoot sympathy, fer what does a devil know of mercy? Aye, I am a cold-hearted beast whose name alone strikes terror in the hearts of his enemies. Save fer one.

Kate Campbell is the granddaughter of the man who imprisoned me. A woman I should despise. I took her from her home with the intention to lure her uncle, the current Earl of Argyll, to me. I didna expect her to slice me with her blade or to awaken a part of me I thought long dead with her saucy mouth and tantalizing curves. But most of all, I wasna prepared to find atonement fer my sins in the bonny eyes of a Campbell lass. And now, instead of killing my enemy, I must do all I can to keep her alive.

Callum MacGregor

Clan chieftain of the MacGregors, and Laird of the Mist.

Dear Reader,

I am neither man nor monster, and yet I am both. Killed by a chupacabra four-hundred years ago, I died and rose again as a vampire.

I killed friends and family before I learned to control the blood-lust. I killed for food, taking lives so that I might live. But no more. Now I kill others of my kind to protect the human residents of Hocksley, England.

I still reside in the Winslow family castle and have watched each generation of my brothers' descendents come into this world. I've watched them grow and trained many to become vampire slayers. Their time upon this earth is far too brief, and when they pass each one takes a part of me with them.

Over the years, I've lived a thousand lives and died a thousand deaths. There are times when I long to meet the sunrise and end it all, but my responsibilities are too great. Should I die, who would protect my family from the scores of vampires not even they know exist? And who would protect my friends from the Winslow slayers?

Yes. I have friends. Michael, Sedrick, and Ty Ellington—my best friends in life—and better friends in death. Killed by the same chupacabra that killed me, we have endured the test of time. Michael runs the local lair and I control the slayers. Together, we rule the night.

This arrangement has worked well for years.

Now things have changed.

Sedrick is dead. I found his body the other night cut down by the blade of a slayer's sword. But not by a Winslow, for all three—Gerard, Jess, and Kacie—are out of town. This is a new player and his actions will not be tolerated. He will pay for his deed—with his life. This I have vowed to Michael, lest he turn his lair of vampires loose on the innocent residents of Hocksley.

I have lost a great friend and the tenuous balance between vampires and humans that I've worked hard to maintain is threatened. I can't imagine how the situation can get any worse.

Then, I run into Kacie Winslow in the streets of Hocksley, her sword still dripping red with the blood, and I know I'm wrong.

Erik Winslow
Earl of Hocksley, Lord of the Night

Lord of the Night Notice

I hope you enjoyed *Lord of the Night*.
Be sure to look for the rest of the
books in the Night Slayer series. If
you want to learn more about me, the
Night Slayer stories, and what might
be coming next, please visit my Web
site at www.robintpopp.com.

Robin Popp

Thirsty for more dark and sexy
paranormal romance?

Demon's Kiss

by Eve Silver

"*Demon's Kiss* is a lush, sensual, and compelling
read. Eve Silver makes magic in this novel about
sorcerers, demons, and dangerous desires."
—Cheyenne McCray,
USA Today bestselling author

"Hot romance . . . Silver is a welcome addition to the
genre."

—Kelley Armstrong,
author of *No Humans Involved*

AVAILABLE NOW FROM
GRAND CENTRAL PUBLISHING

*Want to know more about romances at
Grand Central Publishing and Forever?
Get the scoop online!*

GRAND CENTRAL PUBLISHING'S
ROMANCE HOMEPAGE

Visit us at www.hachettebookgroupusa.com/romance
for all the latest news, reviews, and chapter excerpts!

NEW AND UPCOMING TITLES

Each month we feature our new titles
and reader favorites.

CONTESTS AND GIVEAWAYS

We give away galleys, autographed copies,
and all kinds of fun stuff.

AUTHOR INFO

You'll find bios, articles, and links to personal
websites for all your favorite authors—and
so much more!

THE BUZZ

Sign up for our monthly romance newsletter,
and be the first to read all about it!